Aristide Pompasse stood in his apartment in Florence, staring out into the street below, well pleased with his life. He was the world's greatest living artist, and his paintings were worth millions. True, he hadn't been painting for the past few years. And no wonder—he'd lost his light, his muse, his inspiration.

But all that would change. Charlie would be back soon. He should have realized how much he needed her, but Pompasse was not the sort of man to need people. He was accustomed to being the center of the universe, and the thought that someone could actually, willingly leave him still managed to astonish him.

But now that he admitted how much he needed her, it would be simple enough to get her back. And then he would paint once more. He should have taken care of that ugly little detail years ago—he'd allowed sentiment to rule him. But with Charlie back he could start again.

The bells of the city rang out over the noise of the traffic. Two o'clock. He needed a glass of wine to celebrate his new life. He went out into the hallway, heading for the curving marble stairs. There was a bounce in his step, a lightness in his heart. The deed was done, a new life was beginning, and he felt like a young man. He would paint again, and he would live forever.

He was whistling under his breath, but the sound stopped as he halted at the top of the stairs.

And came face-to-face with his murderer.

THE WIDOW
ANNE STUART

MIRA

ISBN 1-55166-813-0

THE WIDOW

Visit us at www.mirabooks.com

Printed in U.S.A..

To my mother, Virginia Stuart,
a writer and a role model who finally gets a book
dedicated to her. It's long overdue. Thanks, Moo.

Prologue

Aristide Pompasse stood in his apartment in Florence, staring out into the street below, well pleased with his life. He was the world's greatest living artist, and his paintings were worth millions. True, he hadn't been painting for the last few years. And no wonder—he'd lost his light, his muse, his inspiration.

But all that would change. She would be back soon. He should have realized how much he needed her, but Pompasse was not the sort of man who needed people. He was accustomed to being the center of the universe, and the thought that someone could actually, willingly leave still managed to astonish him.

But now that he admitted how much he wanted her, it would be simple enough to get her back. And then he would paint once more.

He should have taken care of that ugly little detail years ago. It was nothing more than housekeeping. He'd allowed sentiment to rule him. Others might call it vanity, but he knew he wasn't a

vain man. He simply understood that the preser-
vation of his gift was worth any sacrifice. Even if
most of those sacrifices were made by others, they
were blessed to be part of a greater calling.

It should be almost finished by now. And once
Charlie knew what he had done for her she would
come back to him and all would be well.

He looked around him, savoring the beauty of
the elegant old apartment. Maybe Charlie would
be happier here in Florence, rather than at the villa.
There were too many memories, too many people
there. He would keep her here, away from everyone, keep her all to himself. And she would never
try to leave him again.

He turned from the window to stare up at the
painting over the marble fireplace in his bedroom.
A masterpiece—one of his very best. But with
Charlie back he would start again. She was his
light, his inspiration, and he'd been arrogant not to
admit it. From the first moment he saw her he
knew he had to possess her, and as long as he'd
held on to her all had been well.

Five years later he still couldn't quite understand
how she could have left him. How anyone could
leave him. Didn't he shower her with money and
jewels and all the things young women usually delighted in? But Charlie hadn't cared about the gifts.

He'd made her image world-famous, immortalized her in his art. He'd never hit her, abused her. He wouldn't have minded if she'd taken lovers—he certainly had. All he'd wanted was for her to stay.

She would come back now, he knew it. She'd become stronger—strong enough to leave him—but she wouldn't be able to resist. His charm was legendary, and he would use all of it. And she would return to him.

The bells of the city rang out over the noise of the traffic. His ancient, beloved city of Florence. Pompasse was French, but he had the soul of an Italian Renaissance master. Tuscany was in his blood, and as he looked out over the rooftops of the city he could see the Arno gilded in the sunlight. Two o'clock. It should be done, then.

He needed a glass of wine to celebrate his new life. He went out into the hallway, heading for the curving marble stairs that led to the first floor of his duplex, and there was a bounce in his step, a lightness in his heart. The deed was done, a new life was beginning, and he felt like a young man. He would paint again, and he would live forever.

He was whistling under his breath, but the sound stopped as he halted at the top of the stairs.

She was standing there, the last person he ever expected to see. And he knew he was going to die.

1

Finding a dead body wasn't Connor Maguire's favorite way to start the day.

He'd been breaking into an apartment in Florence, planning on a little discreet research, when he discovered the corpse of its owner. And not just any corpse. The apartment belonged to the great Aristide Pompasse, the world's most famous living artist. Or at least he was, until maybe an hour ago, Maguire guessed. It didn't take any great powers of observation—he'd spent years as a war correspondent, in the Middle East, in Africa, in Kosovo. He knew a dead body when he saw one, and Pompasse was most definitely dead, though he hadn't been for long. Maguire closed the door with a silent click and leaned against it.

"Well, hell," he said mildly enough. Somehow the situation called for stronger language than that, but all he could think was what a stinking mess he'd gotten himself into.

He was planning to write the tell-all book of the millennium. He'd spent the last five years grinding out stories for *Starlight,* Marc Gregory's internationally sleazy tabloid, but in Pompasse he'd found not only his meal ticket but his raison d'être. Pompasse was a man with enough skeletons in his closet to support Maguire quite nicely. He'd been working on the story for weeks, and it was going to be his ticket back to Australia.

The body was lying on the marble floor in the foyer, at the bottom of the curving staircase that led from the bedrooms above. His dark, intense eyes were blank, his skin as cold and lifeless as the marble floor. There was no blood.

Maguire made himself cross the floor and squat down beside the old man. He didn't want to touch him. It wasn't squeamishness. He'd lost any sensitivity years ago—a life spent in the news business tended to wipe out any tender sensibilities. The more he'd learned about Pompasse the more contempt he'd felt for him—Maguire assumed it was the last ounce of idealism in his own, otherwise tarnished, soul. The old man had deserved what was coming to him, and Maguire didn't give a damn who had dished it out. Except, of course, that it would sell more copies of the paper and, eventually, his book.

He put his hand against the old man's neck. Cold, flaccid, dead skin. Maybe he'd been dead for more than an hour. He glanced back up at the winding stairs. It would have been easy enough for an old man like Pompasse to make a misstep, particularly if he'd had too much wine. One little slip and down he would go.

Maguire sat back on his heels, reaching in his pocket for his cigarettes. That was one thing he liked about Italy—he could smoke anywhere he damn well pleased, probably even in the Duomo itself if he had the insane urge to go there. No one to frown at him and lecture him on the dangers of smoking.

He lit the cigarette and took a deep drag, blowing it at the old man's still form. Yes, it was an accident, easy to explain.

So why did it feel like murder?

He rose abruptly, glancing down at his hands. It had been a simple enough plan to break into the elegant apartment. He wasn't hampered by too many scruples, and he'd assumed Pompasse was back at his villa outside the tiny village of Geppi. He'd simply been planning to search the apartment for anything that might be useful, shocking, shameful in Pompasse's life. In particular, the diaries that Pompasse had kept over his long career, detailing his paintings, his models and, Maguire devoutly hoped, his love affairs. There were volumes and volumes of the stuff—Pompasse had an exalted opinion of his life and work, and was known to document everything. Getting access to those diaries would make all the difference. He just hadn't counted on finding a corpse.

He stared down at Pompasse, coolly calculating the impact this could have on his future. On the one hand, a dead artist was worth a hell of a lot more than a live one. And a scandal involving young girls and one very dirty old man, who happened to be world-famous, would pretty much guarantee a solid income for the next few years to anyone who knew enough to write the story.

On the other hand, he wasn't sure he was pleased to find himself at the scene of a death, particularly as he had strong motives not to like the old bastard. Pompasse had gotten wind of Maguire's interest, and he'd had his lawyer try a little intimidation with Gregory. It had backfired, of course, but the hostility between the two camps was now on record.

None of this mattered if Pompasse's death had been an accident. But Maguire knew damned well why he had this itchy feeling at the back of his neck, why all his nerves were alert, why he wanted to get the hell out of that place before someone could prove he'd been there.

He'd been a journalist for fifteen years, straight out of college, and his instincts had been honed over those years, particularly in war zones. He not only knew a dead body when he saw one—he knew a murder when he saw one. He'd be willing to bet that's what this was, even though there was no sign of a struggle or foul play. The sooner he got the hell out of this apartment, the better.

He moved through the rooms, his reporter's eyes cataloging everything, storing it in the back of his brain for future reference. Only one bedroom was used, the sheets tangled, but there was no way to tell if it had held more than one person. The air smelled stale, dead.

The kitchen had dishes stacked in the sink, crumbs and cheese on the wooden chopping block. Either he'd given his maid some time off or no one knew Pompasse had been there. He glanced in the empty living room, then stopped, staring at the huge portrait.

It was the same woman whose picture hung in the bedroom. There was a sketch of her on the wall of the upper balcony, and a watercolor in the foyer, looking down at Pompasse's body. For a moment he was paralyzed, transfixed. Staring at the portrait.

The woman in the painting was little more than a child. Curled up in a tight, protective ball, the girl stared out at the world with a mixture of hope and defiance, her odd golden eyes full of raw emotion, her tawny hair almost obscuring her delicate face. He recognized the painting of course, as well as the others. He'd done his research—they were from Pompasse's Gold Period, his most famous stretch of artistic endeavor. He'd become more abstract since then, harsher, the various models no longer recognizable. But he knew this model. Knew the haunting expression, the delicacy of her long legs and narrow, bare feet. It was Pompasse's child bride, his muse and his inspiration, though for the life of him he couldn't remember her name.

At the moment it didn't matter. He skirted Pompasse's body in the foyer, stifling the regret that he hadn't brought one of the high-tech cameras he usually carried with him. He'd only been interested in the diaries, and he hadn't thought there'd be anything worth photographing in the apartment. Molly would have been ashamed of him for being so shortsighted. It just went to show that a reporter, even a hack like he'd become, needed to be prepared.

He wiped the doorknob with the tail of his shirt. He didn't have time to do more, and while he didn't think he'd touched anything else, he figured getting out of there was more important than trying to wipe out any trace of fingerprints. There was no reason why anyone would think he'd been there. Sure, he had a grudge against Pompasse for getting in the way of his story, but it wasn't a killing grudge.

Maguire was out of the building and halfway down the street before he breathed a sigh of relief, certain no one had seen him. Maybe his luck was going to hold, after all. He had no reason to feel guilty—just because he despised the old man didn't mean he'd killed him. He despised most of the people he wrote about. Besides, he could come up with a pretty good argument that Pompasse's death would hurt his book deal, not help it. Now that Pompasse was dead, maybe there would no longer be a market for his salacious history.

Maguire knew otherwise, but he could probably convince the police of it. He'd always been good at talking his way into and out of any difficult situation. Assuming no one thought he had anything to do with the old man's death, a murder was the best possible thing that could have happened. The old man deserved it, and it would sell books. Maguire was nothing if not pragmatic.

The café near his run-down apartment was empty in the middle of the afternoon, and he had the place to himself. He was halfway through the pack of cigarettes he'd sworn would be his last when he remembered the paintings in the apartment. The young bride—he still couldn't remember her name. She'd left him years ago, or else Pompasse had tired of her. He no longer painted women with luminous eyes—his models were younger still, pale and frightened-looking creatures.

So who had killed him? He was willing to bet it was one of the women that Pompasse always had around him. The old man had liked his harem—during his research Maguire had found out that he had mistresses from all periods of his life still in residence out at his countryside villa. Any of his castoffs would have had reason to push the old man down the stairs.

He stubbed out his cigarette, then lit another one. He was smoking too much and he knew it, but right now he had more important things to worry about than the state of his lungs. He was putting his money on the one with the golden eyes. The widow, Madame Pompasse herself. She lived in the States, but that didn't mean she couldn't have come back and killed him. If she was the one who did it he could find proof easily enough—he wasn't constrained by the kinds of rules that hamstrung the *polizia*. And it would make one hell of a final chapter.

But for now, he was going to finish the crumpled pack of Gitanes and his cup of coffee, and then put in a call to Gregory. And maybe tomorrow he'd quit smoking.

Charlotte Thomas was in the midst of kneading bread dough when she first heard that her husband had died. It had been a peaceful morning—in the sweet-smelling environs of her apartment kitchen she'd been immersed in dough and yeast and cinnamon, and the calm, rhythmic slap of the dough against the marble counter. She loved making bread—it was a form of meditation, done in an early-morning kitchen with only the sound of birds outside.

She lived in the middle of Manhattan, and the sound of the birds was usually overlaid by the noise of traffic, even at six o'clock in the morning. But serenity was only a state of mind, and she ignored the rumble of engines and the shriek of tires, concentrating on the imperceptible noise of the pigeons that nested in the crevasses of the old prewar building on East Seventy-third Street.

If she'd been listening to the radio she probably would have heard the news, but she didn't like reality to intrude on her baking time. When she was kneading dough she could close her eyes and imagine she was in a different time and place, where nothing mattered but getting the dough to rise. She didn't answer the phone's insistent ring, but the answering machine outwitted her, and within moments she heard her fiancé's voice, stoic, calm, aristocratic, telling her that Pompasse was dead.

Henry Richmond was a lawyer, and while he was devoted to her, he was also slightly lacking in imagination and sensitivity. He left the brief message on her machine, changing her life, and then hung up.

Charlie pushed against the bread, curiously detached. Pompasse had been seventy-three years old, and not in the best of health. He loved his wine and his French cigarettes, his rich food and his indolent lifestyle. When he was painting he was like a man possessed—tireless, energetic, full of youth and life. When he wasn't working he was a querulous old man. And now he was dead. Probably his heart, Charlie thought, turning the dough over and punching it.

Her rings were in a little Limoges dish beside the marble counter she used for working with dough, and she could see the huge canary-yellow diamond Pompasse had given her when he'd married her. She had been barely seventeen. He had been sixty.

He'd been everything to her. A father, a protector, someone who worshipped her, someone who needed her. He gave her a home and stability after years of trailing around after her rootless mother, and he'd used his legendary charm with devastating effect. And she'd loved him.

Knead, push, pull. Turn, slap, punch. The newspapers would start calling again. She kept changing her number—they didn't have her most recent one, but she knew it wouldn't be long before they tracked her down. They'd be lying in wait outside her restaurant, with film crews shoving microphones in her face and lights blinding her. The world's most famous living artist was now dead. What did his former wife think of it all?

She didn't want to think at all. She was strong, a survivor, and she'd learned to put the pain into separate compartments in her brain so she could concentrate on the job at hand. Denial was an underrated tool for coping, and she used it well. Turn, slap, punch. The dough was developing a nice elastic sheen—the kneading was almost finished. She didn't want to stop. Didn't want to put it in a bowl to rise on the back of her six-burner stove, didn't want to wash the flour and butter from her hands and put the canary diamond back on her slender finger.

She'd tried to give it back to him when she'd left him, but he had refused to take it. He had insisted it was only hers, it matched her mysterious yellow eyes, and in the end she couldn't say no to him. So she'd worn it for him, even though she never saw him. In fact, she hadn't seen him once in the five years since she had left him. And she'd wear it today, in his memory.

The shrill ring of the telephone made her jump, and she grabbed it, holding on to her self-control by a thread. It was her mother.

"You've heard?" Olivia said abruptly, her voice cool and controlled on the transatlantic phone call.

"I've heard." Charlie could be equally cool. She'd learned long ago that it was the only way to survive her overwhelming mother.

"I'm coming to New York. You'll be needing me."

"I don't see why." Fat lot of good needing her mother had ever done her, Charlie thought as a shiver of emotion sliced through her icy calm. Olivia wasn't the type to be around when the going got tough. Charlie was certain she'd never understood or forgiven her daughter for realizing how empty her life was and walking away from Pompasse. Or for walking off with him in the first place.

"For the memorial service, Charlie," Olivia said with veiled patience. "There'll be tributes in Manhattan, and then he'll be buried in Tuscany. At La Colombala. You'll want to be there."

The memory of the farmhouse swept over her with blinding clarity—the clear light, the smell of the vineyards, the warmth of the sun. Filling her with both dread and longing. "I don't think so," she said.

"Baby," Olivia drawled, "you're still his executrix, not to mention one of his heirs. The lawyers haven't tracked you down yet, but they got in touch with me. He never changed his will."

"Shit."

Olivia's amused snort carried across the Atlantic Ocean. "I'm glad money means so little to you, darling. Trust your mother—there's no such thing as too thin or too rich."

Trust your mother. Charlie had made any number of mistakes in her thirty years, including marrying an old man, but that wasn't one of them. She had learned early whom she could trust in this life, and Olivia Thomas wasn't one of them.

Charlie took a deep breath. "Look," she said, "it's early in the morning and I've just barely heard. Why don't you call me back in a few hours and we'll discuss—"

"I'm already at the airport. I'll be on the next flight and we can discuss it in person." And she hung up before Charlie could form another protest.

She set the phone back in its cradle. The bread dough lay on the marble counter, a round, plump mass. She picked it up and tossed it in the trash, then washed her hands, scrubbing at them. She had flour beneath her short fingernails, and she kept scrubbing, mindlessly. Her hands were raw and red by the time she finished. She dried them quickly, then reached for the dish of rings. She put the silver rings on her right hand, the gold on her left. Then she slid the huge, winking yellow diamond onto her ring finger, staring down at it blindly.

And she began to cry.

24   The Widow

2

***

He shouldn't have listened to Gregory. He seldom did—his own instincts usually served him
well—but this time his editor had been adamant,
and he *was* footing the bill, as well.

"You've got to get to New York for the memorial service," Gregory had insisted. "Just to
check out the lay of the land. You can stay undercover—we have camera crews and reporters there
to do the main work. But you need to see what's
going on firsthand. How the widow's bearing up.
Whether any former lovers decide to appear out of
the woodwork and make a scene."

"What if someone sees me? How the hell can I
talk my way into the villa when someone might
remember me from the service?" he'd argued.

"I don't need to tell you how to do these things,
Maguire," Gregory had replied. "You're an old
pro—you can talk your way into and out of anything."

"I'm planning on passing myself off as an insurance adjuster once I get to the villa. Why would I be in New York?''

''Afraid you can't handle it, Maguire? Lost your nerve?''

''I can handle it,'' he'd drawled. ''I just don't like needless complications.''

''Consider this a needful complication. Pompasse was a famous man, and there'll be media from all over the world looking for a story. We've already got an inside edge—you've been working on him for weeks now. But we can't afford to let anyone else get the jump on us.''

And so he'd gone. He'd stayed in the background, watching, blending in with the ability he'd perfected over the years. And everything would have been fine, if the widow hadn't looked up at one point and, as luck would have it, met his gaze.

He'd ducked behind a pillar in the huge, crowded church a second later, and by the time he dared emerge her attention was once more on her lap. The place was jammed—with mourners, with curiosity-seekers, with paparazzi like himself. She probably hadn't even focused on him in that split second. There'd be no way she'd remember him after all those people.

He'd stayed in the background just to be sure, listening to the tributes that sounded more suited to Mother Teresa than a monstrously self-indulgent artist, and Maguire took note of several key phrases for later use. He'd get the full transcripts eventually. Right now he only needed local color, impressions. Like the widow's firm step and straight, narrow back. Like the fact that for all the flowery tributes, there wasn't a damp eye in the house. As far as he could see, no one mourned the old man.

Least of all Connor Maguire.

He didn't dare spend more than a few minutes at the private reception afterward. He had no trouble talking his way into the place despite the tight security, but he couldn't risk running face-to-face with Pompasse's widow. Not if he planned to pass himself off as someone else later.

He paused near the crowded entrance of the determinedly upscale La Chance for one last look at Charlie Thomas. He couldn't quite figure her out. On the one hand, he knew all the statistics. Married Pompasse at seventeen, left him at twenty-five, came to New York and opened a trendy restaurant that actually thrived in the competitive world of New York eateries. She was a self-made woman, calm, determined, eerily serene and in charge of her life. And yet, even from a distance he could sense the streak of fragility that ran through her, surrounding the iron core that kept her going.

It would be interesting to find out which was the

more influential, the strength or the vulnerability. Right now she looked as if she was protected by a coat of ice. What would it take to smash that frigid defense?

He had every intention of finding out.

The worst part wasn't the memorial service or the desperate paparazzi, Charlie thought. The worst was the reception.

"That's my brave, darling girl," Henry said, patting her hand as it rested on his impeccably tailored arm. "You've been an absolute brick through all this."

Charlie managed a faint smile. Henry was doing his best to be sensitive and soothing, and she could see the strain it was having on his usual imperturbable calm.

"I'm fine, Henry," she said in a low voice. And indeed, she was surprisingly calm. The reception was going well, but how could it do otherwise, since it was catered by La Chance, Charlie's own restaurant? Maurice had gone out of his way with the food. The various mourners who'd fawned over Pompasse in life now gossiped viciously about him as they ate and talked and drank and sent covert glances Charlie's way. She didn't mind. As long as they didn't plague her with anything more intimate than the prescribed words of sympathy, she could move through this day, this endless day after a series of endless days, with Henry's strong, elegant arm beneath her hand.

Her mother was across the room, her flame-red hair tossed back, brown eyes sparkling. She looked magnificent, as usual, and Charlie wondered whether she'd had any more cosmetic surgery done. If so, she had had plenty of time to heal, and Olivia was looking like the legendary beauty that she was.

Her only child was a pale substitute for Olivia's dramatic charms, but Charlie had always counted that as a blessing. Until she met Pompasse, a man who preferred subtlety, and then she was lost.

No, marrying Pompasse hadn't been a loss, she reminded herself sharply, her fingers tightening on Henry's sleeve. He wouldn't like her wrinkling his impeccable suit, but he wouldn't say anything. Henry was always the gentleman.

Unlike Pompasse, who could throw a hysterical fit with the best of them. He'd chosen wisely when he'd married her. She was already adept at dealing with temperament—her mother had taught her well. After Olivia's histrionics, Pompasse was a lamb to deal with—for the simple fact that Pompasse, unlike her mother, had loved her.

Henry loved her as well, with dignity and affection and admiration. He was everything she wanted and needed in a man—tenderness, charm, sophistication, maturity. He would take care of her when she needed to be taken care of, and let her fly free when she needed her wings. She would take off the canary-yellow diamond and put on the antique Venetian pearl ring that Henry had searched high and low for, claiming it matched her serene beauty. And this time her husband would only be twice her age.

"I wish you'd let me come to Tuscany with you, darling," Henry murmured in her ear. "It's too much for you to take on."

She looked up into his solicitous gaze. "I told you that you could come, Henry. As soon as you're able. I just don't want to wait until you can free up your schedule. I want to begin dealing with the estate as soon as possible, get it into the right hands. The longer I put if off the more it will prey on my mind."

"But surely you can wait a week? Your mother won't even be able to come with you."

Charlie didn't blink. Olivia's hectic schedule was one of her own reasons for haste. The more time she had at La Colombala without her mother's overwhelming presence, the happier she'd be.

But of course, Henry would be horrified if she said any such thing. Olivia seemed to approve of Henry as her second son-in-law, and he was determined to keep that approval. He would never even begin to comprehend the tension that lay between mother and daughter, and Charlie had no interest in enlightening him.

"But she'll be following soon," she said in her calm voice. "And really, I don't know why you think I'm such a fragile creature. I've been an independent woman for years now, and I'm perfectly capable of taking care of things. Lauretta is still there, and so are most of the others. They were always devoted to Pompasse, and he looked after them. He'll have left them well-provided for. I think they'd want his estate settled quickly."

"You'll be selling the villa," Henry said, only the trace of a question in his voice. "You could get a pretty penny for it, given how popular Tuscany is nowadays. And even that ruin behind the farmhouse will add to the value."

"Of course," she said. There was no alternative—it was hideously expensive to keep up, and her life was in New York now. With Henry. What did she need a rambling farmhouse in Tuscany for?

For the light, a tiny voice whispered inside her. For the scent of the air and cool evenings and the luscious grapes. For the first place you ever felt safe.

But she was a practical woman now, and she made practical choices. "Of course," she said again, trying to convince herself. "As soon as the estate is settled."

Had she imagined it, or was there a tiny sigh of relief from Henry? It didn't matter. He smiled at her approvingly. "And I'll do everything I can to help you, darling. We might even get married there, if you'd like."

She'd rather eat fried tarantulas, but she wasn't about to say so. She'd married Pompasse in the grape arbor in the hot Italian sunshine. She wasn't going to start her life with Henry the same way.

But Henry was looking at her as if he'd offered her a great treat, and she remembered his almost childlike awe of Pompasse, combined with a lawyerly disapproval of Pompasse's flagrant lifestyle and his own protectiveness toward Charlie. He'd like nothing better than to marry Pompasse's wife in Pompasse's vineyard, and it would take everything she had to convince him it was a bad idea.

"We'll talk about it," she said. And then she tensed.

Her mother was bearing down on her, a determined expression marring the perfect planes of her face. Her green gown flowed around her model-thin figure, but for once Olivia wasn't concentrating on her performance. Something unpleasant had happened, and Charlie held her breath, half waiting for Olivia to make a dramatic announcement.

"Did Henry tell you?" she hissed. Only her mother could manage to hiss a sentence without any esses in it.

"Tell her what?" Henry demanded.

"That bastard Pompasse," Olivia said bitterly, snagging a glass of wine from a passing waiter.

"He's dead, Mother," Charlie said calmly.

"But he's not finished messing up my life," Olivia said, with a blatant disregard for her own daughter's well-being.

"What's happened now?"

"He never divorced you," Olivia said flatly. "He never signed the damned papers." She drained her champagne glass and set it down hard on the marble-topped credenza. "Here's to Charlie, the happy widow," she muttered. "Looks like this time she hasn't landed on her feet."

"And this is a problem?" Charlie asked.

"You're inheriting his debts as well, darling. Which might amount to a hell of a lot more than his meager estate, since a number of his most important paintings are missing. He always lived the high life, and now it looks like you'll be paying for it. You'll lose the restaurant."

"Don't be absurd, Olivia," Henry said after a brief silence. "Even if they were never divorced they were legally separated. There's no court that could hold her—"

"You're an expert on Italian law, Henry?" Olivia demanded.

"Are you?" Henry shot back.

"I've got a headache," Charlie broke in, trying to keep calm. For five years she thought she'd managed to break free of Pompasse, only to discover that he'd never let her escape, after all. She should have known. He never let anyone leave, not willingly. Those few who had managed to leave him had simply disappeared with no warning, wise enough to sneak away before he could stop them.

"Don't worry, Charlie," Henry murmured. "You'll just put off your trip to Italy until I can come, and we'll settle this very smoothly."

"Pompasse needs to be buried."

"He doesn't need you there." Henry's voice took on a brittle tone.

"I'm leaving tomorrow," Charlie said.

"I can't possibly be ready by then," Olivia broke in.

"You can both join me when you're able. In the meantime the funeral is set for Saturday morning, and I intend to be there."

And "be there" she was. By the time she stumbled off the small commuter flight in Florence she was beyond exhaustion and into a strangely dream-like state of denial. All that mattered was that she got back to the villa, to the warmth and sunlight.

And then maybe things would begin to make sense.

It was a perfect autumn day in Florence. The sun was shining down, gilding the Duomo, and the Arno River moved through the city like an elegant serpent, twisting and turning in the light. It was the scented air that got to her first, though. The unmistakable fragrance that was Italy, even with the smell of the city. Charlie took in a deep breath and closed her eyes in momentary pleasure.

Renting the right car had proved more difficult than she expected. She deliberately hadn't let the people at La Colombala know when she was arriving. She knew from Henry that Pompasse's servants were still in residence, including Tomaso, the combination handyman and chauffeur, and she wouldn't have been surprised if he still drove Pompasse's beloved Rolls-Royce.

But she didn't want to return to La Colombala in a Rolls. For some reason it was important for her to come back on her own terms. Besides, she'd learned to drive on the narrow roads leading to the villa, and she wanted the rare pleasure of traveling them again.

She hadn't wanted to come back in a stodgy old Fiat, either. She'd wanted a sports car, something fast and dramatic, and it had taken her too much time to find one. But the Alfa was perfect, fast and sleek and powerful. The way she wanted to be.

She put the top down on the small Alfa, and the radio blasted passionate Italian pop music. She tied a scarf around her head, Audrey Hepburn-style, and put on her oversize sunglasses. She drove fast and well, out of the city, into the countryside, heading northeast to the tiny town of Geppi. La Colombala, Pompasse's sprawling estate, lay just beyond the town limits, and Charlie had always loved it there. In truth, it may have been harder to leave Tuscany than to leave her difficult husband.

She was in a hurry to get there. The roads were empty, winding through the hills, and she knew all the shortcuts. Tomorrow, or later, she would go out again in the car, taking her time, revisiting the countryside that she'd loved so well. For now it was La Colombala that mattered, and the people there who depended on her.

The town of Geppi hadn't changed in the years since she'd turned her back on it, but then, why should it? It had stayed the same for hundreds and hundreds of years—why should she think it would fall to pieces because she'd abandoned it? It was midday when she drove through the perfect little medieval town, peaceful in its serenity. All was still and quiet. The people of Geppi still observed the ancient custom of the midday rest, unlike their more cosmopolitan brothers.

The long, twisting road up to La Colombala hadn't changed, either. The ancient cypresses must have grown taller, the stone fences must have crumbled further, but if so she couldn't tell. The road was bumpy, rutted, with weeds growing in the middle—that was a change she recognized. Pompasse had adored his Rolls-Royce, and he'd loved his low-slung Ferrari. He always insisted the drive be kept in impeccable shape so as not to damage the delicate undercarriage of his sports car. The Alfa scraped bottom at one point, and Charlie winced in sympathetic pain. Why had he stopped caring?

She realized she was clutching the small steering wheel so tightly that her hands hurt. She loosened them, taking a deep, calming breath, and turned off the radio. The sudden silence was shocking—just the sound of the wind through the olive trees, riffling the leaves.

She drove past the stone cottages, the farm buildings and winery that had been abandoned before the war. And then up and around the curving drive until she came to the villa itself, bathed in warm, golden light. La Colombala. The towers of the abandoned church loomed behind it, casting shadows in the bright Tuscan sunlight. It took her breath away.

It was the same, and yet different. The main section was two storeys high, made of a whitewashed stone, and two single-floor wings spread out on either side. One was for the kitchen and the servants, the other was Pompasse's studio. The doors and windows to the house stood open, but the studio was shut tight, and Charlie felt a tiny clenching in her heart.

He'd been an old man. A difficult, impatient, tempestuous old man, who'd never paid any attention to his health. He'd smoked like a chimney, he'd drunk too much, and his formidable temper had set his blood pressure soaring. She'd loved him once, and she could mourn the loss of his talent. Although, there had been times when she suspected he'd lost his talent long ago.

She switched off the car and sat there in the stillness. No one had heard her arrive, which suited her. Whoever was in residence was sleeping off the heat of the midday sun like all good Tuscans.

She climbed out of the car and stretched in the sunlight like a cat, pulling off the scarf that had restrained her hair. She was wearing jeans and a merino wool sweater. Pompasse would have been horrified. He'd always preferred to see her in designer clothes. He would take some comfort in the knowledge that the sweater was Versace.

She was about to head toward the house when something caught her eye. She looked to the left, where the vineyards stretched out in the sunlight. It was October—it should be harvest time, or past, yet the grapes still hung heavy on the branches. Pompasse had been dead for less than a week—the neglect around the villa had been going on for far longer.

Someone was moving out there among the vines. Pompasse used to love to walk among the grapes, pretending he was a master winemaker. It always used to amaze Charlie—that one of the world's great artists would want a fantasy life as another kind of artist.

It wasn't Pompasse out there, she told herself. Pompasse was dead, gone forever. But it was definitely a man, and even though he'd disappeared around a corner she knew it hadn't been Tomaso. This man was younger, taller. And Pompasse had seldom tolerated any men in his household of women.

Without stopping to think about it Charlie headed into the vineyard. She followed the scent of fresh cigarette smoke. Cigarette smoke was an odd thing—dead nasty when it lingered, but actually pleasant when it was fresh. Only Pompasse had smoked at La Colombala, though Tomaso occasionally indulged in a pipe. Pompasse had considered it a filthy habit, but he himself was above his self-imposed rules. But he was dead now and she no longer had to live in a haze of smoke. Still, the fresh scent of it made her feel oddly nostalgic.

The sun was hot overhead, despite the fact that autumn was well advanced. The merino sweater was too warm, the sun too bright, and she'd left her sunglasses in the rented Alfa. She was half tempted to go back for them, when she turned the corner to come face-to-face with a mysterious stranger.

3

Charlie stopped short of barreling into him, just barely, doing her best to put a pleasant expression on her face. If she'd learned anything from Olivia it was perfect manners.

"Jesus! You scared me! Who the hell are you?" the stranger demanded.

She halted, astonished. "Charlie Thomas," she said politely. She held out her hand, and the rings glinted in the Tuscan sunlight as she peered at him. "And you are?"

The stranger's manners left something to be desired. He just looked at her, and at her proffered hand, before he finally reached out and took it in a quick, bone-crushing shake. "Connor Maguire," he said in a cool voice. "Insurance consultant."

"I didn't realize they'd sent someone out already," she said. Italy must have changed more than she'd realized in the past five years. Business in Tuscany usually moved at a snail's pace.

"With an estate of this complexity they wanted someone on the scene as soon as possible," he said. It was reasonable enough, and yet she wasn't sure she believed him. He had some sort of accent—Australian or New Zealand rather than British. Odd, but she'd assumed the insurance people would be Italian. On top of that, he looked strangely familiar. She'd never met the man before in her life—she knew that with a gut-deep certainty. He wouldn't be a man who was easy to forget.

"That's good," she said vaguely. "I haven't been to the house yet so I hadn't realized anyone was here."

"You're the widow," he said.

"We were separated," she said, determined to be pleasant. She was still having a hard time dealing with the fact that she'd never been divorced at all, but she wasn't about to share that information with a stranger. "But apparently I'm the executor of his will and as such you'll be dealing with me."

He simply raised an eyebrow at that. Connor Maguire was a far cry from anything she'd imagined an insurance adjuster to be, and she wondered how the household had reacted to him. He was young—mid-thirties, Charlie guessed, with shaggy dark hair that was badly in need of a cut, several days' worth of stubble, and a rumpled suit on a strong-looking body. Just the sort of man she found least attractive. He couldn't be much more than six feet tall—she liked men who towered over her own substantial height. She liked slender, elegant men with long, narrow fingers and ascetic faces and cool, charming voices. She liked men with experience and patience and charm, men who didn't demand or paw. The man in front of her didn't look like he possessed any of those finer qualities. She found him…unsettling.

"Apparently?" he echoed. "I would have thought someone would have figured that out by now."

Charlie's smile stiffened. "Pompasse was an artist, not a business man. Apparently he had a lawyer here in Tuscany…"

"There's that 'apparently' again."

Charlie's smile vanished. "If this is an inconvenience you could always return once the estate is settled," she said, her voice cool. She didn't like men like him, men so bristling with masculinity that they positively reeked of testosterone.

"My schedule doesn't work that way," he said. "I'm here now, and I'll leave when I'm finished."

He had very dark eyes in a tanned, lined face. He looked like a man who worked for a living, worked hard, and the eyes were those of a much older man. One who had seen too much and wished he hadn't.

"And exactly what is your job, Mr. Maguire?"

"Cataloging his paintings, his drawings, anything of value. The usual," he said vaguely.

"And how long do you anticipate it will take you?"

He didn't even blink. "As long as it needs to. The government doesn't like to be cheated of inheritance taxes, and the estate needs to be properly valued. Of course, there's that small complication that you're no doubt aware of. A number of your husband's most valuable paintings have vanished, as well as all the records he kept of his work. The government is very interested in finding them as soon as possible."

"Which government?"

He shrugged. "Take your pick. There are at least three involved in your husband's estate. Italy, France and the U.S., and probably others besides. What is this, a job interview?"

Charlie blinked. Maguire's attitude was bordering on rude—surprising for someone in his position. "I beg your pardon?"

He snorted with amusement. "What, you don't like my manners? Sorry, but I'm not about to waste my time on polite chitchat. I've got a job to do, and you're not the one who hired me. I'm staying here at the villa until my work's done and then I'll be out of your hair. In the meantime, just ignore me."

Charlie took a deep, calming breath. She didn't want or need this complication, but she'd survive it. She'd survive anything. "I'm sure we'll manage to get along just fine. As for ignoring you, that'll be pretty much impossible. It's going to be a full house in a couple of days, and you'll have to make the best of it. My mother and my fiancé will be arriving soon and they'll each need their own rooms. As I remember, the villa isn't equipped for that many visitors."

"Your fiancé? You're not wasting any time, are you?"

"Mr. Maguire…"

"Just Maguire, sweetheart," he said. He cocked his head, looking at her, and she felt an odd little shiver of discomfort slide down her backbone despite the heat of the sun overhead. "It's none of my concern. I just wonder why your fiancé doesn't share your room."

"If that were any of your business I'd be certain to tell you," Charlie said. "In the meantime, why don't you attend to your business instead of wandering through the vineyard?"

"Can't a man take a break?" he inquired in a low growl. "All work and no play makes Jack a dull boy."

She looked at him. Connor Maguire was never going to be considered dull by any stretch of the imagination. "Please play on your own time, not mine," she said in a cool voice. "What's your estimate on the value of his estate?"

"What's the big hurry?"

"I just want to get the estate settled and go back to New York."

"That's where you live?"

"That's where I live. I own a restaurant there," she added, then could have kicked herself. What in heaven's name was she doing volunteering information to a man like him?

"You cook?" He sounded completely skeptical.

"As a matter of fact, I do," she replied. "On my chef's days off."

"Fancy that," he murmured, clearly unimpressed. "Somehow you don't strike me as the practical type." He dropped his cigarette and stubbed it out beneath his scuffed shoes. He glanced up and met her gaze. "I suppose you're going to tell me you don't want me to smoke?"

"How did you guess?"

"You look the type," he said enigmatically.

"What type is that?"

"Someone who doesn't want a stray ash marring the perfection of her existence."

She smiled wryly. "La Colombala has fallen to pieces in the last few years, Mr. Maguire, and even before then I hardly expected perfection. I live in

Manhattan, remember? Full of dirt and drugs and crime.''

''But I imagine you're safely isolated from all that. You strike me as someone who keeps herself well guarded from the ugliness of real life.''

''I wish.''

''Well, Mrs. Pompasse, you happen to be in luck. I was planning on quitting when I finished the pack, and that's just happened. You see before you a changed man.''

Mrs. Pompasse. It certainly wasn't the first time she'd heard that, particularly in the last seventy-two hours with the god-awful press hammering at her every chance they got. But it sounded strange, hostile, terribly wrong in Maguire's rough voice.

''We were separated,'' she said again. ''I go by my maiden name.''

His entire bearing suggested he wasn't particularly interested, but he simply nodded. ''I'll go back to work, then,'' he said finally.

A relief, and she should have let him go. But some inner demon stopped her. ''How long do you think it will take you?''

''What?''

''To catalog his estate,'' she said patiently.

''If I could find your husband's records I would be out of here already. At this point, it appears that as few as three paintings are missing, maybe as many as a dozen, but without the journals I can't tell for sure. He may have sold some. There may be others the art world isn't even aware of.''

"I doubt it," Charlie said. "Pompasse didn't believe in hiding his light under a bushel. When he completed a painting the world was informed."

"Didn't care much for the old geezer, did you?"

Charlie repressed her start of surprise. Maguire was rude and abrasive—hardly the type of man suited for this kind of diplomatic work.

"I loved my husband, Mr. Maguire. I don't care much for you."

If she'd hoped to annoy him even half as much as he was annoying her, she was doomed to failure. He merely nodded, but there was a faint gleam of amusement in his dark eyes.

"So where do you think his journals are?" he said.

"I haven't the faintest idea. If I were you I'd be more interested in the lost paintings than the journals. They're worth more."

"Maybe," Maguire said. "I asked the housekeeper, but she says she has no idea where they could be. As far as I can figure out either he destroyed them, or one of his harem did." He let his dark eyes sweep over her. "This place is full of women. No one ever leaves him, do they?"

"I left him," Charlie said, knowing her voice sounded hollow.

"But you came back."

"To bury him, Maguire. And then I'm gone once more."

"Who's his heir?"

"Presumably his widow."

"You?" he said.

"Me."

"You don't sound very excited about the idea. Which is a good thing—at this point it doesn't look like you're getting much. Any reason why he might have been selling things off? Giving them away?"

"Not that I know of."

"I guess I can assume you didn't have anything to do with the disappearance of his valuables. Since I got here before you."

"His valuables?" she echoed, startled. "What about the silver? And I left behind a fair amount of jewelry—it must still be here."

She'd managed to startle him. "The jewelry's already yours. You don't need to pay inheritance tax on it."

"I gave it back to him."

"Tell it to the tax people, lady. Not me."

"I thought you were the tax people."

"I'm an independent insurance consultant. I just make lists."

"You don't look like a list-maker to me."

She could have bit her tongue the moment the words were out of her mouth. His eyes met hers, and for the first time she realized they weren't brown, but a very dark green, so dark they were almost black. He took a step closer to her, and the bright sun overhead seemed to dance behind a cloud.

"What do I look like to you, lady?" His voice was soft, rough, earthy, and he was close enough to touch. She didn't like touching people. Especially not men like Maguire.

But she wasn't going to flinch. "A man of action," she said coolly. "Not a man of words."

His laugh was short, abrupt. "Now, that's where you couldn't be more wrong, Mrs. Pompasse. I'm very much a man of words."

"Don't call me that," she said.

"Bothers you, does it? You call me Maguire, I'll call you Charlie. When's the funeral?"

"We already had one service in New York, and I believe there was one in Florence and Paris as well. We'll be having a simple committal service here on Saturday."

"He's not buried yet?"

"His ashes will be buried in the vineyard as he requested," she said stiffly.

"I thought the old man was Catholic. No cremation, no unsanctified ground."

"You're Catholic, Maguire? Somehow that surprises me."

"I'm about as lapsed as you can be, lady."

"So was Pompasse. If his life hasn't condemned him to an eternity in hell then I doubt simply being buried the wrong way will do it. At least, not in my beliefs." Again, she'd said too much to a stranger.

But he simply nodded, seemingly unsurprised. "I'll tell you what. I'll try to have the inventory done by Saturday. That way I'll leave right after the committal service and you won't have to put up with me anymore. Of course, then you'll be dealing with the tax people and you might end up thinking I wasn't so bad, after all."

"Saturday?" she echoed. "I'm expecting a full house by then. My mother, my fiancé..." The words trailed off before his implacable gaze. He really was the most annoying man, Charlie thought, and that was saying a lot, considering she'd lived with Pompasse for eight years. And she couldn't get over the irrational feeling she'd seen him before.

"If things get too crowded I can always camp

out in the studio. Or the ruins of the old church. I'm an amenable guy.''

Charlie resisted the impulse to snort. ''The studio is too crowded...''

''The studio is empty, lady. Haven't you seen it? I can just drag a mattress in there and be fine.''

She stared at him, knowing she should say something. Anything. But she couldn't. The studio was more than just the room where Pompasse had worked—it was the heart of the house.

''It can't be,'' she said in disbelief. Suddenly Maguire was no more than a perplexing annoyance in the whole scheme of things. If the studio was empty then something was definitely very wrong at La Colombala, more than just the loss of its owner. ''Ex-excuse me,'' she stammered. ''I have to go.''

And she left him without another word, heading straight for Pompasse's deserted studio.

4

Charlie moved by instinct, avoiding the center of the house as she headed straight for Pompasse's old studio. She half expected the French doors to be locked, but they opened easily enough, letting light and Charlie into the gloomy interior.

Dust motes sparkled in the shaft of sunlight that lit the huge room, and the smell of turpentine and paint flooded her with memories. But it was overlaid with something else, something disturbing, and it took her a moment to recognize it.

It was the smell of neglect. Cobwebs stretched across the inside shutters, dust was thick on the floor, and she could smell the unmistakable odor of a resurgent mouse population. Even the cats hadn't been allowed into the atelier. Which meant that Pompasse hadn't worked in a long, long time.

Maguire had been right, though she hadn't really doubted him. There were no canvases in the room. No sign of his art at all. He'd had periods of inactivity in the past, but never long enough to allow his studio to deteriorate into this. And where were his current paintings?

He must have been working elsewhere. Astonishing as that notion might be, he had to have found another place to paint. Pompasse had lived at La Colombala for the past thirty years, and he'd always insisted that nowhere else had the same perfect light. But the idea of him not working at all was even more preposterous.

She moved to one window, about to push open the shutter, when the room suddenly darkened as something filled the doorway, blocking out the sunlight. "What are you doing here?" a voice demanded in Italian.

It was a young voice, full of shaky bravado, and Charlie pulled open the shutters, letting the light stream into the abandoned workroom before turning to face her questioner. It had been a rough day already, and she wasn't really in the mood for another confrontation.

"Hi, Gia," she said pleasantly enough. She didn't make the mistake of crossing the room and pulling the girl's slight figure into her arms in comfort. Giavianna Schiavone wouldn't accept comfort from the likes of Charlie—she'd always been too jealous.

Gia Schiavone was a slender, olive-skinned Modigliani sort of girl—with huge dark eyes and all the dubious wisdom of her twenty-some years heavy on her face. She had taken Charlie's place as Pompasse's model when she was fourteen, and taken her place as Pompasse's lover when she was seventeen. Pompasse had always been fond of seventeen-year-olds, Charlie thought grimly. When she'd last seen Gia she'd been rebellious, devoted to Pompasse and utterly without humor. It still astonished Charlie that Pompasse could have painted such a shuttered, brooding soul in the translucent Tuscany light.

As expected, Gia made no move toward her. She'd never disguised the fact that she despised Charlie, and Pompasse had actually encouraged her animosity. It suited his vanity to think that women fought over him, and it didn't make any difference that Charlie had conceded the battle long ago.

"What are you doing here?" Gia demanded.

She'd lost that dewy-eyed innocence, Charlie thought critically. But then, Pompasse stripped the innocence off most people.

"I thought you knew I was coming," she replied. "I'm the executor of Pompasse's will. I'm supposed to oversee the disposal of his things…."

"He didn't leave you anything!" Gia cried. "He told me he didn't. He said you abandoned him, and you would have nothing."

"It doesn't really matter," Charlie said in a

soothing voice. "I'm just here to meet with the lawyers and insurance people and make sure things are in good hands. I owe Pompasse that much."

"You owe him more than that. You owe him everything," Gia said wildly.

Charlie had never particularly liked Gia, though she'd always felt sorry for her. It had been overwhelming enough for Charlie, falling under Pompasse's spell when she was seventeen. Gia had been only fourteen—she'd never stood a chance.

"We'll get everything sorted out quickly," she said. "I can't stay away from my restaurant for too long, anyway, but I promised I'd see things settled...."

"He gave you that restaurant," Gia taunted her.

In fact, he hadn't. She'd bought it with the remnants of her inheritance from her father once she'd managed to break free from Pompasse's controlling spell, but she didn't feel the need to defend herself with Gia.

Instead she moved to the next flank of shutters and opened them, letting the midday light stream into the deserted room. She'd have someone sweep out the place, or maybe she'd do it herself. She couldn't stand to see it so dusty and abandoned. "How is Madame Antonella? I haven't seen her yet."

Gia was obviously torn between the need to gossip and her desire to stay aloof and disapproving. "She's still alive. She's senile—doesn't recognize anyone nowadays, but she's comfortable enough in her little cottage."

"That's good to hear. I'll have to go pay her a visit."

"She won't want to see you," Gia snapped. "Emmanuelle was here but she left, which is just as well. I doubt you'd get along with her, either." If Gia's voice had been hostile before, it was now filled with pain.

"You'd be surprised how easily I get along with most people. Who's Emmanuelle?"

"Pompasse's new model."

"I see," Charlie said gently. So Gia had already been replaced. No wonder she was in such a torrent of pain. It should have come as no surprise—Pompasse never stayed with one woman for long, though he never abandoned the others.

Antonella had been his first model, an early mistress, and she'd held a place of honor in his life and his household, even though she held no place in his bed. She had been a few years older than Pompasse, and now she was lost in the vagueness of the past, victim of the early stages of senility.

Lauretta was a remnant from one of his middle periods, and she had run his household ever since. There had been others, of course, young women, old women, fat women, skinny women, who'd come and go; he'd sleep with them, but never paint them. Most of the ones he'd painted, he'd kept, unless they slipped away in the middle of the night without a word.

Except for Charlie. She'd escaped, the first and last ever to simply walk out on him. She now had a life of her own, a man who was devoted to her, and Pompasse couldn't touch her from beyond the grave. Couldn't hold on to her, the way he was obviously still holding on to Gia.

She looked into Gia's narrow, bitter face, and she didn't know what to say. Had Pompasse provided for his women, his castoffs? Surely he must have. Gia had turned her back on her disapproving family, with no assets but her beautiful, mournful face.

Charlie suppressed a sigh. It had been hard enough to break free from the old man—now she had suddenly become responsible for the others, as well.

The sooner she saw the will, the better.

"I met Maguire," she said. "He's the one who told me the studio was empty. Where has Pompasse been working? There's nothing here."

"You'll have to ask Lauretta. For all I know he may have burned his current work."

"Burned it?" Charlie echoed, horrified.

Gia shrugged. "He had the wrong model. That little girl could never inspire an artist like Pompasse. He was a fool to think she could."

So Pompasse had moved on to another teenager, Charlie thought. No wonder Gia was so bitter. It was hard to be considered too old at her young age.

"I'll go find Lauretta," Charlie said.

"Fine," Gia said with a toss of her head. "We'll make a pact—you keep out of my way and I'll keep out of yours." And she stalked from the deserted studio, impressive and indignant.

Charlie suppressed an irritated sigh. So this was Pompasse's ultimate revenge. She may have escaped, but he'd left her his damaged castoffs. It was going to be a horrendous few weeks getting things settled.

She moved toward the door, and the soft light washed over her. She could smell the pine resin and the wild rosemary, the tang of the lemon trees. No, *horrendous* was not the right word. A week or so at La Colombala was worth dealing with Gia and the insurance adjuster and dotty old Madame Antonella. She would take her joy from the place, do her duty, and then turn her back on it once more, closing that chapter in her life for good. Gia's hostility would only make things easier.

She glanced over at the vineyard. There was no

sign of Maguire's rumpled figure, and she breathed a small sigh of relief. He made her nervous, though for the life of her she couldn't figure out why.

Once Henry was there she'd feel safer. Why she would think a man like Maguire would be any kind of threat was something she didn't want to consider.

At least Lauretta and Tomaso were happy to see her. The plump, middle-aged housekeeper greeted her like the prodigal son, with tears and cries of joy and so many hugs and kisses that Charlie felt winded, while her husband Tomaso beamed with pleasure. She dutifully plowed through half the wonderful food Lauretta placed in front of her, drank the strong, bitter coffee and laughed about the past. There was no mention of the present—the shadow of Pompasse loomed over all of them, and it was too soon to speak of it.

"I was going to put you in the master's room," Lauretta said apologetically, leading the way up the narrow stone stairs. "No one's used it in a long time, and of course I kept it clean, but I decided you'd be happier in your old room." She pushed the door open. "It seemed best."

Charlie froze, not making any effort to enter the room. "It's still the same," she said in a hollow voice. Except for her suitcase which Tomaso had already carried up for her.

"The master would never let anyone else use it. That Gia wanted to move in, but he wouldn't let her. Everything is just as you left it, though of course it's been dusted every other day. All your clothes are still in the closet, all your jewelry is in the jewelry box. Your makeup and perfume were too old, so Pompasse had me buy new ones every year, to keep them fresh. He also had me keep fresh flowers in here. Wildflowers in the summer, as you liked them. Yellow hothouse roses in the winter. He said he wanted it to be welcoming when you came back home."

Charlie stared at her in bewilderment. "I had left him, Lauretta. I'd filed for divorce. Surely he knew I wasn't coming back?"

"He always hoped," Lauretta said calmly. There was no censure in her voice, no judgment. She had spent her life serving Pompasse, could imagine no reason not to, but she'd served Charlie in her own right, as well. She had lent Charlie her own money to make her escape that night seven years ago.

Charlie walked into her old room, trying to shake off the peculiar sense of foreboding. It was like stepping back into her past, back into the old emotions. Fear, anger, resentment, all the feelings she'd pushed away from her were back in force, overlaid by guilt at the sight of the wildflowers blooming cheerfully in the terra-cotta vase.

She moved to the window, looking out over the view she had loved so much. The windows were spotless, and she pushed them open to stare at the rolling countryside and the tangled gardens just beneath her. That was another thing Pompasse had let slide. While her room had been kept as a shrine, the precious formal gardens had been allowed to turn into a jungle. No more neat, weed-free rows pruned into submission—they were wild and uncontrolled. And for some reason Charlie liked them better that way.

She could still see Maguire out there, moving through the tangle. "For an insurance adjuster he certainly doesn't seem that interested in work," she muttered.

Lauretta leaned past to look out into the garden. "You met him already? He's been working very hard searching for those old books and paintings, *signora*. Going through papers and notes and things since he arrived. He showed up yesterday afternoon and I put him in Pompasse's room. It was the only one that was ready, but I'll move him if you wish."

"I'm surprised no one told us he was coming," Charlie said. The villa was large and rambling, but not limitless. And she'd been planning to put

Henry in Pompasse's room when he arrived. She knew it would please him, and she needed his presence nearby. "I suppose we can move him later if we have to. Tell me, how is the old church? Has it fallen in completely?"

"It's falling in, as it has always been," Lauretta said genially. "Things don't change much around here."

"You're right, of course," Charlie said. "It just seems like centuries since I've been back, and yet nothing has really changed. Everyone's still here— Madame Antonella, Gia, you and Tomaso."

"Not everyone, Signora Charlie. Pompasse is gone."

"Yes," Charlie said, knowing she should weep. Knowing that Lauretta would clasp her to her massive bosom and comfort her. But also knowing she just couldn't do it. She'd shed her tears for Pompasse in New York. Back in Tuscany, she remembered the bad parts all too well.

She glanced back at her bed. She was jet-lagged, exhausted, and a midday nap would have done wonders. But the thick damask coverlet was the same one she'd slept under. The same one under which she'd accepted Pompasse's straining flesh. She wasn't going to lie down on it if she could help it. "I think I'll just strip the bed and then take a little nap. Those coverings are too heavy for me—I like something a little lighter. Surely there must be a duvet in the place.''

Lauretta didn't blink. "Of course, *cara*. I was planning roasted chicken for dinner, but if you have any other preference...?''

"No, that's fine," she said absently. "My fiancé will be coming in a couple of days, as well as my mother. I hope that won't be too great an inconvenience?''

"It's what I'm here for, Signora Charlie. Will your fiancé be sharing your room?''

"No," Charlie said flatly. She was half tempted to launch into a dozen explanations, of how she and Henry had chosen to wait, how it might be disrespectful to Pompasse's memory, how she liked her personal space. She resisted her need to explain.

Lauretta simply nodded, accepting the answer. "Would you like me to strip the bed for you, Signora Charlie? I'll be happy to.''

"That's all right, Lauretta. It's easy enough for me to do. Do you want any help in the kitchen? I still love to cook, you know. I even have my own restaurant in New York.''

"I know," Lauretta said, beaming proudly. "But today is your first day back at home, and you need to rest. Tomaso and I will cook dinner, and all you will have to do is enjoy.''

Looking at Maguire and Gia across the table, no doubt, Charlie thought. It wasn't an appetizing thought, but she smiled at Lauretta, anyway. *"Grazie,"* she murmured.

"Have a good rest, *cara.* Sweet dreams."

Charlie looked at the bed. For some reason nightmares seemed more likely in a massive old bed that held so many memories.

But she was back, and Pompasse was gone. There would be no one left who could hurt her, not anymore. All she needed was a little nap and then she could deal with anything, including Pompasse's angry women and the annoying Maguire.

Anything at all.

5

So that was Madame Pompasse up close, Maguire thought, watching her race out of the vineyard as if the hounds of hell were after her. She wasn't what he'd expected—he thought she'd be prettier. She was too tall, too thin for his tastes. Years of living in Italy had made him appreciate buxom women, and Charlie Thomas Pompasse was built like a model. She needed to be fattened up.

Her face was narrow, angular, with those strange golden eyes that had been so luminous in Pompasse's paintings. They were less vulnerable now, more guarded, and the tawny hair had been pulled back from her face in a sleek chignon. She looked like what she was—the wealthy widow of a world-famous artist.

For some reason he thought she'd be different face-to-face. When he'd looked at her from across the crowded church he'd felt an odd connection. Even attraction. He reached in his jacket and pulled out the mangled postcard. He couldn't figure out why he was carrying it with him—it wasn't his

style to be impulsive or sentimental. But the re-
production of the portrait fascinated him. He'd
done a blitz of research before showing up at the
villa, and *Charlie When She Left* was legendary.
He stared down into Charlie's lost golden eyes, so
different from the cool gaze he'd just looked into.
And then he shoved the postcard back into his
pocket, crumpling it further.

He'd had a busy few days. First the rushed trip
to New York, then a flurry of last-minute research
when he'd gotten back. For once Gregory had
come through with a decent amount of information, including a packet of postcards with Pompasse's work on them dating back to his early years
in Paris. Including three postcards featuring the
most well-known portraits from Pompasse's Gold
Period.

Two of which were hanging in Pompasse's
apartment. One he'd never seen before, and he'd
been half tempted to crumple up the shiny print
and toss it. He stopped himself, staring down at the
tiny rectangle of glossy color.

Mrs. Pompasse again, older this time. She was
wearing some sort of ratty sweater, though he suspected Pompasse had dressed her in designer
clothes, and her luminous golden eyes were no
longer innocent. Still wary, but by the time this
portrait was painted she had known what to be

wary of. There was a "to hell with you" twist to her soft mouth, a firmness to her jaw that hadn't been there before. But he could still see the warmth in her shadowed eyes.

He turned it over to read the back. *Charlie When She Left* was the name of the painting, and it was quite recent. Only five years old. And according to Maguire's expert sources, everything since then had been garbage.

Had the old man just let her go, or had he tried to get her back? Maybe he had hoped Gia would provide a suitable distraction and he wouldn't miss Charlie. If so, it hadn't worked. The last Maguire had heard, Pompasse had moved on to someone even younger, more innocent.

Charlie's eyes still haunted him. The real ones, with their defenses in place. He wanted to spark some kind of emotion, and he'd been as obnoxious as he could be when she'd found him in the vineyard. Well, maybe he was capable of being even more obnoxious, but it would have been a stretch. She was the most self-contained ice princess he'd ever met, an anathema to him. She should have been a Nordic blonde, not a tawny cat.

He could exert considerable charm when he chose to, but he'd known instinctively that someone like Charlie would be immune to something as facile as charm. He wouldn't be able to lie and flirt and flatter his way into her confidence—she was too well guarded. The best angle of attack was to act as if he didn't give a shit.

He would have to walk a fine line if he was going to carry off his impersonation. He knew as well as anyone that he wasn't the typical insurance type, and he had to remember to tone down his natural instincts just enough to keep her from throwing him off the property.

But he still wanted, needed, to keep her off guard. She was a strong woman, a survivor—he could tell by the way she carried herself, by the determination in her generous mouth. She had all her defenses and boundaries in place, and it was going to require a concerted effort on his part to break past them.

He hadn't even been able to annoy her, though for some contrary reason he'd done his best. He'd annoy the hell out of her once she found out why he was really here. Of course, he expected to be long gone by then, so he wouldn't have the pleasure of watching Madame Pompasse explode. He'd have to settle for his imagination.

Maguire stripped off his jacket and tossed it over his shoulder. It was October, for Christ's sake. Why the hell was it so goddamn hot?

And why was he feeling guilty? Mrs. Pompasse could take care of herself—beneath that cool exterior he suspected that she was as tough as nails. But he'd looked into her remote golden eyes and suddenly felt like a piece of dog shit, forcing his way in here under false pretenses, lying, as he always lied. He'd looked at her and had wanted to tell her he was sorry. Tell her he wouldn't use the dirt he'd been amassing so steadily. He'd wanted to...

He wasn't going to think about the crazy things he suddenly wanted to do with the ice princess. He was staying put. No way would he miss the story of his lifetime. No way. Gregory would kill him. His old pal Molly would rise up in her grave and kick his sorry butt. He'd spent ten years moving from war zone to war zone, cataloging horrors and tragedy and disaster and the deaths of innocents. And then he'd turned his back on it, burned out so profoundly that he wasn't sure he could even keep living. When what little money he'd saved had run out he'd hooked up with the first dirty job he could find, one that happened to be for Marc Gregory's sleazy tabloid.

Dealing with the lives and deaths of the selfish rich was a walk in the park compared to the horrors of war, and he intended to use everything he could find and then get the hell out. Gregory had promised him the moon and more, and if there was one thing Gregory was willing to pay for, it was sleaze.

He could see a book, excerpts in tabloids all over the world. He could see a bloody fortune coming his way.

And he told himself he didn't give a rat's ass if the way to riches was strewn with the bodies of Pompasse's castoffs. Including the self-controlled, luminous widow who for some goddamned reason he wanted to touch.

He started back toward the house, taking his time. He had the perfect excuse for ferreting around the place. There were valuable paintings missing, as well as important records, and as a so-called insurance consultant it was his duty to find out what had happened to them. He already had a pretty clear sense of Pompasse's financial picture, and it wasn't good. The widow was going to be damned unhappy when she discovered what kind of mess the old man had left her. Too damned bad he wasn't going to be around to comfort her in her distress.

But then, she'd have her fiancé. He didn't know why that annoyed the hell out of him, but it did. She'd left Pompasse years ago—a woman like that wouldn't be long without a man to look out for her. He wondered what kind of man she'd chosen this time. A Euro-stud with rippling pecs and not much brainpower? A New York stockbroker dressed in Armani who'd made his first million by age thirty?

He was betting on the stockbroker. Someone young and ruthless, as Pompasse had been old and ruthless. A worthy adversary for someone like Maguire.

Though there was no damned reason why he'd have anything to do with Charlie's fiancé. Charlie's intended wouldn't have had anything to do with Pompasse.

Maguire reached in his pocket for his cigarettes, only to come up with a crumpled, empty packet, and he began to curse with the fluid invective he'd learned on a thousand battlefields. The only one who could swear better than he could was Molly, his old photographer, and she was dead. She'd laugh if she saw the mess he'd gotten himself into, and a reluctant, wry smile curved his mouth.

It was a helluva time to give up cigarettes, right when he was in the middle of the story of his lifetime. He'd already given up drinking a couple of years ago, finding he couldn't control it. It wasn't fair that he had to fight still another addiction. On top of that, now he had Charlie Thomas floating in his subconscious, getting on his nerves as well. It was going to be one god-awful week.

He should be used to it by now. The best stories never came easy, and he ought to count his bless-

ings. He was living, if not in the lap of luxury, at
least in beautiful surroundings. Lauretta was a
good cook, Tuscany was gorgeous, and something
was making him feel more alive than he'd felt in
years.

It was the promise of a good story, he told himself. It was the thought of all the money he'd make
from it, after too many lean years.

And it was the challenge, the temptation of
Charlie Thomas, shut off from everyone and everything. She held secrets even he couldn't begin
to guess at. Hell, he'd slept with women before for
the sake of a story. Women liked to talk when they
were in a postcoital daze, and he was very good at
getting them into that place. With any luck, all he
had to do was fuck Charlie's brains out and she'd
tell him everything she knew about Pompasse.

He could do it. He could rise to the occasion,
he thought with a wry smile, and enjoy seeing if
he could make the ice princess scream.

Hell, he ought to sleep with all Pompasse's castoffs if he were going to be really thorough, though
he drew the line at senile Madame Antonella. And
he could probably get just as much information out
of Lauretta if he simply complimented her cooking. That way he wouldn't have to risk Tomaso's
ire.

He didn't want to sleep with Gia, either. She'd

already dismissed him as not being worth her time, but it wouldn't take much to convince her otherwise. She was young and healthy, and it would be a piece of cake to appeal to her animal nature.

But the problem was, she didn't appeal to his. And he doubted she'd know much, either—like most beautiful young women she was completely self-absorbed. Probably anything she knew about Pompasse would have only been in relation to herself.

And he doubted that she'd blurt out that she'd killed him when she came.

No, he had other ways of pumping Gia than the old-fashioned way. He didn't think she was the one who killed Pompasse, but she might very well know who did. Or at least know something that could lead him to the killer, assuming one existed. He still had no proof other than his own sure instincts. It would be a damned shame if it were an accident, after all. Nothing sold books so well as murder.

He'd work on Gia if he had to, and even sleep with her if it was necessary.

But in the meantime he was more interested in seeing what he could get from the widow.

He skirted the building, moving around back to the narrow path leading up to the abandoned church. He could hear voices from the studio, women's voices, and he leaned against the back of the building, well hidden, trying to make out their words. It was too good a chance to miss. He recognized Gia's strident tones even through the thick stone walls, and the soft responses could only belong to Charlie.

But a moment later he heard the slamming of the studio door, and then nothing but silence. A missed chance, but there would be others. It was Wednesday—by Saturday Pompasse's ashes would be buried and Maguire would be out of there. Much longer and he'd be caught, and Charlie Thomas wouldn't be the sort to take kindly to a viper in her midst.

If he couldn't find out who killed Pompasse and why in the next four days, then he wasn't the reporter he thought he was.

And he had no illusions. He was a ruthless bastard, a heartless user when it came to people. He cared about no one and nothing, but he was a damned good reporter, whether it was dealing with international conflicts or Euro-trash. He already knew a great many of Pompasse's dirty little secrets, his obsession with young girls, the disturbing number of suicides and disappearances among his former models and lovers, the games he'd played and the astonishing amount of money he'd squandered.

But he still didn't know where the missing paintings were. And of equal importance, who killed Pompasse and why. Once he discovered the answers he could leave, with or without nailing the repressed Charlie Thomas.

Hell, maybe she wasn't repressed, he thought, climbing up the narrow, twisting path by the olive grove. Maybe she just hated him at first sight and didn't mind showing it. He was used to rubbing women the wrong way when they first met. He was hardly the lady's type—he was brash, working-class, no-bullshit and no-charm. She probably saw him as some kind of lower-class oaf.

And he saw her as the lady of the manor. Just the sort of thing to incite his distrust of class issues. He wondered whether her old man had given her a good time in that bed upstairs. Or whether her new one did.

He knew he could. She'd tell him about Pompasse, once he had her underneath him. She'd tell him anything he wanted to know. She was that kind of woman—she held everything in reserve, wary, protected, until she finally gave in. And then she'd give it all.

And he would be a right bastard to take it. But take it he would, before she even realized what she'd lost.

It wasn't the first time he'd climbed up the hillside to the ruins of the old church. Tuscany, and indeed, all of Italy, was littered with churches, from huge cathedrals to tiny little wayside chapels. The chapel had served the farmhouse that was now La Colombala, as well as the surrounding countryside, but World War Two bombing had put an end to most of the building, including a good portion of the roof and two of the walls. There were still remnants of the place left—some underground storerooms, a couple of hallways, and half the sanctuary sheltered under the remains of the old roofing, while the rest of the building was open to the stars.

He liked the place, particularly at night. For a lapsed Catholic he had a curiously sentimental attachment to the ruins, and it had nothing to do with the strict Jesuit education he'd had in Australia.

No, stretched out on the remnants of a battered old pew that had somehow survived the bombing, Maguire could tilt his head back and look at the stars and remember the lost smell of incense and the lost faith that had once been a false comfort. The car crash that had killed his bickering parents had ended all that, though his kid brother still believed.

Except for his brother, Dan, Maguire had been alone in the world since that day, and the only one who'd ever gotten past his shell was Molly, with her tough talk and her soft heart. She'd been his best friend, his mother, his sister, his lover, until the day he'd seen her blown to pieces by a land mine in Kosovo.

But lying back on the hard wooden pew, he could almost see her up there in the stars. That's where she'd be—not in some traditional heaven wearing white robes and playing a harp. For one thing, the lady was tone deaf. For another, she didn't believe in that sentimental crap.

No, she'd be up there in the stars, looking down at him, telling him what an asshole he was for being sentimental about her. Telling him what a bastard he was for even thinking about using someone like Charlie Thomas. Telling him to stop wasting his life with trashy tabloids and get back to work on a real paper.

He wouldn't listen, of course, but then, she'd been used to that in life. It wouldn't come as any surprise in death. But she'd still be watching, nagging at his conscience. And maybe once he managed this final, monumental score, maybe he'd leave Europe, go back home, find himself a small-city newspaper and a plump wife and forget all his demons.

Maybe.

In the meantime he was going to do one more search of the church ruins. There were all sorts of nooks and crannies, hidden places where someone might stash a fortune's worth of paintings. Finding out where those paintings had gone was at least as important as finding out how Pompasse really died. Given the monetary value, it was probably even more important to his pragmatic public.

One thing, though—Maguire needed to concentrate on the task at hand and keep his mind off the widow. There'd be time enough to deal with her.

Even with the heavy damask cover stripped from her bed, the old room still brought Charlie almost suffocating memories. The windows, wide open to the warm autumn air, did nothing to make the room inviting—it felt both cold and claustrophobic.

She swept the makeup and perfume into the trash, not even hesitating, and by accident some of the scent spilled, filling the room with its cloying fragrance. Pompasse had had it blended especially for her on her eighteenth birthday, and it had never suited her. It was too heavy, too sophisticated a scent for the child that Charlie had never really been, and now it was too strong and melodramatic. She put the waste bin in the hall and closed the door, then moved to the window to breathe in the fresh air.

The perfumer who'd made the scent had been

one of Pompasse's lovers, she remembered. A thin, secretive woman who'd watched her out of dark, hungry eyes. Pompasse had insisted she accompany him to Rosa's shop. "How else will she know what will be the right scent for you?" he'd said, and Charlie had already known it was useless to argue. Pompasse had always gotten his own way.

So his former mistress had blended a fragrance for the cherished wife, and Charlie used to dream that Rosa had put poison in it, to eat into her skin and her soul. Not that Rosa would have hesitated, had she had the ability, but she was no medieval poisoner, and the thick scent of her perfume was the only revenge she could take.

Charlie was jet-lagged and worn-out. And she really didn't want to lie down on that bed. It was a huge, carved affair, brought from some *castello* in the north. She pushed against it with all her might, but it wouldn't budge—it might as well have been nailed to the floor.

On impulse she walked through the adjoining bathroom and knocked on the door that had once led to Pompasse's bedroom. It now housed the unsettling Mr. Maguire, but she hadn't heard or seen him come upstairs, and she expected the room was abandoned.

She knocked again, then pushed it open, wondering what she'd do if Maguire were standing there.

The room was deserted. But that wasn't what surprised her. If the studio had been a shock, the bedroom was even more so. It had been stripped of everything—including the paintings that Pompasse had surrounded himself with. His own, of course. Pompasse had firmly believed that no artist even came close to his own talent, and he insisted he found other painters boring.

He'd even done a mural on the far wall, one of delicate charm. It was gone, painted over with a flat white paint, as were all the walls. Pompasse's bed was gone as well, replaced by a utilitarian double bed with plain sheets and blankets. All the antique furniture had vanished, and in its place were cheap IKEA knock-togethers. Pompasse would never have slept in such a place.

But Charlie would. It looked cool and peaceful and entirely new, and she would have given anything to stretch out on that bed and sleep.

But she was no Goldilocks, and Maguire had more of the makings of a Big Bad Wolf than a displaced bear. She could just imagine his reaction if he walked into the bedroom he was occupying to find her asleep in his bed. It would seem like an invitation.

She started to back away when something

caught her eye. The duffel bag under the window was hardly the type of luggage she would have expected an insurance adjuster to use. As a matter of fact, Maguire hadn't seemed like any kind of insurance official she'd ever met. Maybe things were different in Italy, but she didn't think so. Bureaucrats and businessmen were the same the world over, and Maguire didn't strike her as either.

She didn't hesitate, didn't think twice. She went straight to the duffel bag and unzipped it, looking for answers.

She only found more questions. Jeans and T-shirts and denim—not the sort of clothing she connected with business consultants. He wore briefs instead of boxers. Typical. There were a couple of books about Pompasse—that was understandable since he was here to catalog his works. If he could ever find them, of course.

She zipped the bag closed again. It wouldn't do any good to be caught pawing through his belongings. It wasn't as if she really doubted he was who he said he was.

Except that she did. Something about Maguire didn't ring true. He was far too brash, too argumentative, too…earthy to be an expert on artworks and dead men's estates. Henry was much more the type. Maguire should be out doing something physical, not chasing ghosts.

And she was letting her imagination run away with her, seeing conspiracies where none existed. Maguire was an insurance consultant, nothing more, nothing less. Even if he seemed just a bit like a pirate.

He must have set up work somewhere else—there was no sign of a laptop or a briefcase. She'd ask Tomaso—he was probably working in the study. Sometime when it was safe she'd take a little peek at what was on his laptop. Just to reassure herself. After all, she had responsibilities. To the estate, to the women whom Pompasse had left behind. It was her duty to make sure that Maguire was exactly who he said he was.

She rose, casting one last longing glance at the small, pristine bed. If she didn't get at least a short nap she'd fall apart completely. She was going to have to put up with her old bed and its ghostly memories, whether she liked it or not.

She closed Maguire's door and the door to the intervening bathroom, and lay down on the mattress, trying not to think about the other times she'd slept there. Just an hour or two of sleep before dinner, and then she'd be able to face anything. The hostile, defensive Gia. Madame Antonella, if she was well enough to leave her cottage.

And Maguire, who for some inexplicable reason was the greatest threat of all.

6

The room was filled with shadows when Charlie awoke. She'd slept heavily, so heavily she hadn't dreamed, but she was disoriented, suddenly afraid, and she sat up quickly, squinting in the darkness, fighting off the panic.

She was back in Tuscany. But Pompasse was dead—she had still managed to escape him. There was nothing to be afraid of, nothing at all.

Her hair had come loose and it was hanging around her shoulders, her clothes felt too tight, and her stomach was growling. She could smell Lauretta's cooking, snaking up from the kitchen through her open window. With luck she'd missed dinner and Lauretta would feed her in the kitchen. And then she wouldn't have to face everyone all at once.

She needed a shower to wake her up. She climbed off the bed and pushed open the bathroom door, then let out a muffled shriek.

At least he wasn't entirely nude. Maguire stood

there, a towel around his waist, equally surprised to see her.

"There aren't any locks on the door," he said. "You're going to have to learn to knock."

The door opened inward, and for her to grab it and slam it shut again, as she desperately wanted to do, would mean that she had to get closer to him. And that was one thing she wasn't going to risk.

"I can have locks put on," she said in a shaken voice.

He seemed absolutely huge in the small, steam-filled bathroom, and yet she knew that Henry was taller than he was. Maguire was muscular, with broad shoulders, the dark hair on his chest and his stomach arrowing down beneath the towel. How could one man be so unsettling, so…there?

"You look like you've never seen a seminaked man before, princess," he said. "You want me to put more clothes on or less?"

"This isn't going to work," she said abruptly. She was struggling for that center of calm that had served her so well, but in her half-asleep state it seemed to have deserted her.

"What isn't?"

"You'll have to sleep elsewhere. I need that room, and I'm not going to share a bathroom with you."

"Honey, it's Europe. Everyone shares bathrooms. There are only two in this house, and there are too many people. Why do you want my room?"

"Then one of the bathrooms will be for the women and one for the men," she said stubbornly. The steam from the bathroom was wafting out toward her, an unnerving combination of fragrances. Soap and shampoo, though he hadn't bothered to shave.

"How Victorian. I thought Americans were more relaxed about these things. You still haven't told me why you want my room."

"There are too many memories in this one." It was the honest answer, telling him far more than he had any right to know, but she was too shaken to be guarded. Besides, what did it matter what he knew or didn't know? He was just a surprisingly ill-mannered stranger. In a few days he'd be back in his office at some international insurance conglomerate and the twisted history of Aristide Pompasse and his women would be nothing more than a good bar story.

"I'd offer to share mine but the bed's too small," he said.

"Thanks, but I prefer to sleep alone," she said. "We'll find you another place to sleep."

She half expected an argument, but she didn't

get one. He was watching her out of half-closed eyes, a dreamy, speculative expression on his face. He was good-looking, she suddenly realized. In a rough-hewn, craggy sort of way. Most women would find him quite attractive. But then, she wasn't most women. She liked older men, secure, gentle men who never made demands.

"All right," he said finally. "I'm yours to command. And I don't blame you for not wanting to sleep in that room."

She shouldn't have fallen for it, but she did. "Why?"

"According to Lauretta, once you left the old man moved in. He slept in your bed, usually with one of your nightgowns in his arms. Hell, maybe he even wore them."

"You're disgusting."

"Hey, I didn't break the old goat's heart."

"He wasn't an old goat. He was a great artist."

"He liked little girls, love. Calling him an old goat is giving him the benefit of the doubt."

It was like a dash of ice water on a hot day. She opened her mouth to protest, then closed it again. "He slept with my mother," she said abruptly. "She was hardly a little girl."

"Did he? He probably did it just to get back at you."

Why the hell had she told him that? At least he

seemed almost bored by the information, and for some reason she couldn't keep from talking. Maybe it was all that hot, damp flesh filling the doorway. She was babbling to keep her mind off it.

"It was before we...before he painted me."

"Then he slept with her to get to you. Your mother must have loved that once she figured it out."

It hadn't taken Olivia long to realize Pompasse wasn't interested in painting her mature charms—he was mainly focused on her seventeen-year-old daughter. Charlie still didn't like to think about that horror scene in the hotel in Venice, when she told Olivia she was going to marry him.

"My mother was more concerned about me than about her own ego," Charlie said smoothly. It was a good lie, the right lie, and she'd practiced it for the last thirteen years. It was even the same lie Olivia had told her, but Charlie had never been able to believe it.

"Yeah, sure," Maguire said.

"And what the hell business is it of yours? Why am I telling you these things?" She didn't know who she was madder at—Maguire or herself.

His grin was slow, wicked and devastating. She'd never had a good-looking, mostly naked man grin at her, and her stomach knotted. "Maybe I'm just a good listener," he said.

"Could you at least put some clothes on?" she said irritably.

"Sure thing, lady." He reached for the knot of the towel, but she spun around before he could drop it.

"And close the damned door."

"Sure thing," he said again. "Next time knock and you'll preserve your maidenly blushes."

She waited until she heard the door close. Maidenly blushes, my ass, she thought. Just because she didn't like muscle-bound men swaggering around in skimpy towels...

Not that he was actually muscle-bound. He was definitely strong, but not like some of the men she'd seen on the beaches, with their carefully delineated muscles. Maguire just looked like a man who'd done hard, physical labor for a good portion of his life.

She looked back at the bed. Why hadn't Lauretta told her about Pompasse? That he'd ended up crawling into her bed, wrapped in her clothes, mourning her desertion? But then, what good would it have done? She was beyond feeling guilty. Pompasse had been like a huge, devouring spider, and most of the women who'd been caught in his web were still there, numbed, no longer struggling to break free.

At least she had gotten away. Even if she was back now, she was no longer trapped. Pompasse was dead—he couldn't reach out from beyond the grave.

She sank down on the small wooden bench beneath the window, staring at the bed. She couldn't wait until this was finished—until Pompasse's ashes were buried in the gardens of the place he'd loved, until the will was read and the estate settled. If it was like America it would take forever for the financial details to be worked out, but once she could put it in the hands of the lawyers she could forget about it. Go back to Manhattan, to her East Side apartment and her lovely little restaurant. Go back to her safe, secure life where no one could hurt her, no one could break through her iron calm. She'd marry Henry eventually—though she was in no hurry. For now she just needed her safety back. The cocoon of a life she'd built for herself, which Pompasse's death had ripped open once more.

The sharp rap on her bedroom door tore her from her abstraction. "Bathroom's clear, princess. I'm heading downstairs."

She took the fastest shower on record, both because she was afraid he might come back, and because he'd used most of the hot water in the old house's outdated water system. She grabbed the first thing she could find in her suitcase—a pair of jeans and a T-shirt, and leaving her hair hanging wet down her back she raced barefoot down the wide stone stairs in the center of the farmhouse, knowing that if she had hesitated she'd never have left her room.

The main floor of the house consisted of four main rooms—the huge living room, with its massive fireplace, rustic furniture and windows, the formal dining room with a table that could easily seat twenty, the large kitchen and the smaller study. Everyone was gathered in the living room, and when she appeared in the doorway a sudden hush fell over the ill-assorted group.

Maguire was there, of course, watching her. Gia was beside him, dressed in a clingy silk dress that displayed her angular charms. Madame Antonella sat by the empty fireplace, dressed in voluminous black, a lacy shawl around her hunched shoulders, her white hair piled artfully on her head. She gazed up at Charlie with a blank, disapproving gaze.

"Who are you?" she demanded in soft, querulous French. "Are you one of the servants?"

"That's Charlie, *madame*," Lauretta said patiently. "She was the master's wife."

Madame Antonella let out a genteel snort. "At La Colombala we dress for dinner."

Gia's malicious laugh floated over the room.

"Now, Madame Antonella, you know that's not polite," Lauretta said, casting an apologetic glance in Charlie's direction.

"I'm old. I don't have to be polite," Antonella announced smugly.

"You haven't changed, *madame*," Charlie murmured. Thirteen years ago she'd been wary of the old lady, and the last five hadn't improved her manners.

Antonella's eyes were mere slits beneath the crepey wrinkles, but they summed up Charlie with one disparaging glance. "Who are you?"

"It's Charlie," Lauretta said again. "You remember her."

"Don't tell me who I remember! I don't remember a damn thing!" She pushed herself out of her chair, with more strength than Charlie would have suspected. In her youth Antonella Bourget had been a spectacular creature—tall, voluptuous, powerful. Now that power had degenerated into fat as her mind had slipped into forgetfulness, but she was still surprisingly agile. "Young man!" she called out to Maguire. "Come here and take my arm. You're dressed in rags as well, but you may as well prove yourself useful. At least you have better manners than she does."

Under any other circumstances Charlie would

have laughed at the absurdity, but for some reason her sense of humor had fled.

Maguire moved to Antonella's side, proffering his arm, and he gave Charlie an ironic grin. "Cozy little house party, isn't it?" he muttered under his breath.

"What did you say?" Antonella demanded. "I hate it when people talk behind my back."

"No one's talking behind your back, *madame*," Lauretta said calmly, taking her other arm. "I've prepared something lovely for dinner. You know how you love my gnocchi. The best in Tuscany, you've always told me."

Antonella's response was an unimpressed snort. She clung tightly to Maguire's arm as she tottered into the dining room, the rest of the mismatched house party trailing after her. She went straight for the head of the table, but Lauretta caught her arm, pulling her back.

"You sit here, *madame*," she said.

"What do you mean? I always sit at the head! Except when Pompasse is here. Where is he?"

"He's dead, *madame*. You remember. And now Charlie is here. She is the master's wife. She takes precedence."

"Oh, for God's sake, let the old witch sit where she wants," Gia said bitterly.

"Madame should sit at the head…" Charlie began at the same time, but Maguire had already seated the old lady at the foot of the table. He looked up at Charlie and smiled wickedly.

"You're the matriarch now, Mrs. Pompasse," he said. "Might as well enjoy it."

"I don't want…"

"Will you sit down, for Christ's sake!" Gia said, grabbing the chair on Maguire's left. "I'm starving, and we've already spent too long waiting for you."

There was nothing she could do but sit. Madame Antonella sat at the foot of the table, Gia on one side and Maguire on the other. Charlie grabbed the chair and sat.

It had always been Pompasse's chair, huge, oversize like the personality of the man himself. She felt small, trapped, and for a moment she half expected the arms of the chair to wrap around her, holding her prisoner. But of course it was only a chair—there were other things that were keeping her trapped.

The dinner was miserable, despite Lauretta's excellent cooking. The majority of Gia's conversation was directed at an unresponsive Maguire, although occasionally she sent out a barb in Charlie's direction. Madame Antonella said nothing, eating everything in sight and dribbling half the food on her massive, black satin bosom, and

Maguire simply watched them all out of his cool, dark eyes.

It was amazing to Charlie that she could manage to choke down anything.

"This is an inferior wine," Antonella announced at one point after downing her fourth glass. "Where is Pompasse? He never would have allowed such garbage to be served at his table. It's your fault," she said, glaring at Charlie.

Five years ago Charlie might have been tempted to argue—but now she was past the need. "We'll have Tomaso see if there's anything better," she said.

"I like it," Gia pronounced. "Don't you, Maguire?"

Maguire hadn't touched his wine, a detail that hadn't escaped Charlie's attention. In fact, she'd been watching him too much. It was purely for lack of something better to look at. Antonella's table manners were far from appetizing and Gia was too hostile. And the walls were bare.

"Where did the paintings go?" Charlie asked abruptly.

Gia didn't even bother looking around. She had managed to down a fair amount of wine herself and, if anything, her malicious mood had only deepened. "You mean your portraits? They've been gone for a long time. I don't know whether he burned them or sold them, but your glorious face hasn't been seen anywhere around here for the past five years.''

"Burned them?" Charlie echoed, horrified.

"Don't be ridiculous!" Antonella piped up. "He knew the value of his work—he would never have burned anything. And why do you think he would, you stupid little tramp?"

Since that had been Antonella's form of address to every one of Pompasse's models for the past fifty years, Gia didn't bother to take offense. "Because he loved Charlie and she abandoned him, you old bitch," she shot back.

Charlie set her fork down. She'd barely eaten a thing since she'd heard of Pompasse's death, and this kind of atmosphere wasn't doing much for her appetite. "Could we not fight…?" she began in a faint voice.

"Don't be ridiculous. All we ever do is fight in this household," Gia snapped. "That's the way Pompasse wanted it. Or have you forgotten that along with everything else?"

"He wouldn't have burned his paintings, even those of that whore," Antonella said flatly. "Someone must have hidden them."

"And where would that be?" Maguire broke in softly. He'd been watching, listening to the ensuing conversation with all the rapt attention of a gossip-monger.

Madame Antonella shrugged her massive shoulders. ''Ask Pompasse.''

''He's dead, you old witch!'' Gia snapped, her voice ragged.

''Of course he is.'' Antonella's voice was wasp-ish. ''I know that. The question is, who killed him?''

7

The crash that followed the old lady's question couldn't have been timed worse, Maguire thought irritably. One bombshell was perfect—he could have sat there and watched everyone's expression once Antonella had brought up the idea of murder, and within a matter of moments he would have learned a great deal. Maybe even who could have done the deed.

But Lauretta was on her way out to the kitchen, and the plate she was carrying smashed to the floor, drawing everyone's gaze, giving them all a chance to hide their initial reaction. A moment later Tomaso appeared behind her, looking unnaturally disturbed.

Maguire was fast enough, well trained enough to have caught lightning-fast impressions. Gia must have suspected he'd been murdered—she barely blinked when Madame Antonella asked who killed him.

There was no doubt about Lauretta's reaction, of course. Shock and horror made her drop the platter, and she stepped over the cake to Antonella's side, an angry expression on her plain face. "You shouldn't say such things, *madame*," she said fiercely. "Pompasse's death was an accident. Who would want to kill him?"

"Probably everyone who ever met the man," Maguire said, just to see what kind of reaction he would get.

Lauretta turned on him in a fury. "How would you know? You didn't meet him, did you?"

"Never had the pleasure," he said. "If I had, I'd probably be a suspect along with the rest of you." He was doing a piss-poor job of acting like an insurance investigator but he didn't care. He'd be gone before they figured it out, and in the meantime he liked putting the cat among the pigeons.

His pronouncement made up for any lost ground. They all stared at him in shock, even crazy old Antonella.

After a moment Charlie rose. She was pale, visibly shaken. He'd been watching her carefully all through dinner, and she'd barely touched her food. It was no wonder she looked half starved. Give her another twenty pounds or so and she'd be an impressive figure of a woman. Right now she seemed barely female. And yet, female enough to distract him more than he was willing to be distracted.

"I think we've had enough of this conversation," Charlie said in her deceptively calm voice.

Lauretta and Tomaso were already hustling Madame Antonella away from the table, carrying on a muttered, hectoring conversation in colloquial Italian that Maguire couldn't understand a word of, no matter how hard he tried.

"You don't really think he was murdered, do you?" Gia asked him.

"Enough!" Charlie said again, this time sounding a little ragged around the edges, and before he could respond she left the room, closing the French doors behind her as she disappeared into the warm Tuscan night.

He turned to look at Gia. She'd been paying him far more attention tonight than she had previously, and he wondered whether she'd suddenly realized what a handsome, charming bloke he was, or whether Charlie's entrance into the house had anything to do with it. Gia had taken Charlie's place with Pompasse, or at least she'd tried. Maybe she needed to make sure that no man looked at her nemesis while she was around.

Not that Maguire was interested in Gia, with her morosely beautiful face and her skinny little butt. He'd flirt with her a bit, see what kind of information he could pry out of her, but he didn't expect much. Gia Schiavone was too self-centered to notice much outside her own orbit, and if the old man really had been murdered, she wasn't the one who killed him. At least, that's what his instincts told him, and he'd been relying on his instincts for most of his thirty-five years.

But she might know something and not realize it. A little judicious flattery might get him some useful information. Particularly since his time here was limited. Sooner or later, someone was going to figure out that he wasn't who he said he was and he'd be out on his ass. He just had to make sure he had enough for a book before they caught on to him.

Gia could wait. But Charlie was a different matter. She was out alone in the night air, she was exhausted and jet-lagged and upset. In a perfect condition for him to work on. She'd be vulnerable, and no reporter worth his salt would let an opportunity like that slip by.

Not that he considered himself much of a reporter these days. Gossip hound, paparazzo, the epitome of yellow journalism, and proud of it. Charlie Thomas didn't think much of him at this point. By the time she found out who he really was, her contempt would know no bounds.

He could only hope she wasn't the one who'd killed Pompasse. Because by the time he was done with her, he'd give her more than enough motive to kill him as well, and he preferred his mortal enemies to be nonviolent. He didn't want to be next on her list.

It was a beautiful night, one of a thousand beautiful nights in the countryside. He'd gotten to the point where he seldom noticed his surroundings, but tonight it got through to his jaded senses. There was a soft breeze riffling through the olive trees, and in the distance he could hear the baying of a sheepdog. The scents were strong in the air, as well—the fragrance of the grapes and the olives, the fall flowers that lined the stone wall of the terrace. And he could smell Charlie—the fresh scent of some subtle perfume, or maybe it was just her shampoo.

She was over in the corner of the stone terrace, hidden from view by the shrubbery that had been too long between prunings, but he had eyes like a cat, and he started toward her, taking his time, giving her the chance to run if she wanted. Her need to escape would have told him almost as much as he expected to get from talking to her.

But she stayed where she was, watching him. In the darkness he couldn't see her strange-colored eyes, but he had the momentary conceit that they could see in the dark as well as he could, that they could read every expression that crossed his face.

Not that he ever allowed himself a betraying expression. He kept his face bland, polite, as he came up to her, wishing to God he had his cigarettes. He found he wasn't craving the nicotine as much as wanting to have something to do with his hands. Something to keep his hands off her.

She spoke first, which surprised him. "I'd forgotten how hellish those dinners could be," she said with a stray shiver that he knew wasn't caused by the temperature.

"There weren't usually that many people, were there?" he asked. "He wouldn't have had Gia there while you were still married...."

He didn't have to see her ironic expression to know it was there. "Don't be naive, Maguire. Pompasse's affairs were legendary—he always had his women. The ones he slept with, the ones he painted, the ones who'd outlived their usefulness, but he wouldn't let any of them go. And one of his favorite occupations was to set them off against one another. He loved the idea of women fighting over him. It's probably one reason why he kept his castoffs around."

"Nice guy," Maguire said.

Charlie shrugged. "I didn't mind. My infatuation with him died quickly, but I recognized him for what he was."

"And what was that? An egocentric pervert?" Maguire offered.

"A great artist," she said in a calmly reproving voice. "Great artists don't have to be decent human beings, you know. There's a price to be paid for brilliance, and Aristide couldn't be a good man and a great artist."

"That's just so much bullshit and you know it," Maguire said bluntly. "He used his art as an excuse to get his own way, and idiots like you let him get away with it. Would you have sat around and let another man parade his mistresses and castoffs in front of you? Will you let your fiancé do it?"

"Henry would never do anything like that," she protested. "He loves me—he'd never hurt me."

"Lady," Maguire said, "then he's not the man for you. Love is pain. It's betrayal and hurt and passion and joy. What you're talking about is simple affection."

"Then maybe simple affection is highly underrated."

"It doesn't go very far in bed, now, does it?"

She didn't answer him, of course. He was surprised she was making no effort to get away from him. But then, he suspected that she was just the tiniest bit fascinated by him, rather like a doe in the headlights of an oncoming tank. She wasn't going to be too pleased when he flattened her with the great tell-all.

"So what did you think about all that?" he said after a moment, sitting on the stone wall beside her. "You think the old guy was murdered?"

"How would that affect his estate if he was?" she countered.

He was about to say "beats me" when he realized he was supposed to know such things. "Depends on who did it, what the will says, that kind of stuff," he said instead. "I know that in most countries people can't profit by a crime, so if you're his heir and you offed him then you're shit out of luck."

She swung her head around to stare at him. "I didn't kill Pompasse. I hadn't even seen him for years."

"And where were you the day he died?"

"In my apartment. As a matter of fact, I spent last week alone in my apartment, no phone calls, no visitors."

"No alibi?" he said.

"I don't know. Maybe the doorman saw me. Besides, it doesn't matter. It was an accidental death—there hasn't been even a suggestion that it was anything but. Madame Antonella is old and quite…forgetful. It's ridiculous to pay attention to anything she might say. She likes to be outrageous to get attention. She can't even remember that

Pompasse is dead—how would she know he was murdered?''

"Maybe she knows who did it?" he suggested.

"I think we'd be hearing from the police if there was any suspicion surrounding his death."

"You'd think so, wouldn't you," Maguire drawled.

"Anyway, they've released the body and he's already been cremated. If they start thinking that he might have been poisoned or something it's a little too late to check."

"Poison? Interesting thought. It's known as a woman's weapon."

"Don't be sexist, Maguire," she said with a spark of life. "Frankly, when I look at you I tend to think of a gun rather than poison."

He resisted his impulse to smile. He liked it when he could get her to fight back. "Do you know how to use a gun?" he asked.

"As a matter of fact, I do. Pompasse insisted I learn. He said there were too many stalkers, kidnappers and the like who might try to break into the villa. For that matter, what if one of those stalkers or kidnappers killed him? Some random, deranged art collector?"

"Or maybe a deliberate, sane art collector who knew his works would be more valuable once he was dead," Maguire countered. "But I don't think Pompasse was killed by a stranger."

"I don't think Pompasse was killed at all," she shot back.

"You don't think he's dead?"

Her reaction was fascinating. She shivered in the warm summer night. "He's dead," she said in an equally lifeless voice. "I'd know if he wasn't. I just don't think he was murdered."

"Why not? Because it's inconvenient?"

She turned to look at him, and in the shifting moonlight he could see her golden eyes quite clearly. "Because the police haven't indicated they have any suspicions," she said flatly. "And because I don't want it to be true."

He'd pushed her far enough, gotten more honesty out of her than he had expected. But then, that was his stock-in-trade, his ability to make people reveal things they'd never usually tell strangers. "Fair enough," he said. "You look beat. Why don't you go up to bed? You don't need to waste your time worrying about this stuff tonight."

"Damnation!" she said, pushing away from the wall. "I forgot to ask Lauretta to find you another room. It's too late now."

"Not a problem. You can sleep in my bed."

"Maguire..." she said in a warning voice.

"Without me, angel. It's too damned small a

bed, anyway—I like to spread out. You sleep in my room, I'll spend the night in yours with the ghost of Pompasse lurking beneath the sheets. Imagine the old goat's reaction when he finds me there instead of you.''

Her soft laugh was reluctant and oddly stirring. ''I can't...''

''Of course you can. It's your house, at least until the will is read. You're the widow, after all. You can even wedge a chair under the door handle to make sure I don't creep in in the middle of the night. I don't know if it would keep Pompasse's ghost out, but you could probably find garlic in Lauretta's kitchen....''

''That's for vampires, not ghosts,'' she said. ''And Pompasse is dead and gone. He's not coming back to haunt anyone.''

''Not even you, Charlie? The one woman who escaped?''

She turned to look at him, a stricken expression on her face. ''I don't believe in ghosts,'' she said.

''And besides, you never escaped, did you? He still owns you, body and soul. I'm going to be interested in seeing this fiancé of yours. I was figuring he had to be some up-and-coming Wall Street shark, but now I'm thinking you'd probably be looking for another Pompasse. Some randy old

man who'd take care of you. Another father figure.''

"You're disgusting, Maguire.''

"It's one of my many charms. So is he like
Pompasse? Your Henry?''

"Not in the slightest. He's a lawyer, he's well
bred, well behaved, thoughtful, considerate, kind
and restrained.''

"Doesn't do it for you in bed, does he?''

He'd pushed her too far but the temptation was
irresistible. "Go to hell, Maguire.'' Her voice was
fierce. "I don't care how many governments you
work for—I don't have to put up with this.''

"How old is he, sugar? I don't suppose you
stole this one from your mum as well?''

"You can leave, Maguire. Right now.''

"On Saturday. After the committal service. I've
got a job to do and I'm going to do it. Don't mind
me—people say I'm a royal pain in the butt. I
never did learn not to speak my mind.''

"It's never too late to master new skills,'' she
said sharply.

"Tell you what—you can have first crack at the
bathroom while I move my stuff out of the room.
Then you can settle down all safe and sound knowing that no one's going to bother you, either from
this world or the next. Okay?''

She still wanted him gone, he could see that. He

had to remember that there was a limit to how far he could push Charlie Thomas. For all her desire to keep the peace, she wasn't going to let him go too far.

"I don't want you here," she said in a weary voice, knowing it was a losing battle.

He knew she didn't. But she would, sooner or later. He had three days to get her in bed, the one place where she'd have no defenses left at all, the one place where he could find out everything he wanted to know about Pompasse and his strange marriage and his kinky tastes. It was a dirty job but someone had to do it.

"I'm sorry," he said, all false earnestness that she probably didn't believe. "I'll behave myself. I didn't mean to upset you. You go on up, and by the time you're ready for bed the room will be deserted. Unless that room gives you the willies, too? You must have slept there with the old guy as well...."

"It's been changed," she said. "It's all new furniture. And no, he always came to my room. And why the hell am I telling you that?"

"You need a sympathetic ear?" he suggested.

"I need my head examined," she shot back, suddenly fierce. "I want you out of here, Maguire. I want you to spend tomorrow getting your work done. The sooner the estate is cataloged and appraised, the better my peace of mind.''

''I've got to find the paintings and the journals first, love.''

''We'll find them,'' she said grimly. ''I'll help you.'' She turned toward the house, dismissing him.

Before she could see his triumphant grin.

How in God's name was she going to survive the next few days? Charlie thought desperately. Pompasse's harem was bad enough—with Antonella's crazy accusations and Gia's rampant hostility. Throw Maguire on top of that volatile mix and she was ready to run screaming into the night.

Now that she was finally alone Charlie was famished. She found cold chicken and carrots in the huge steel refrigerator that Pompasse had ordered from Rome. The kitchen was deserted, and spotless, of course. Lauretta prided herself on both her cooking talent and her cleanliness, and Charlie had learned everything from her. She sat at the scrubbed table, eating the cold chicken and gnocchi with surprising relish. It seemed like years since she'd been hungry.

Lauretta seemed to have survived Pompasse well enough, Charlie thought, reaching for her glass of wine. Of course, she had Tomaso to help, and she was a practical country woman. Her affair with the great artist had only lasted a year, and while the paintings from that period were considered some of his best early work, she'd gone from being model and lover to housekeeper and cook with no difficulty as far as Charlie could tell. Of course, it had all been way before her time, but Lauretta and Tomaso had served Pompasse long and devotedly, seemingly happy.

There'd been Luisa's disappearance, of course. Their only child had run away when she was sixteen, never to be heard from again, and the shadows of that loss still lingered. Lauretta would never speak of it, or of her child at all, though she had become even more fiercely religious. Tomaso would talk quietly about his lost daughter when his wife was nowhere around, taking comfort in telling Charlie about the young girl who'd run away long before Charlie and her mother had ever come within Pompasse's orbit.

And Madame Antonella was senile, cranky, but hardly ruined. She'd lived her life in comfort, enjoying the respect and awe of the art world and Pompasse's household, and Aristide himself had always made it a duty to have afternoon tea with her when he was in residence.

No, Pompasse wasn't a destroyer, just, as Maguire had said, a selfish man.

She washed her dishes and set them in the wooden drying rack, then headed up to bed. The door to Pompasse's old room stood open when she reached the top of the first flight of stairs. The door to her room was solidly closed.

She approached the open door hesitantly, peeking inside to make sure it was deserted. There was no sign of Maguire, and her suitcase was sitting on the low table. He'd propped a chair under the knob of the adjoining bathroom door.

Smart-ass, she thought to herself, closing the door behind her and surveying the strange, denuded room. She didn't like the idea of him having access to her belongings, but at least she could comfort herself in the knowledge that he'd have no interest in her utilitarian white cotton underwear or anything else. Thank God she hadn't let Lauretta unpack for her. The thought of Maguire's big, strong hands picking up her clothes gave her the shivers.

She undressed, pulled on the cotton nightshirt she slept in and climbed into bed. It wasn't until she was drifting off to sleep, in the strange room, in the strange bed, that she remembered that Maguire had been sleeping there. That she was sleeping in Maguire's bed, between Maguire's sheets.

The chair was still propped under the doorknob,

keeping monsters at bay. It could only keep Maguire out if he tried to come through the bathroom.

But what would keep Aristide's memory from haunting her? Ghosts could wander through walls, invade dreams, torment the living. But she didn't believe in ghosts.

And when she slept, she dreamed of Maguire.

8

Maguire settled down in the big old bed, the Day-Timer in his hand. He'd struck pay dirt, and not where he'd expected it. He'd searched Charlie's suitcase with the care and thoroughness of a professional, coming up with little of interest. She favored jeans and sweaters and T-shirts, though they all had impressive labels. She wasn't sleeping with anyone—the plain white underwear simply solidified his belief that she was either celibate or uninterested. Sex clearly had no part in her life right now.

He'd found her leather-bound Day-Timer and filched it, knowing he'd have to slip it back into her suitcase before she noticed it was gone. It made dry reading. No emotional outbursts—it was a record of her appointments, work schedule and social engagements, mostly with the mysterious Henry. She worked surprisingly hard—she kept meticulous track of the time she put in at the restaurant, both cooking and overseeing the operation. He couldn't imagine a skinny, chilly creature like

Charlie being able to cook. It was too physical an occupation for someone out of touch with her body.

Then again, he couldn't imagine her making love, either. Couldn't imagine her doing anything but sitting behind a desk in her designer sweaters and staring at him out of her exotic eyes.

He was particularly interested in the week of the nineteenth, when Pompasse died. Her schedule was devoid of an alibi—there were no dates, no work, no appointments during the five days surrounding her husband's death. He wondered if anyone had bothered to ask her where she was when the old man bit the big one? He had every intention of doing so when he got the chance.

The rest of the room had proved to hold little of interest, despite the fact that it had been kept like a shrine to Charlie's lost memory—the five-year-old clothes still hung in the closet, the drawers were still full. She used to favor a different sort of underwear, he'd noticed with great interest. Aristide's wife had worn silk and lace, in exotic colors. Aristide's widow wore cotton.

Of even more interest were the paperback romances stuck in the drawer of the bedside table. They were a greater contradiction than the silky underwear. Charlie must have once believed in passion, or at least been vaguely interested.

He turned off the light, sinking down in the bed. He didn't like the idea of Charlie and the old man doing the nasty in this bed, and he couldn't blame her for preferring the other room. He just wished he had a good excuse to join her there.

He was running out of time. It was Wednesday night—he had until Saturday at the latest to find out all the dirt he could dig up on Pompasse, Charlie and the myriad of women who still clustered around the villa. He needed to find what had happened to the lost paintings, and who had murdered the old goat. If he could come up with that information he'd be set for life.

It was possible a real insurance adjuster would appear on the doorstep, in which case he'd just have to get the hell out of there before Charlie went after him with a shovel. He had to admit the thought of seeing her startled out of her unruffled calm, blazing mad, was tempting. But he was counting on the notoriously slow workings of the Italian bureaucracy to keep him safe for a long enough interval. By the time a real insurance adjuster showed up he'd be gone.

Besides, if he had to choose between seeing Charlie lose her self-control and the big bucks that would be coming his way when he finished the book for Gregory, there was no contest.

He didn't need much sleep, and he worked best

in the early hours of the day. He'd catch a few hours, then head down to the study he'd claimed as his work space and get more written. He was a journalist—he could work fast under pressure, and the bigger the delay on this the less valuable it might turn out to be. He wasn't the only tabloid reporter on the trail of this story, though he had the inside track. But in the news and trash business, timing was everything. He needed to capture Charlie on paper, now that he'd met her. He needed to describe her eyes, the long, slender body, the touch-me-not calm to her that needed to be shaken free. He needed to understand both her mysterious strength and her indefinable uncertainty. He needed to capture her in words.

And then maybe she wouldn't haunt him.

Charlie woke early, before anyone else. She showered quickly, half-afraid that Maguire would wander in while she was undressed, but the room beyond the adjoining bathroom door was silent. She thought he would have been the kind of man who snored, but the night had been pleasantly silent.

Even Lauretta and Tomaso were still asleep—a small blessing. She loved them dearly, but she liked to make her own coffee, and Lauretta would want to weep and talk about Pompasse, and at least for one morning Charlie didn't want to talk about her dead husband.

Where the hell had those paintings disappeared to? Had he sold them? He couldn't have—his work was highly valuable for a living artist, and the kind of money they'd bring in would make news. Would he have given them away? Not Pompasse. He reveled in the fame and money—he knew his own worth to the last penny and cherished the power it brought him. He wouldn't have given anything away unless he'd had an ulterior motive.

She had no idea what he'd been painting in the last five years. Probably dour portraits of Gia.

She'd done her best to avoid news of the art world, but there'd been no new records set for a work by a living artist. Not since *Charlie in Her Dressing Gown.*

It should have embarrassed her, but then, Pompasse had painted her in every state of dress and undress. She remembered sitting for the damned thing, out on the terrace with the sunlight caressing her damp skin. He'd seen her coming from the shower and insisted she pose for him when she hadn't posed in months. He wanted her skin and hair wet, the robe falling off her shoulders, exposing her tanned skin. And she'd complied, even to the point of letting him spray her with water when the sun dried her hair and face.

It had been a masterpiece, they said. The skin tones were worthy of a Renaissance master. If it hadn't been for that painting she might never have left him.

But she had been young, and still capable of being childishly flattered by all the attention it got. She'd read the newspapers, the magazines, the fawning praise and learned critique, and she'd preened like a teenager—until she'd read the description in the *Art News of Italy*.

"Much has been made of the glorious use of texture in the model's skin tones, but what truly makes *Charlie in Her Dressing Gown* a masterpiece and Pompasse the foremost living painter is the expression in the model's eyes. Pompasse has captured her doubts, her sexual ambiguity, her desperate attempts at serenity. It has always been said that the eyes are the window to the soul, and the soul Pompasse has captured is empty, helpless, completely dependent on whoever views the painting."

She'd left the next morning.

They all assumed it was because he'd left her bed for Gia's a year earlier. Her mother thought her pride was damaged, Pompasse was certain he'd broken her heart and pleasure warred with panic inside him. He'd been trying to make her jealous for years, and now he thought he had succeeded beyond his wildest dreams.

But Pompasse's infidelities had nothing to do with it. She hadn't cared when he left her bed, she'd been desperately relieved. She hadn't cared when he brought Gia into the household.

His betrayal had been far worse. She kept remembering the old story about primitive people who were afraid of cameras. They thought the photographer stole their souls.

That's what Pompasse had done. Not stolen it, exactly—she'd handed it to him on a silver platter and he paraded his trophy for the world to see. Anyone who looked at that painting would see what a lost, empty shell of a human being she'd become. But far worse was accepting the knowledge herself. That she'd given herself away, till there was nothing but a pretty shell remaining.

So she'd run. It was past time to reclaim her life, her soul, and she'd found them in New York. Nothing on earth could lure her back, not threats, not her mother's constant phone calls, not Pompasse's pathetic suicide attempts. Gia would take good care of him. So would the other women who still surrounded him. She was the one who escaped and she would never go back, even if a part of her soul still remained in Tuscany. The part that Pompasse had stolen from her.

She shook herself, as if to rid herself of the power of memories. That was one painting she never wanted to find. Fortunately, or unfortunately, Pompasse had sold it to a private collector, and she had no idea where it was now. At least it wasn't on view for the world to stare at and judge, though photos of it still cropped up in articles about Pompasse. Some twisted soul could gloat over it in private, and she could forget that lost little girl ever existed.

Even if she knew that she was still hiding, somewhere deep inside her cool defenses.

She liked her coffee strong, black and sweet, and she poured herself a mug, shoving her still damp hair back from her face. One of her favorite things to do at La Colombala was drink coffee on the terrace, but this morning the memories were too strong. She would curl up in one of the huge leather chairs in the study and drink it there, looking out the back windows up toward the ruins of the old church.

She moved silently along the stone floors on bare feet. The door to the study was half closed, and she pushed it open, then paused. She'd forgotten that Maguire had claimed the space for his own. The intruder sat at Pompasse's desk, hunched over a laptop computer, his face intent in the glow from the screen, his fingers flying. He wasn't a touch typist, but he was incredibly fast, which seemed odd to her.

He had headphones on, and the music was so loud she could hear the muffled strains. Rock and roll. Loud, noisy rock and roll as he pounded on the keys of the laptop.

He didn't even notice her, he was so intent on whatever he was typing. She took a sip of her coffee, watching him. He was rumpled, unshaven, totally lost in his work, and he reminded her of someone. It took her a moment to realize who it was. He was young and good-looking in a rough sort of way, she supposed, and Pompasse had been old and elegant. And yet Maguire had something of the same expression Pompasse had had when he was in the midst of painting. Yet insurance reports were a far cry from creativity. How could a man get lost in something so dry?

She pushed away from the door and entered the room, but he was still unaware of her presence. He didn't even realize he was being watched. His attention was elsewhere as he stared intently at the computer screen. She came up behind him.

She saw her name on the screen. Others as well, words that didn't seem to belong in an insurance adjuster's report, but a second later he slammed the lid down on the computer, ripped off the earphones and turned to glare at her.

"What the hell do you think you're doing, sneaking up on me like that?" he demanded.

"Walking through my husband's house," she replied, taking a sip of coffee. "And I made plenty of noise. What is that awful stuff you're listening to?"

"Metallica. I work best listening to heavy metal."

"Writing insurance reports?"

"Something's gotta make them interesting," he replied. "Is there any more of that coffee?"

"In the kitchen. Help yourself." Anyone else, even Gia, and she would have offered to get it for them. But not Maguire. Besides, she wanted to see what he was writing.

He moved back from the table, pushed a button on the portable compact disk player and the noise stopped. "Have a listen if you've a mind to," he said cheerfully, and left the room. Leaving her alone with the computer.

The kitchen was a good ways from the study, but Charlie didn't hesitate. She set her half-empty cup of coffee down and moved behind the desk, lifting the lid of the computer.

Cartoon figures danced across the screen. Wile E. Coyote and the Road Runner in their endless chase. Odd that Maguire would have that as a screen saver, but then, Maguire was a difficult man to figure out.

She pushed a key, but instead of bringing the text back she was rewarded with a blank screen. And a demand for a password.

By the time he returned she was curled up in the leather chair, both hands wrapped around her coffee mug, wishing it were Maguire's neck. He sat back down at the closed computer. "Find out anything interesting?" he asked lazily.

She considered denying everything but Maguire was doing his best to unsettle her, and the least she could do was respond in kind.

"That you like Warner Brothers cartoons and you're paranoid enough to need a password," she said. "I didn't have enough time to get any further."

"You think you can crack my password? I doubt it. I change it every day or so," he said.

"Why?"

"To keep nosy little girls like you out of my business."

"I'm not little, I'm not a girl, and it happens to be my business as well, doesn't it?"

"Honey, you're like Peter Pan. I don't care how old you are, you've never grown up."

She managed a very convincing laugh. "If you

think I'm childish then you haven't been in this household very long.''

''You're not childish. You're a child.''

''Fuck you.'' The words came out totally unexpected, shocking her.

It only seemed to amuse him. ''You ever said that to anyone before?''

''No,'' she admitted.

''You ought to. Starting with me, and going right on down the line to anyone who annoys you. You're someone who hasn't told the world to piss off, and you need to.''

''Thank you for that sensitive analysis of my character,'' she said in an icy voice. ''Anything else you want to add?''

''You make a great cup of coffee.''

''Yes, I do,'' she shot back. ''I'm also an excellent cook.''

''You'll have to convince me on that one.''

''I'm not cooking for you, Maguire. I want to get you out of here as soon as possible.''

''Why? Do I bother you?'' he asked in his soft, rough voice.

They both knew the answer. He bothered the hell out of her, but she wasn't about to admit it. ''I need the space. I'm expecting a full house for the funeral.''

''Then help me find the journals. They'll tell me

what paintings are missing, and they may even reveal what he did with them. The sooner I find them the sooner I'm done.''

''I've got things to do....''

''You want me out of here? I'm not leaving till I catalog everything Pompasse owned. Including his women.''

''He didn't own me, Maguire.''

''Body and soul, babe.''

She stared at him stonily. ''All right,'' she said. ''We'll start in the old church.''

He started to protest, then nodded. ''When?''

She set her empty mug down on the delicate French table that had come from an old château. The table was spindly, just a bit unsteady, and the earthenware mug looked out of place on the intricately painted top. ''There's no time like the present,'' she said. ''If we find them right away you can have them cataloged and be gone by nightfall.''

''Honey, I'm good but I'm not that good,'' he said. ''I like to take my time when it comes to beauty. Give it all the attention it deserves.''

''Is that a sexual innuendo?'' She was getting tired of his double meanings.

''Only if you see it as one, babe. Sex is in the eye of the beholder.''

''Is it?''

He came around the table, moving toward her. He hadn't shaved in several days—obviously he was one of those men who didn't think daily shaving was necessary. Henry didn't even have much of a beard and yet she knew for a fact that he shaved twice a day. He was a very fastidious man.

Maguire probably knew that his stubble only made him more attractive. He leaned over her, and she could see the green in his eyes. Annoying, she thought. She'd always liked green eyes.

"Then you're a blind woman, honey," he said in a soft, seductive voice.

She didn't move, trapped by his voice, his eyes, his body. He was too close, looming over her, and she felt the familiar tendrils of panic start to build inside her. Combined with something else, something odd and clenching that had nothing to do with fear.

"Back off, Maguire," she said in a cool voice.

To her amazement he did. But the wry smile on his face was even more disturbing. "I'm ready if you are, Charlie," he said.

"For what?" she snapped.

"For searching the old chapel. Isn't that what we decided to do?" he asked innocently.

She stood up, but he didn't back away, and she was much too close to him. He was taller than she was, but not by much, and their eyes were almost level. She had to get him the hell out of there, as fast as she could. She had enough stress in her life right now—she didn't need a testosterone-poisoned Australian making her even more unsettled.

"Yes," she said. "And we won't stop until we've found them."

But Maguire only smiled.

9

In centuries past La Colombala had been the center of a thriving little hamlet, complete with its own marketplace and church. But time had eroded the stone buildings. The people had left, for war, for factory work, for more prosperous times. When Pompasse had bought the place in the 1970s he'd had most of the ruined old houses torn down. He'd kept the sturdiest ones, turning one into a cottage for Madame Antonella, another a place for Lauretta and Tomaso. He'd left the church to tumble into disrepair and decay. It amused his artistic, atheistic sensibilities, he often said. He saw it as the forced faith of his childhood tumbling into ruins.

But Charlie had always loved the place. The path that led up to it was steep in places, though there was a more winding way that looked like nothing so much as a goat path. If goats went to mass.

When Charlie was young she would wait until Pompasse was occupied with something before she could escape. Even when he no longer painted her, no longer slept with her, he kept close tabs on her, and it was only on rare, precious occasions that she managed to slip away. Charlie had always hiked the steep trail through the towering cypresses and she would sit beneath the open roof and feel safe, protected.

She never considered how odd that was. In Pompasse's home she was so protected that she was practically smothered. He allowed no one to talk to her, he wanted to know where she was and what she'd been doing, what she was reading, what she was buying, what she was dreaming and what she was thinking. And she'd told him.

Some of it.

The rest she kept for the empty church with the shattered windows letting in the clear Tuscan light.

The early-morning air was cool and damp, and she took Maguire the steep way, hoping his affection for cigarettes would have him wheezing before they were halfway there. He was disgustingly fit, and if she hadn't been so set on ignoring him he would have probably kept up a running conversation.

She hated having to bring him up here. Hated to spoil the ruined sanctity of the place with his annoying presence. But it was a small price to pay to get rid of him. Once they found the journals and the missing paintings, and once he left, then she could reclaim it. At least for the short time she was here.

"What's that over there?" he demanded. He wasn't even panting—he must be in better shape than she'd realized. And then she remembered what he looked like in a towel, and she realized he was in very good shape indeed. And she didn't want to be thinking about that.

Charlie took a surreptitious gulp of air. She'd forgotten how steep it was on this rocky path. She really should have taken him the longer way, but that would have meant more time in his company, and she wanted to avoid that.

She glanced toward the little cottage. "That's where Madame Antonella lives."

"The old bat? How long's she been there?"

"Since Pompasse bought the place. She was his first model, and she never left his side."

"Not many women did," he said. "He must have been quite the stud. Ruined you for other men, did he?"

She turned. The path fell away beneath him, and she could look out over the rich valley. "One push, Maguire, and with luck you'd break your neck."

"Is that how Pompasse was murdered?"

It was like a slap in the face. "He wasn't murdered, Maguire. He fell. Madame Antonella is senile—she doesn't know what she's talking about.''

"She may be senile but she makes sense. Admit it, Charlie. There are too many people who wanted Pompasse dead. Including you.''

"I didn't want him dead. I didn't care. I'd left him. Divorced him, or so I thought.'' The moment the words were out of her mouth she could have bitten her tongue, and of course he was on them immediately.

"So you thought?'' he echoed. "He never signed the papers? Sounds like the Pompasse we all know and love. So he kept you on a string, after all, just like all the others. Now, why doesn't that surprise me?''

"Leave it, Maguire,'' she said wearily. "All that matters is that I thought I was divorced. I hadn't seen him in five years—he was part of my past.''

"Not yet, he isn't. Maybe when you bury his ashes in the vineyard he will be. Or maybe he'll never let you go. You'll be like Madame Antonella, crazy as a loon, wandering around mourning your lost Pompasse.''

"At least you won't be around to witness it,'' she said in her calm voice. "Do you want to keep baiting me or do you want to look for the goddamned paintings?''

He grinned, and she cursed herself for letting

him see that he'd gotten to her. But the fact was, he had. Easily. He knew just what buttons to push to make her say and do things that she was usually too self-contained to do.

"We'll look for the goddamned paintings," he said.

The church hadn't changed much in the last five years. The early-morning sun cast a warm, rosy glow over the pale stone, and it sat there in the tangled underbrush, a simple country chapel with no airs or graces. Farmers and peasants had worshiped there for centuries—the upper classes had driven down into Geppi to attend the huge cathedral. Whenever practicing Catholics had joined their transient household, they, too, would drive down to Geppi, and Lauretta, Tomaso and Madame Antonella never missed Sunday mass.

But this was a different kind of church. One that belonged to the earth, to nature, to the sky pouring in from the open roof, to the smell of leaves and dirt and the warmth of the sun. And Charlie always used to think that if God wanted to hang out anywhere, he'd be close to the earth in a place like this, rather than in the stultified, incense-laden air of Our Lady of Geppi Cathedral.

She paused in the entryway. The wooden doors were long gone, leaving the building open to the elements and whatever wild animals happened to wander by. Maguire was just behind her, not even short of breath, and she realized with a start that she'd never come here with anyone. She'd always been alone.

Just as she would have preferred to be alone now. The church was her secret, sacred spot—she didn't want to be sharing it with the interloper. Particularly one as disturbing to her equilibrium as Maguire was.

Maguire, with his usual sensitivity, simply walked past her into the interior. "Where do you think he might have hidden them?"

She had no choice but to follow. "I didn't say he'd hidden them. He must have had some reason for removing them from the farmhouse, and this is a logical place to have put them."

"I wouldn't think so. It's damp and exposed up here. Not the best place to keep oil paintings. Wouldn't he be more likely to have kept them in the apartment in Florence? Or rented some kind of storage facility?"

"But that would have required getting help, and no one in the household has any idea what happened to the paintings. According to Lauretta, they just seemed to vanish one by one. Pompasse had to carry them someplace, and this is about as far as he could have managed."

"Maybe. Who says Pompasse did it?"

"Because he would have raised holy hell if anyone else had tampered with his precious paintings," she said. "It's only logical."

"Good point. But then, life isn't always logical."

"Tell me about it," she muttered.

The sun was streaming through the open roof, and dust motes danced on the beams of light. Maguire had moved on ahead, and she saw that the hole in the center of the floor had caved in, making passage impossible. Except for the board that someone had placed across it, and Maguire was already navigating it with careless speed. He stopped at the other end, looking at her quizzically. "Are you coming? There's no other way around it."

"What about the back entrance? There used to be a door...."

"I've already poked around here and there's no other way. Just rubble. You've got a choice, lady. Either walk the plank or go back to the farmhouse."

"Walk the plank," she repeated. She looked across the great gaping hole at him. In the sunlight he looked very much like a pirate, with his unshaven face and shaggy hair, his piercing eyes and rumpled clothing. No peg leg or eye patch or parrot on his shoulder, though. Maybe being a pirate was a state of mind.

"Are you afraid of heights?" he taunted her when she still hesitated. "You were scrambling up the hillside like a mountain goat—I wouldn't think a steep drop would make you nervous."

She was tired of arguing with him. She started across the plank, too fast, and it wobbled beneath her. For a moment she froze, terrified, only to have Maguire step onto the end, grab her and haul her to the other side.

He didn't let go of her, not for a moment, and she was still too shaken from the experience to notice that his hands were on her. Touching her. And then she did.

She jerked her face up to his, and then stepped away. He let her go, of course. But she could still feel his hands on her arms. She didn't like to be touched. Not by men like him.

"I assume you've checked this level," she said, refusing to show how shaken she was, "but we may as well go through the rooms again, just to be on the safe side."

"Lead on," he said amiably. "I just hope we don't find anything."

"I thought we wanted to find the paintings? Otherwise why are we here?"

"I do. But not here. It's cold and damp, and God

knows what kind of damage they could have incurred. Pompasse's estate is already looking shaky—if those paintings don't show up then you're going to have a rough time of it. They were some of his most valuable pieces.''

''Do you know which ones are missing?''

''As far as I can tell there are three famous ones that are unaccounted for. *Charlie When She Left*, *Awakening* and *Amber Moon*.''

''Those are all of me,'' she said, uneasy.

''So they are. The question is, are any later ones missing, as well? Lauretta and Tomaso say no, just those three. I'm not convinced.''

''Why would my paintings be the ones that were taken?''

''I can think of a number of reasons. Maybe somebody doesn't like you,'' he suggested cheerfully. ''Or maybe they're worth more than the others. Money talks, you know.''

''I don't like it,'' she said.

''Neither do I. That's a lot of money unaccounted for.''

''Sweet of you to worry. If the paintings are here they wouldn't have been here long enough for them to be destroyed. I'll worry about the estate— your job is simply to detail the assets. Isn't it?'' She kept thinking about that computer screen, with her name on it. Not the widow, not Madame Pompasse or Ms. Thomas. Charlie.

"Sure thing, love," he said.

She turned. "You want to stop calling me that? Love, honey, sweetheart? It's condescending and annoying. You know perfectly well I'm not your love or your sweetheart."

"Maybe it's wishful thinking."

"Yeah, right," she scoffed. "And don't call me lady, either."

"Ah, but there's no doubt that's exactly what you are. An overbred lady faced with a down-and-dirty bloke like me. It obviously drives your fastidious soul crazy."

"I couldn't care less about you!" she snapped.

"Glad to hear it, love."

Charlie turned from him with a suppressed snarl, giving up.

She hadn't really expected to find anything on the first floor—Maguire struck her as a thorough man, and he would have searched the place. Not that he couldn't have missed something, given the rubble of stonework that cluttered the shattered ruins of the building. But he hadn't found the stairs to the lower level, the old catacombs. It was blocked by fallen roof timbers, hidden in the shadows, and he hadn't even realized there was a door there, one of the few still in existence in the old church.

Together they cleared the way, the dust rising around them. The door was stuck, but Maguire used brute force, yanking it open, and another shower of dust covered him. He looked less like a pirate and more like a ghost, and in other circumstances Charlie might have been amused. Not here, not now.

"Watch out for the rats," she said as she started down the dark, winding stairway.

"Don't you think we need an electric torch or something?" he asked, not moving. "It's dark as pitch down there."

"You want to go back and get one? I'm not afraid of the dark, but if you have problems..."

He started after her down the narrow stone stairs, and she let herself grin in the darkness, feeling childishly smug. In the end Maguire was simply a man—easy enough to bait when his pride was involved.

"Your eyes get used to it," she said as she felt her way down the uneven stone stairs. In fact, it was darker than she remembered, and she kept thinking her foot was going to connect with something long and skinny and furry. She couldn't imagine why rats would live in the old church—

there was nothing to eat there, but she knew for a fact that they did.

By the time her foot reached the rough flooring of the bottom level her eyes had begun to adjust. Light filtered through the hole in the floor overhead; beams of light from the warm Tuscan sun that flowed through the nonexistent roof. Originally the area had been a large open space, but now it was filled with rocks and rubble.

"As I remember there are storage rooms all around the sides," she said. "Why don't you go that way and I'll go this way?"

"Because it's too bloody dark to see which way you're pointing," he said. "And I think we ought to stick together. There's a lot of junk around here—you may need my help clearing the way."

"I'm quite strong, Maguire."

"Okay, let's just say I don't trust you. You could find the paintings, tell me there was nothing there, and then once I left you could sell them to private collectors without paying estate tax."

"But then I couldn't get rid of you as quickly. Trust me, Maguire, when you weigh the thought of millions of dollars against getting you out of my hair a couple of days early then it's a small price to pay. Money's overrated."

"You know, I'm touched. I don't know that

anyone's ever found me that annoying. I'm damned near priceless.''

''Damned near,'' Charlie said agreeably. ''There's also the fact that I happen to be an honorable person.''

''Are you?'' He sounded genuinely surprised by the notion.

She glanced back at him, but in the murky shadows she couldn't see his expression. It didn't matter. For some obscure reason he was going out of his way to annoy her. He'd say anything he could to get under her skin.

''You don't like me very much, do you?'' she said, not moving.

''What makes you say that?''

''Oh, I don't know, maybe it's your delightful manners,'' she said. ''Did I do something terrible to you in a former life? Do I remind you of your mother or ex-wife or something?''

''Honey, my mother is the last thing I think about when I look at you,'' he drawled. ''And why do you care what I think about you? Looking for my good opinion, are you?''

He was having a very negative effect on her equilibrium, she thought, trying to stifle the little surge of irritation. She worked hard at being calm, unruffled, and Maguire seemed adept at stripping away her hard-earned serenity.

"Not particularly," she said, making an effort not to grit her teeth. "I just don't like being baited and I wonder why you seem so determined to do it?"

"Partly it's my charming nature," he said genially. "And part of it is simply third-grade dynamics."

"Third-grade dynamics?"

"Remember the little boy who sat behind you in third grade and dipped your pigtails in the ink?"

"I never had pigtails, children haven't used ink in schools in ages, and for that matter I never went to school. I had private tutors. I don't know what you're talking about."

"Private tutors? La-di-da. You have led a charmed life, haven't you?"

"Absolutely peachy," she replied. "Are you going to explain yourself?"

"Nope."

Maguire was wrong about one thing, she thought as she turned from him and picked her way over the rubble to the first storeroom. He'd said everyone who'd ever met Pompasse had reason to kill him. She'd never, in her life, felt even the slightest murderous impulse. Until she'd had to spend time with Connor Maguire.

Fortunately Maguire kept relatively quiet during the next hour, hauling stones and debris out of the way with deceptive ease, following behind her as she made her way systematically through the cells. At one point Pompasse had kept his wine here, but that chamber was equally empty, devoid of even a broken wine rack or an empty bottle. Whatever had been up here was long gone. Including the paintings.

"All right," she said finally. "They're not here. They probably never were."

"What's down that way?" Maguire demanded, gesturing toward a huge pile of wood and rubble.

"If anything's behind there, no one's seen it in years," Charlie said. "It's been that way for as long as I can remember. As a matter of fact, the whole area looks on the verge of collapse. There's no way anyone would be able to get inside there. They must be somewhere else."

"So why did we just spend the last hour grubbing in the dirt looking for them?" Maguire grumbled.

"To be certain. Those are three good-size paintings. They couldn't have just disappeared without anyone noticing. If a delivery truck had carted them away someone would have seen it. They had to have been moved one at a time, which means they couldn't have gone far. This was a logical spot."

"So where do we look next? I'm putting my

money on Madame Antonella. She's so dotty she wouldn't even notice if someone stashed the paintings in her bedroom. Hell, she may have carted them off herself.''

''She's an old woman, Maguire. In her seventies at least.''

''She looks like she's as strong as an ox. Pompasse liked his models big and strapping, didn't he?''

This time she didn't rise to the bait. ''Sometimes,'' she said evenly. ''I'm heading back. I was planning on stopping in to visit Madame Antonella, anyway. I'll take a look around.''

''I'll come with you.''

''I don't think so. You look like you took a bath in flour. Madame Antonella has strict standards. She wouldn't want a gentleman calling on her in your condition.''

''Hell, she should be lucky any man calls at all. And sweetie, I'm no gentleman. I thought you'd figured that much out.''

''I have,'' she said dryly.

By the time they reached the main floor of the church the place was flooded with sunlight. Maguire looked ridiculous—dust everywhere, in his dark hair and his rough clothes. She glanced down at herself and realized she must look equally absurd.

Maguire had already crossed the makeshift bridge, and he turned back to look at her. "You coming?"

She took a deep breath, trying not to look down into the gaping hole beneath. "Give me a minute."

"The longer you hesitate the worse it's going to be," he said, stepping back onto the plank and holding out his hand. "Just do it."

She wasn't sure which was more threatening— the hole beneath her or the strong hand reaching out for her. "There's got to be another way out of here…" she began.

"Quit whining and start moving," Maguire said. "Or I'll come back there and carry you."

That was enough to make her move. She practically sprinted across the narrow plank, but the damned man didn't move, didn't get out of her way. She had no choice but to barrel into him as he pulled her to safety on the other side.

This time he held her, looking at her.

And this time he kissed her. As somehow she knew he would.

10

Charlie wouldn't have thought a kiss would be earth-shattering. But then, she would never have let anyone like Maguire kiss her if she had had half a chance to avoid it.

But she didn't. He wrapped one arm around her waist, pulling her up against his dusty, sweaty body, put a hand behind her head to hold her still and simply kissed her, openmouthed, using his tongue.

She stood frozen in his arms, trapped, unable to move. It felt as if she were still dangling over the precipice, ready to drop into some dark hole of oblivion. He took his time with the kiss, and there was nothing rushed, nothing brutal, nothing emotional. Just a kiss, thorough, territorial, and when he released her he didn't even look shaken.

"Not much experience with men, right?" he drawled.

She went at him like a football player, plowing her shoulder into his stomach. He had a hard stomach, but he wasn't expecting her sudden move, and he fell backward with a grunt of pain as she sprinted over him, down the narrow aisle of the church and out into the overgrown countryside.

She was rubbing at her mouth while she ran, but she couldn't wipe away the taste, the feel of him. Why the hell had he kissed her—he didn't like her, and she despised him. So why had he pulled her up against his body and…

She slid once, going down hard, and she let out a stifled sob that horrified her. She kept going, heading toward Madame Antonella's tiny stone cottage, looking for some kind of safety.

She scrambled up the steps to the terrace. It was deserted—no one to ask unwanted questions. She threw herself into one of the old iron chairs, taking deep, shuddering breaths as she tried to control herself.

She was being ridiculous. Absurd, to react like a hysterical virgin because Maguire had decided, in a moment of complete insanity, to kiss her. She'd been kissed a thousand times, by a thousand men….

Well, no, she hadn't. There had been a few boys before she met Pompasse, but those had been messy, awkward, fumbling occasions, their idea, not hers. Pompasse had never kissed her on the mouth—not even at their wedding. He thought kissing unsanitary and overrated.

And Henry was a cuddler, not a kisser. When they kissed it was closed-mouthed, brief, affectionate. Nothing like Maguire's animal pawing.

It hadn't been animal pawing, she corrected herself, making an effort at fairness. It had just been a kiss, nothing more. Nothing to make such a fuss over. Just part of his strange need to unsettle her, though she couldn't begin to guess why. Third-grade dynamics, he'd said. The only thing she knew about third grade and boys dipping girls' braids in ink pots was that it was an early, fumbling attempt at flirtation.

If that was Maguire's way of flirting then he was doing a piss-poor job of it.

But he wasn't flirting with her. He couldn't be. She'd worked very hard at keeping her defenses about her, and with her hard-won serenity, her height and her cool politeness, she usually managed to keep unwanted men at a safe distance.

And, in fact, they were all unwanted.

It was just a shame she didn't want women, either. She'd grown to adulthood in Pompasse's bohemian household and she had no provincial concerns about sexual preference. It would have made life so much simpler if she preferred women. People would accept her choice and leave her alone.

They usually did, anyway. But not Maguire. He

was like a nasty rash—raw and irritating—under her skin. And she still couldn't figure out why.

"What are you doing here?"

She looked up. Madame Antonella loomed over her, huge in the bright sunlight. She was very tall, and massively built, and despite her age she was surprisingly strong and agile. It was only her mind that was prematurely weak.

"Good morning, *madame,*" Charlie said, starting to rise from her seat politely. Madame Antonella had always expected to be shown the courtesy her age and position deserved, and Charlie had never hesitated. Pompasse had made it clear that Antonella, as his first model, held a place of honor, and Charlie had been dutiful.

She didn't get far this time. Antonella put a strong, gnarled hand in the middle of her chest and shoved her backward into the chair, with such force that the iron legs skittered across the flagstoned terrace.

"Whore," the old lady spat at her. She spoke in the guttural French of her youth, and Charlie could barely understand her. "You think you can get away with it, spreading your legs for everyone, when you didn't even deserve the blessing of…"

"Antonella?" Charlie stammered, trying to move out of her way. "*Madame*…I don't know how I've offended you…."

The iron chair was pushed up against the low stone wall. Behind it, the path fell away steeply, and for the first time Charlie realized what a precarious position she was in. With the demented old lady leaning over her, one more push and she could topple down onto the rocks below, with only the iron chair to cushion her fall.

"Bitch," Antonella spat. "Slut." She put her big hands on Charlie's shoulders, squeezing hard.

"Madame!" The sound of Lauretta's voice was a blessed relief. Antonella's face fell, and she looked like a naughty child caught with matches. She released Charlie, then turned to look at Lauretta.

"She has to be punished," she said plaintively, her aging voice sounding eerily like a child's.

"There's no need to punish Charlie, Madame Antonella," Lauretta said sternly. "She's done nothing wrong."

"Charlie?" the old woman echoed in a puzzled voice. She swung around to look at her. "Is that Charlie?"

For a moment Charlie had been too shocked to move, but she scrambled out of the chair, moving out of Antonella's reach, absently rubbing her shoulders. The old lady's grip had been fearsome.

"Yes, Antonella. It's Charlie. You remember me, don't you?"

The old woman's milky gaze sharpened for a moment behind her thick, distorting glasses, then she nodded. "He married you," she said in a tone of disbelief. "He never married the others."

"He's dead now, *madame,*" Lauretta said soothingly. "He's at peace now."

"But what about the rest of us?" Antonella said bitterly. She tilted her head to stare at Charlie. "So you're Charlie. How very strange. I thought you were dead...." The sentence trailed off.

"You thought I was dead?" Charlie repeated, slightly queasy.

But Madame Antonella didn't answer. She turned and wandered back into the cottage, her tuneless hum floating back to the terrace.

"I'm sorry, Charlie," Lauretta said earnestly. "You aren't hurt, are you? She gets odd ideas at times, thinks someone is going to hurt her. She must have thought you were someone from the past."

"Maybe," Charlie said, rubbing her shoulder. In fact she could have almost kissed the old woman. The pain in her shoulders had obliterated the feel of Maguire on her body. At least temporarily.

She glanced at the low stone wall. "Is she quite safe up here? I didn't realize how steep the slope is. Wouldn't she be better off in the main house?"

"She won't come. Pompasse had tried to get her

to come down in the past, but she barricaded herself in the cottage and refused to come out. He even threatened to put her in a home if she didn't behave herself.''

''And did she?''

Lauretta shrugged. ''When has the old woman ever behaved herself? And she gets worse every year. Pompasse finally gave up arguing. He said if she ended up falling to her death then it would be a fitting end, and we should let her be. I bring her meals when she's too tired to come down to the main house, and I help bathe her when she lets me. Tomaso and I take her to mass and to the doctor's when she needs to go, but otherwise she's happy enough up here in her little house, as she has been for all these years.''

Charlie looked back over the wall, to the steep path below. ''I hate to think of her falling, lying there helpless....''

''We check on her several times a day. She wouldn't be there long. And if she dies that way, so be it. She's an old woman. Death is part of life—you Americans have a hard time realizing it.''

There was no reproof in her gentle voice, but her words still startled Charlie. She wasn't used to thinking of herself as an American, despite her birth, despite the last five years. She and her

mother had always been rootless, wandering, and
Pompasse had considered himself a citizen of the
world, rather than from one country. She must
have unconsciously adopted that notion.

That, and her love of this small piece of land,
which had always felt more like home than any
place in the vast United States did, including her
cozy apartment and her restaurant.

But for some reason it was no longer feeling like
the home it once was.

She wasn't about to argue. Not with Maguire
coming up the path, heading straight toward them.

It was too late to escape—if she took off, he'd
simply catch up with her. The sooner she faced
him the better, to prove how completely unmoved
she was by his kiss. And Lauretta's beaming presence would provide some measure of security.
Though why she should be smiling at Maguire was
beyond Charlie's comprehension.

Charlie sat back down in the iron chair, sliding
away from the wall a little bit, and waited for him.
He was taking his time, looking entirely unruffled.

"Ah, that explains it," Lauretta greeted him ob-
scurely.

"Explains what, *bella?*" he replied, mounting
the stone steps, barely glancing at Charlie. She
wasn't reassured, though. He was as aware of her

as she was of him—he was just playing more games. God, she had to get him out of here!

"Why Signora Charlie is covered with dust. The two of you look like you've taken a bath in plaster. Were you up in the old church?"

"Looking for the missing paintings," Maguire said amiably. "We didn't find a trace of them. And you're certain you have no idea where he took them?"

"I've told you over and over again, Signore Maguire, that I have no idea where they are. Aristide Pompasse was a law unto himself—it wasn't up to me to ask questions."

He looked down at Charlie, a deceptively mild expression on his face. "Did you check the old lady's house?"

She gave him her best stony-faced look. If he was going to ignore the fact that he'd kissed her in the old church then she could ignore it, too. She just had to make sure he never got a chance to do it again.

Not that he'd want to. Not that she could figure out why he wanted to in the first place. And she had more important things to concentrate on than the strange wanderings of the Australian male mind.

"You think the paintings are here?" Lauretta said. "You haven't been inside, then. It's so cluttered you can barely move—you know what old ladies are like. There's no place she could hide them, even if she wanted to.''

"She's right," Charlie said. "I'd forgotten what a pack rat she was.''

"So you're telling me we aren't going to look?'' Maguire growled.

"She just about pushed me off the terrace, thinking I was someone else," Charlie said in a sour voice. "Feel free to risk life and limb searching her place. I think I've had enough for today." She rubbed her aching shoulder.

"Had a rough day, love? Something unsettle your equilibrium?" he asked innocently.

She looked him in the eye quite calmly, as something clicked into place. He hadn't kissed her because he wanted to. He hadn't been overcome by lust or desire or passion or, God knows, affection. It had simply been one more way of baiting her, the most effective way he could find.

"Just a rat in the church," she said. She turned to Lauretta. "Mr. Maguire will be leaving us today. If he needs help with packing—"

"I don't think so, sweetheart," Maguire interrupted her.

"I don't have to put up with you...."

"Yes, you do."

"If Madame Antonella hears you two arguing she'll get upset again, and I'll have a hard time calming her.'' Lauretta's voice was stern. ''You go somewhere else and argue.''

''I'm not going anywhere with him,'' Charlie shot back.

''And I'm going to see if the old lady is hiding the paintings.''

''You are going to go back down to the villa and work out your differences. I don't think you can get rid of him, Signora Charlie, and expect to get the estate settled any time soon. And Signore Maguire, you leave Charlie alone. She's just lost her husband, and this is a hard time for her....''

''She dumped her husband years ago, even if she didn't bother to divorce him,'' Maguire said. ''She doesn't strike me as someone who's particularly brokenhearted.''

''Enough!'' Lauretta said, with even more majesty than Madame Antonella could summon. ''Go back to the villa and behave yourselves.''

Charlie opened her mouth to protest once more, then shut it again as color flooded her face. Lauretta was absolutely right—she was behaving like an adolescent, angry and hostile and defensive. She could blame Maguire all she wanted, but in the end she was the one responsible for her actions and reactions. And from this moment on Maguire was not going to make her jump to his bait.

''You're right, Mama Lauretta,'' she said, using the old term of affection from her youth. ''I'll behave myself. But Mr. Maguire has to find another room—we're expecting more guests.''

"Not to worry, Mrs. Pompasse," he said in that ironic voice that made her want to hit him. "I'm already packed. I'm planning on bedding down in the studio. Tomaso found me an old bed and I'll be perfectly comfortable.''

"No," she said flatly.

"Yes. You can't get rid of me, babe. Not until I'm good and ready to go.''

Charlie looked at Lauretta for help, but there was none. Maybe Henry would figure out a way to dislodge him, but she had no idea when he'd be showing up. Sometime before the service on Saturday, but when was anybody's guess.

"Very well," she said. "In the meantime, keep out of my way.''

"Signora Charlie!" Lauretta said, shocked at her rudeness.

It shocked Charlie herself. She hadn't allowed herself to display open hostility in years. If ever. And yet Maguire seemed to drag forth all sorts of unnerving reactions and emotions she'd thought were long buried. It was an unpleasant reminder that she was still occasionally vulnerable and all too human.

"Sure thing, sweetheart. As soon as I find the paintings. I told you, I don't trust you. If you run across them when I'm not around you might just forget to mention them to me, and therefore to the tax bureau.''

''And I've told you, Maguire, that getting rid of you is worth far more to me than a few million dollars' worth of paintings,'' she said wearily.

''Flatterer. Are we going to force our way into Madame Antonella's house or wait for another time?''

''You'll wait for another time,'' Lauretta informed them. ''She'll go to confession tomorrow—you can look then. Unless, of course, the two of you feel the need to purge your souls of sin.''

''I'm lapsed, *bella*,'' Maguire drawled. ''And it would take years for me to list all my transgressions to the good father. I'll just stay in my sinful state. As for Charlie here, I don't imagine she could drum up even five minutes' worth of misdemeanors.''

''You underestimate the effect you have on me, Maguire,'' she said in a cool voice.

''Turn you on that much, do I? Well, control yourself, babe. We've got more important things to take care of right now than our libidos.''

She stared at him in shock. He was being completely outrageous, with Lauretta as a witness, and he didn't seem to care. ''I'm going to hurt you,'' she said in a dangerous voice.

''No, you're not. Let's go back to the house and...''

"I'm not going anywhere with you."

"Hey, I promise. Hands off." He held out his hands in a gesture of innocent surrender. The hands that had touched her. Held her.

"Go along, Charlie," Lauretta said fondly, totally oblivious to how dangerous Maguire really was. "The *signore* will make sure you don't stumble again. He's all talk, aren't you, *signore?* He flirts with everyone but he doesn't mean a word of it. Just ignore him."

"I'm trying," she muttered.

Maguire, in true gentlemanly fashion, had already started down the narrow path, not even bothering to see whether she was coming. She considered hanging back, waiting on the terrace until he was back at the house, but Madame Antonella was moving around in the cluttered cottage, muttering angrily in a mixture of French and Italian, and in a few moments she was likely to erupt onto the terrace again. And who knew who she'd think Charlie was this time?

"Go with him, Charlie," Lauretta said in a slightly urgent tone. "I'll take care of the old lady. But go now."

And she had no choice but to follow him down the narrow path, as the sound of Antonella's voice trailed after her.

11

One thing was for certain, Maguire thought as he picked his way down the pathway. Charlie Thomas didn't like kissing.

Or maybe it was more obvious than that. Maybe she just didn't like him. But he didn't think that was the problem.

Well, of course she didn't like him—that went without saying. He'd gone out of his way to get under her skin—the fastest way he could think of to get information out of someone with defenses as strong as hers were. It was a delicate balance. He had to be just obnoxious enough to get her to react, but not so bad that she kicked him out of the house. He was walking a fine line, and he'd almost fallen over the edge today.

She was following behind him—he could hear the rattle of loose pebbles as she walked down the path. He made no effort to slow down, and she wasn't about to catch up with him. They marched down the hillside to the villa, single file, and if he was half tempted to stop and turn, so that she'd have no choice but to barrel into him, he resisted the impulse. He'd pushed her enough for now.

No, she didn't like him, and she didn't like kissing. But there was definitely more to it than that. She was fascinated by him; he recognized that without any false modesty, though he wasn't sure why. It wasn't straightforward sexual interest—he doubted if Charlie even knew what that was like. If she did, she kept it for her fiancé.

Maybe she simply saw through him. Knew him for a liar and a cheat, no insurance bureaucrat at all. But she'd asked him no leading questions, and she seemed to take him at face value. If she had any doubts that he was who he said he was, it would have been a simple enough matter to make a few phone calls and then kick him the hell out of the house. This whole intricate charade was going to collapse soon enough, and all that was needed to hurry it along was the hint of suspicion. And yet as far as he knew she hadn't done anything to check up on him.

According to his early-morning phone call with Gregory, no one had seemed the slightest bit interested in the whereabouts of one Connor Maguire. He probably should have used a different name when he showed up at the villa, but he tended to find it easier to keep his lies to the absolute minimum. But if Charlie decided to start looking into her insurance consultant, it would be easy enough to track down the name of Connor Maguire among the registered aliens working in Italy. And it would lead her to the *Starlight,* not some nice, boring insurance conglomerate.

But apart from Gregory's general antsiness about getting things done, there was nothing to suggest he needed to rush things. He had a few days' grace. And despite his editor's demands for information, he'd told him next to nothing. He'd learned early on that knowledge was power, and that no one could be trusted. He'd fill Gregory in when he was ready to, and not a moment sooner.

In retrospect, he realized he shouldn't have kissed Charlie. He'd been wanting to ever since he'd first seen her—hell, he wanted to do a hell of a lot more than kiss her. And covered with plaster dust, trembling with panic, she'd been damned near irresistible.

But he'd almost overplayed his hand. She stood frozen in his arms like the ice princess he knew she'd be, and the panicked beating of her heart doubled when he put his mouth on hers. He should have pulled back then, feeling the iciness of her skin, but he'd given in to temptation, vaguely aware that she was too frightened to move.

Frightened of what, for Christ's sake? She'd been married to a notorious womanizer. The old goat had gone through some of the world's most beautiful women, including Charlie. And she had a fiancé. It wasn't as if she hadn't been having it regularly.

Maybe he was just too rough and crude for her. Pompasse had been an elegant old man, and if he knew Charlie as well as he was beginning to, then she'd probably chosen another creature of refined tastes for her fiancé, someone just like her. Not a working-class bloke from the outback who...

Who what? Who was out to find out every bit of dirt he could about her marriage, her dead husband, and even about her if he thought it would sell books? Who was entirely willing to sleep with her, and just about anyone else in the household, in order to further his cause? Who could end up turning her over to the Italian police if it turned out she'd killed the old man?

He couldn't see Charlie killing. She was so guarded she didn't allow herself to feel that much of anything. Besides, she was probably the least likely suspect. She'd been in New York—and even if she *had* made a fast trip over to Florence to off her former husband, she would have left a paper trail. And besides, she had no reason to do it.

So then, who did it?

It didn't matter in the slightest that the police didn't seem to suspect a thing. Bestsellers were made of just such stuff. If he was going to present Pompasse's death as a murder, then Gregory would be expecting a suspect. And he still wasn't sure who he liked the best for the role of killer.

Charlie would be the most interesting, of course, but it would be far too easy for her to prove her innocence. He had to preserve the shreds of his so-called journalistic integrity. If he smeared her without reasonable proof, it would destroy what credibility he did have. Of course, he didn't have to outright accuse her in the book—he just had to use enough innuendo to titillate the readers of highbrow trash. He could destroy a life without much effort at all. Not that he particularly wanted to, but he refused to allow sentimentality to get in his way.

He glanced back at her. Her head was down, and she was concentrating on the narrow path beneath her feet. She must have sensed his eyes on her, because she halted, looking up at him.

No, she definitely wasn't happy with him. If he thought her eyes had been cool before, they were now chips of ice.

"It was only a kiss, sweetheart," he drawled. "You act like I took a hammer to the Pietà."

"The subject is not open for discussion."

"Not that I put you up there with Michelangelo. I mean, you're pretty and all that, but you're only a woman, not a masterpiece. Then again, you've been a masterpiece, haven't you? What does it feel like to have your portrait worth millions of dollars? Must be flattering.''

She glared at him. "Don't be an idiot, Maguire. The value of the paintings has absolutely nothing to do with me, and everything to do with Pompasse's brilliance as a painter. Whether or not he was an admirable human being, he was certainly a great artist.''

"I suppose so. But why are his paintings of you so much more valuable than any of the others? Why are those the ones that were taken? Were you that inspiring? The work he did after you left him was shit and you know it. Doesn't that make you feel guilty?''

Bingo. He'd touched a raw spot, an important one. For some crazy reason Pompasse's artistic talent seemed to excuse everything in her mind. If he lost that, then all that was left was a selfish, degenerate old man.

"Not particularly,'' she said after a moment. "He'd stopped painting me several years before I left.''

"Except for the last one. His so-called masterpiece.''

Her laugh was entirely without humor. "Are you talking about *Charlie When She Left*? Pompasse was an excellent manipulator of the media. You're right—it was the final portrait of me. But he painted it two years before I left him, just as he was starting in on Gia. And he called it *Charlie in a Bad Mood* until he decided to show it. No, I don't feel guilty.''

He really wanted to kiss her for that juicy little tidbit, but he wisely kept his distance. ''So you left him because you were jealous? Someone else had taken your place?''

''I left him because he didn't need me anymore.''

''You're that easy? All someone has to do is need you and you're his?'' He didn't bother to temper his disbelief.

''If I loved him.''

For a moment he said nothing. If she loved him? It was almost an alien notion. He wasn't even sure if he believed in love. Lust, yeah, and affection. But not the kind of love she was talking about. Not the kind that required sacrifice.

''So you loved him?''

''I married him, didn't I?''

''Sweetheart, people get married for thousands of reasons, and I doubt if love enters into it much. Besides, when you were eighteen you must have been starry-eyed and romantic. You couldn't have been looking for an old man.''

"When I was eighteen I'd been married to Pompasse for over a year. And he was exactly what I needed."

"An old man. Father figure, right? Whatever happened to Daddy?"

"My father died in a plane crash when I was young. But it wasn't traumatic—I'd only seen him a couple of times in my life. Olivia goes through men rather quickly."

"That was your mother?"

"She still is." She didn't sound particularly pleased about it. "You'll have a chance to meet her soon enough. In the meantime, do you suppose we could get back to the house? I don't know why you give a damn about my life, but it has very little to do with your job. The missing paintings, remember?"

"And those paintings were of you, remember?" he shot back.

"Pompasse did quite a number of paintings of me, and only three are missing. And my childhood has nothing to do with it, thank you very much. Are you going to move or am I going to go around you?"

The path was very narrow. She'd have to brush against him to get past, and while the thought was tempting, he decided to give her a break.

"Sure thing, sweetheart," he drawled, turning

back on the path. "We can continue this discussion later. First dibs on the shower."

"We're not sharing a bathroom anymore. If you really insist on sleeping in the studio then I'll show you the shower down there. Pompasse frequently painted in the nude and then showered afterward."

"I really didn't want to know that," he said.

"Why not? You seem to have an avid fascination for everything involving Pompasse's life. You have tabloid sensibilities, Maguire. You probably read those garbage newspapers for your view of the world."

This was getting too close for comfort. "I don't read newspapers, love. I don't have time."

"Stop calling me that!" she snapped. "You seem to have plenty of time to hang around here and bother me."

"Priorities," he said with a grin. "Simple priorities."

She was going to kill him, Charlie thought, once she'd left him at the empty studio. Tomaso had already brought a double bed down from somewhere and set it up in the middle of the room. The windows were open to the bright sunlight, the dust had vanished, and there was even a vase of wildflowers on the small table beside the bed. The same as the flowers in her room. She wanted to spit.

His battered duffel bag was there, and fresh towels hung in the tiny bathroom off the back of the room. She had managed to escape before he annoyed her enough to do something about it.

She still wanted to kill him.

His unnerving curiosity shouldn't have surprised her. The world had been fascinated with Pompasse—he'd cultivated his outlandish reputation with assiduous care. Never a month had gone by while Charlie had been in exile in New York that she hadn't seen an article or heard a news story about the Great Artist and his eccentric ways. Once people knew who she was they would usually pelt her with questions. What was it like to be married to the great man? How had it felt with all his legendary womanizing? And worst of all, they always wanted to know why she'd married him in the first place. And she could never come up with an answer, not when she wasn't sure of the reason herself.

She'd soon learned to stop telling people about her background. It was a lot easier if they simply thought of her as Charlie Thomas, owner of La Chance, and not the relict of a legend.

So Maguire's incessant curiosity shouldn't surprise her. And he was a man—a rough, no-nonsense type without the sensitivity to realize that there were some questions you shouldn't ask, some subjects that shouldn't be discussed. There was nothing unusual or suspicious about that.

But it didn't feel right.

She needed a shower almost as badly as he did, but she detoured by way of the study. His laptop was still there, unguarded, and she slipped behind the desk and opened the lid.

Once more the cartoon figures raced across the screen, a touch of whimsy that was totally unlike Maguire. She tried a few buttons haphazardly, rebooting the computer to see if it would help, but it just returned to the demand for a password. Charlie groaned.

She typed Maguire. Too easy, of course. What was his first name? Connor, right? She went through the gamut of possibilities, meeting only with an invalid-password message. Why hadn't she spent more time learning how to mess with computers and less time with solitaire and Free Cell, she thought grumpily. There was something that Maguire was hiding in this computer and she wanted, needed, to find out what it was.

But she wasn't going to find out what it was today, that much was certain. Besides, she was dusty and dirty and starving—one always had better luck at spying if one was showered and well fed. Or maybe she could just sneak up on him again when he didn't realize she was there. Have someone call him away and she could race back in. Except there was no one here she could trust.

The shower was a blessed relief, almost as wonderful as finding the door open to her empty room. At least Maguire wouldn't be walking in on her—she could hog the hot water to her heart's content. Despite the fancy improvements Pompasse had insisted on, the supply of hot water was limited, and no one was allowed to shower on laundry day, or when Lauretta had to do the dishes. But for now she could drain the tank and hopefully freeze Maguire in the process.

The windows were steamed up when she stepped out of the huge marble bathtub, and she pushed them open, letting the fresh air in. It wasn't quite as hot as it had been—the air now had a hint of autumn in it, and she shivered in the huge, enveloping towel.

She pushed open the door to Pompasse's old bedroom, only to find Gia sitting in the middle of the bed, pawing through her purse.

She looked up at Charlie's approach but didn't stop what she was doing. She was wearing shorts, and her long brown legs were folded under her. The bed was littered with Charlie's possessions—her underwear, her toiletries bag, even her jewelry was spread out on the plain white coverlet.

"What are you doing in here?" Charlie had

every reason to be proud of her calm tone—not an ounce of her fury showed.

Gia shrugged. "I was bored. I figured you would have brought the latest styles from America, and I wanted to see what you were wearing. But it's just the same stuff you had before. Pompasse was right—you have no interest in dressing for men, do you?"

Charlie took a shallow breath, trying to control her anger. A deep breath would have made her towel fall off, and the last thing she wanted was to appear naked in front of Gia's avid eyes.

She'd forgotten how incredibly intrusive the girl could be. In the time they'd both lived at La Colombala Charlie would come down to find Gia wearing her clothes, her jewelry, her perfume. And she'd smile at Charlie, taunting her, daring her to make a fuss.

And Charlie had never said a word, simply because she knew how much Pompasse had wanted her to.

But Pompasse was dead, and Gia was wearing her canary diamond ring. Despite its value, she was welcome to it, as well as the chaste pearl ring that Henry had given her.

But the plain silver ring that had been her father's was a different matter.

With one hand she clutched the towel together. She strode across the room to the bed, yanked the purse out of Gia's slender hands and tossed it across the room. And then she held out her own hands, much larger, paler than Gia's. "Give them back."

She sounded very calm. A foolish woman might not realize she was shaking with rage, and very dangerous indeed, but Gia had never been a fool. She looked at her with a speculative expression, as if considering the merits of a full-blown catfight. Charlie was taller, stronger than Gia, but she was hampered by the towel. At that moment she was mad enough not to care.

With a lazy shrug Gia stripped the rings from her fingers and dumped them in Charlie's outstretched hand. "You never used to mind when I borrowed your things," she murmured.

"I minded. I just didn't say anything. Would you leave me alone? I need to get dressed."

Gia leaned back against the pillows she'd piled high. "We're just girls here. When did you become so prudish? Half the world has already seen your naked body, me included. Pompasse used to insist we swim naked in the pool, remember. No bathing suits allowed. So you have no secrets from me."

"You and Maguire would make a perfect pair," Charlie muttered, heading for the top drawer of the dresser and dropping her towel. She kept her back to Gia as she pulled on the plain cotton underwear, determined not to let her know how angry she was. Gia would only see her anger as a sign of weakness.

"Why do you say that?" Gia asked in a lazy voice. "Not that I disagree with you. He's sort of rough around the edges, but that can be very... pleasant if you're in the right sort of mood."

"Then go for it, with my blessing," Charlie said, reaching for a clean pair of jeans.

"When did you start wearing underwear? Pompasse..."

"I know. Pompasse didn't want me to wear underwear, or a bathing suit, or a nightgown, even though he kept buying them for me. Pompasse didn't want me to eat or breathe or speak unless he approved of it. But I left him, Gia. I don't have to answer to him anymore."

Gia looked as if she'd been slapped in the face. "You didn't love him enough—"

"I wanted to be free. Didn't you?"

She looked horrified at the notion. "Never."

"Then you got your wish," she said, reaching for the sweater.

"You've gotten fat," Gia said.

Charlie only shrugged. "Maybe by Pompasse's standards. But I don't live by them anymore."

Gia had a desperate expression on her face, and Charlie could see her mentally searching for something to replace it with. ''Maguire thinks you're fat, too,'' she said.

Charlie made the mistake of laughing. ''I don't care what Maguire thinks. I told you, have him.''

''He isn't yours to give. He doesn't want you, he wants me....''

''Wonderful. Then maybe he'll leave me alone.'' The moment the words were out of her mouth she realized what a mistake they were. Gia had wanted everything of Charlie's, whether it was precious to her or not. She wanted Pompasse, she wanted Charlie's clothes and jewelry and bedroom, she wanted the attention of any man in the vicinity. For her to realize that Maguire had expressed any kind of interest in Charlie was to seal his fate.

Though why the hell should she care if Gia attached herself to Maguire? If anything, she should encourage her. The two of them deserved each other, and that way maybe she'd get some peace.

Gia stretched and climbed off the bed with her usual feline grace. ''I'm pleased you approve. I'll go find him.''

''I'm so glad you're not wasting time with an extended period of mourning,'' she called after her.

It was a cheap shot, but Charlie's usual calm had deserted her that day, and she wanted to lash out at someone. Unfortunately it was far too effective. Gia froze in the doorway, and her olive skin paled as her huge almond-shaped eyes filled with tears.

"I shouldn't have said that...." Charlie said, taking a step toward her, but by that time Gia had whirled around and left.

Leaving Charlie alone, guilty and ready to weep herself.

Even beyond the grave Pompasse was having a destructive effect on her life, she thought, throwing herself down on the rumpled bed that Gia had recently abandoned. She'd been in Tuscany less than two days and already she'd turned angry, upset and uncertain.

Though in actual fact, it was Maguire who was disturbing her. Not Pompasse.

Even if he hadn't let her go completely, she'd escaped. She mourned the passing of a great artist, she mourned the death of someone she had once revered. But her heart wasn't broken. He was old and it was his time.

She just wished a bolt of lightning would strike Maguire to make things a little more comfortable.

However, Gia in full form was comparable to a bolt of lightning. He wouldn't know what hit him, and she'd manage to keep him out of Charlie's way for as long as it took him to finish his work.

So why wasn't she feeling happier about it?

12

Maguire wasn't particularly pleased coming out from his shower to find Gia Schiavone in his room, wearing a skimpy outfit of shorts and a halter top. Granted, she was gorgeous enough in a dour, Mediterranean fashion, and normally he would have been tempted, but for some reason all he could think about was Charlie.

Gia pushed back her dark hair and smiled at him, with more warmth than she'd shown so far. "Hi, there," she purred.

He grunted something in reply, about to order her out, when his common sense stopped him. She'd been giving him the cold shoulder ever since he arrived, a fact that had not bothered him in the slightest. But she would know a lot more about Pompasse's recent activities than Charlie would, and he'd be a fool not to find out everything he could, particularly when she seemed so willing.

He summoned a half smile and sat down on the end of the bed, reaching for his shoes. "To what do I owe this honor?" he asked in a wry voice.

"I thought we should be friends," Gia replied. "I haven't been very nice to you. It's been a very sad time for me, losing the great love of my life."

"You mean Pompasse?"

"Of course I mean Pompasse," she snapped, some of her melting sorrow vanishing in irritation. "I adored him, worshiped him, gave him my youth…"

"Honey, how old are you? Twenty? Trust me, your youth isn't gone."

"Twenty-four."

"Still a child," he said. "And don't worry—if you've been standoffish I hadn't noticed. I've got a job to do, remember?"

That didn't sit well, either. She didn't like to go unnoticed. She smiled stiffly, not willing to give up. "And how is the job going? Is there any sign of the missing paintings?"

"Not a trace. I don't suppose you have any idea where they might have gone to?"

"Me? How would I know?" Her innocence was just a bit overplayed.

"Because you were living in the house when they disappeared, and unlike the other members of the household you're neither senile nor busy working for a living. At least, not by most standards."

She missed the veiled insult, which was just as

well. "I'm a student at the university," she said stiffly. "I'm working on my degree."

"In what? Art appreciation?"

"Art history."

"Interesting," he murmured. "So you have to spend a lot of time in Florence for that, don't you? The old man must have missed you."

"He would have, but I took the last two semesters off. He needed me."

Sure he did, Maguire thought wryly. Undeterred, he continued, "So it must be nice living so close to Florence. You get the peace of the countryside and the excitement of the big city nearby. The best of both worlds."

"I'm tired of the countryside," she said frankly, her eyes meeting his. "I'm tired of Italy. I want to travel."

"Then for your sake I hope the old man left you a tidy amount in his will," Maguire drawled. "Travel's expensive."

"Not if I go with someone." She moved toward the bed with a slow, graceful languor, and he noticed her feet were bare.

She had very pretty feet, with painted toenails. Unfortunately feet were not much of a turn-on for him, and neither were manipulative little girls looking for a way out.

"Honey," he said with a laugh, "I can't afford you."

She halted, clearly affronted. "What do you mean?"

"You know exactly what I mean. You need a new sugar daddy now that Pompasse has kicked the bucket, and so far I'm the only male around. But you can do a hell of a lot better. I'm too old for you."

"I like older men," she said. "Besides, Pompasse was probably twice your age." She sat down on the bed beside him, making one last attempt at charming him. It didn't work.

"Then you need someone blinded by your beauty. I'm afraid I'm too much of a cynic for you. I can see right through that manipulative little brain of yours."

She turned off the phony seduction like flicking a light switch, and if her pout was childish it was at least a lot more honest. Not that he was anyone to put much store in honesty, he reminded himself. "But I need someone to take care of me," she said.

"Why don't you go home to your family?"

"I'd rather die," she said flatly. "Don't you like me? Don't you think I'm pretty? Don't you want to sleep with me?"

"Sure I like you, yes, I think you're absolutely gorgeous, and no, I don't want to sleep with you," he said, wondering if he was being noble, stupid, picky or all three. It wasn't every day that women like Gia offered themselves to a battle-scarred soul like himself. He had to be nuts to turn her down. Considering the stories she could tell if properly motivated. But the damnable thing was, he wasn't in the mood. Not for her.

"Tell you what," he added, out of pure malice. "Charlie's fiancé is supposed to be arriving sometime soon. He's a lawyer, he's rich, and he lives in New York. Why don't you try your luck with him? After all, if Pompasse liked you both then maybe this guy will, too. And I get the impression that you wouldn't mind sticking it to Charlie. Am I right?"

He'd struck pay dirt. Her dark eyes lit up with pure malice. "She already told me I could have you with her blessing," she said.

"Did she, now? Well, I'm not so easily had. And if she doesn't care, what's the fun in it, right? She'll think twice about handing her wealthy fiancé over to you, though. I'm a poor man, sweetheart. You need someone to keep you in style. I'm betting Charlie's fiancé is just the man to do it."

She slid off the bed, as sunny-tempered as a child. "You're a very smart man, Maguire," she said. "I underestimated you."

"I didn't underestimate you, love," he replied.

But she'd already left, leaving the studio door open behind her.

He stretched out on the bed that she'd thoroughly rumpled, putting his shower-damp head against the pillow and humming to himself. He was a thoroughly nasty SOB at heart, and he didn't feel the slightest trace of guilt. If Charlie Thomas had found true love in the arms of her lawyer, then a conniving little gold digger wouldn't stand a chance.

And if there was trouble in paradise, then Gia was just the sort of serpent to be tossed into the mix.

Or maybe he was the serpent, and Gia was the forbidden fruit. And maybe he was wasting a hell of a lot of time being biblical. He should save his flights of fancy for the book. Gregory wasn't going to wait forever—he'd been foaming at the mouth already because Maguire hadn't checked in often enough for his peace of mind. He wanted photos, he wanted text, he wanted everything and he wanted it now, but the last thing Maguire was going to do was tie up the villa phone lines e-mailing incriminating photos of the residents. Gregory would just have to hold his horses.

Still, he'd better go grab his laptop and set up shop in here. Pompasse's old study was far too public a place for his scandalous tell-all, even protected by a password. Charlie had been just itching to see what he was writing, and he imagined the rest of the household was just as nosy. He changed the password daily, just to be on the safe side, and Charlie didn't strike him as any sort of computer geek, but you could never be too careful. Closet nerds lurked behind the most unlikely exteriors.

He saw the dusty handprints the moment he entered the study. The laptop was still closed, but on the textured black case he could see the white outline of a woman's hand. She hadn't wasted any time in trying to get back into his computer.

He sat down and opened it, but he already knew she hadn't been able to breach it. If she had, she would have found out exactly what he'd been writing, and he would no longer be here. Hell, he might not still be alive.

He'd bet his life that someone in this household was a murderer. Whoever killed Pompasse would probably have just as strong a reason to kill him, once they found out what he was doing. He was going to have to be more careful.

Not that he imagined he was in any kind of danger from Charlie's slender hands. If killing him meant that Charlie had to touch him, then he knew he was safe. Unless, of course, she was proficient with a gun.

Gia, on the other hand, would have no qualms

about killing, and she'd probably prefer to use her hands. And Lauretta was strong and beefy enough to wring a chicken's neck—she probably could have snapped the old man's without much more effort.

Tomaso was a possibility, though he couldn't imagine why he would care, and he could rule out the senile old lady. God knows who else could have been around with a grudge to settle.

But he needed to watch his back. He wasn't in the mood to find a knife between his shoulder blades.

Charlie stayed in her room the rest of the day. It was nothing but sheer cowardice and she knew it, but right then she needed to give herself permission to be a coward. Besides, this room was one part of La Colombala that was completely different from when she'd lived here. It had no memories, no history. The walls were whitewashed, the bed was small and covered with a plain white duvet. The only color in the room was the countryside beyond the open casement window, and that was color enough.

She stretched out on the bed, alternating between sleeping and daydreaming. It was hard work with so many things she wanted to keep at bay, but she'd learned early on how to keep her mind off things that might disturb her. She lay on the bed and devised recipes in her head, mentally adding the ingredients, stirring a great copper pot with a wooden spoon, visualizing it so strongly she could practically smell the food. Then she moved to setting the table, choosing just the right linens, the proper plates, reveling in the earthen tones and the splash of flowers on the painted pottery dishes. It soothed her, comforted her, and she sat down at the table in the sunshine, peaceful, serene, and looked up to see Maguire's image across from her.

The fantasy was shattered, and she sat up, cursing. The smells, however, were real—Lauretta had set lunch out on the terrace beneath her, and the fragrance of tomatoes and herbs carried upward. Charlie's stomach growled in response, and she realized it was midafternoon and she hadn't had anything but coffee all day.

Her window overlooked the terrace and the valley beyond. The table was deserted—the meal consumed, and all the stragglers were gone. If she hurried down she could snag some of the remains and not have to deal with anyone in the house. Not Gia or Madame Antonella nor the curious Lauretta. And most particularly, she wouldn't have to deal with Maguire.

There was no one in sight when she reached the terrace. A platter still held some bruschetta, a dish of pasta remained, and even the bottle of wine stood open on the table. Lauretta must have been escorting Madame Antonella back to her cottage before clearing up the mess.

She sat down at the table, filled an empty plate with the leftover food, and poured herself a glass of wine. It was a delicious Chianti, and she told herself she should savor it.

But she would have killed for a Diet Coke.

Pompasse had outlawed what he termed "belly wash" from his household. Wine was the only civilized thing to drink with meals, and he'd trained her well. She knew a Bardolino from a Valpolicella, she could even identify what part of Italy the grapes were from. This Chianti complemented the meal perfectly.

And she would have killed for a Diet Coke.

There was no denying that a few sips of wine soothed her jangled nerves almost as effectively as herbal tea. She leaned back in the chair, looking down over the valley, watching the breeze ripple through the olive trees, tossing the changing leaves.

She knew she ought to wonder where everyone else was, but she didn't. She was simply glad to have a moment of peace out on the terrace she'd once loved.

It didn't last long.

He came up behind her. She didn't turn to look, hoping in vain that she could ignore him, but she could feel his presence, the heat of his body, the smell of the soap from his shower. He wasn't touching her, but he was too close, willing her to turn around, and she wasn't going to move. She sat there, frozen, praying he'd go away.

"I doubt that view has changed in the last five years," Maguire said. His voice was low, slightly raspy, though that was probably from all the cigarettes. She still didn't turn, but she knew she couldn't ignore him.

"Probably not in the last five hundred years," she said. "But I haven't been here to enjoy it. Which I prefer to do alone. Go away."

He moved then, taking the chair beside her and straddling it, his arms on the scrolled backrest. "Don't you get tired of telling me that, Charlie?"

"Don't you get tired of staying where you're not wanted?" she replied, still keeping her gaze averted.

"You want the estate settled, don't you?"

"Yes."

"Then you have to put up with me. At least for a few more days. Would it help if I apologized? Said I was sorry I was overcome by the passion of the moment and your rare beauty and kissed you?"

She could see a car approaching, up the winding

road to La Colombala, and she concentrated on it, still refusing to look at Maguire.

"It would help if you never mentioned it again," she said stiffly.

"So you can pretend it didn't happen. What's wrong with kissing, Charlie?"

She turned then, unable to help herself. "Any number of things," she said. "One, I don't like you. Two, I'm engaged. Three, I don't like you. Four, you're supposed to be doing a job here, not flirting. Five, I don't like you. Six, I'm in mourning. Seven—"

"You don't like me," he supplied lazily. "You're trying awfully hard to convince me."

She'd been fiddling with the stem of the wineglass, trying to hide her nervousness, but at that she spilled it, and the red wine spread over the white tablecloth like fresh blood.

"I don't like you," she said, exasperated. "Can't you get it through your thick head? I don't like you, I don't like anything about you. I don't like being pawed, I don't like being mocked, I don't like flirting, and I don't like you."

His shaggy dark hair was still wet from the shower. He was wearing khakis and a denim shirt, far too casual for her taste. He hadn't bothered to shave, and she thought beard stubble was pretentious. He sat there looking at her, that cool, assessing expression in his dark eyes, totally at ease with the world and her discomfort, and she wanted to slap him.

"Convince me," he said softly.

She wanted to cry from frustration, when she hadn't cried since she'd first heard about Pompasse's death. She pushed away from the table, starting to rise, when he caught her wrist, pulling her back. He was very strong.

"Take your hands off me," she said in an icy voice.

"Then tell me why you're so damned interested in what's in my laptop. You left your dusty handprints all over it this morning."

"I wanted to see how you're doing with your investigation."

"You could have asked."

"I don't trust you. Are you going to let go of me?"

"I don't think so, Charlie." His lazy voice sent little shivers down her backbone despite the bright Italian sunlight. He was rubbing his thumb against her wrist, and he could probably feel her pulse hammering wildly. "Not until you tell me the truth."

"You're hurting me," she said, her voice shaking. In fact, he wasn't. He was simply holding her there, his skin against hers, warmth against her icy-cold flesh.

"Sorry," he said. And before she realized what he intended he brought her wrist to his lips, pressing his open mouth against her sensitive skin.

It was like an electric shock, straight to the heart, the caress of his lips, his tongue against the fragile veins of her wrist, and she was too astonished to move. He looked up at her, and his dark green eyes were compelling. "I can taste your pulse," he whispered against her skin, and the electric shock sizzled down between her legs. "Why don't you taste me?"

In a daze she heard a noise, but it was a roaring, rushing sound that simply might have been inside her own head. She could feel her body sway toward him, almost of its own volition, and she couldn't stop herself, she was mesmerized by his eyes, by his mouth on her skin, by the warmth of the afternoon and the drugging effect of the Tuscan sunshine—

"God, I've missed this place!" Olivia's arch tones preceded her through the open French doors. "There's nothing like Tuscany." She paused, admiring the view, giving the two of them plenty of time to admire her if they were so inclined. All Charlie could do was thank God her mother's self-absorption enabled her to escape from Maguire's touch, unnoticed.

"You got here sooner than I expected," she said awkwardly.

"And aren't you delighted, darling?" Olivia demanded archly. "Come give me a kiss, and then introduce me to your gorgeous young man."

"He's not mine," Charlie said, skirting the table to keep out of Maguire's way. Though why she thought she had to worry was beyond her. He'd hardly grab her with her mother watching. Just because he'd kissed her the last two times they'd been together didn't mean she wasn't perfectly safe as long as someone else was around to make sure he behaved himself.

She kissed her mother's smooth, unlined cheek, inhaling the usual sent of Joy. It always seemed such an odd fragrance for her mother to favor, since she spent so much of her life dissatisfied, looking for a joy that always seemed to elude her.

Before she could slide away Olivia's gaze narrowed, and she caught Charlie's hand in her perfectly manicured one. "What did you do to your wrist, darling? Did you burn yourself?"

The mark was red, still damp from his mouth, and without thinking she cast a furious glance at Maguire, sitting there smugly.

A glance her mother didn't miss. "Oh, really?"

she said. "Then maybe now is the moment to tell you that Henry's here, as well. Don't you want to greet your fiancé?"

Escape was the only possible alternative. "Yes," she said, practically dashing into the house.

But not before she heard Olivia's cool voice slither back to her. "So tell me, who are you and what are you doing to my frigid daughter?"

13

Maguire still hadn't moved from his chair. The newcomer was a beauty, with an unlined, flawless face, a perfect cloud of dyed red hair, a ruthlessly thin figure. She looked to be in her mid-thirties, thanks no doubt to a masterful job of plastic surgery.

"You're Charlie's mother?" he drawled lazily. "I thought you were her sister." It was pandering, and it was effective.

"Don't give me that crap," the woman said, but she couldn't hide her pleased smirk. "I'm perfectly comfortable being forty-three years old. I don't try to hide my age."

Charlie was thirty, which would have made the carefully preserved woman in front of him young indeed to have been a mother. He didn't bother pointing it out to her. Not at that point.

He rose, holding out his hand. "Connor Maguire. I'm an insurance adjuster, here to assess the estate."

She looked up at him. She was much shorter

than her daughter, and she had cultivated a kind of helpless female look that Maguire found particularly annoying, when he knew that beneath the slightly fluttery surface she was hard as steel. Unlike her daughter, who tried to present a calm, steady mien to hide her complete vulnerability.

"Olivia Thomas," she said, putting her manicured hand in his big paw. She'd even had her hands taken care of, he thought with distant admiration. You could tell a woman's age by her hands and her neck, but Olivia's neck was swathed in a silk scarf, and her slender hand was spot-free and unlined.

"Thomas? Charlie said you'd been married a dozen times," he said.

"Seven," she corrected him with a touch of that inner steel. "And it makes it simpler to go by Thomas. Besides, I don't have a husband right now. I'm completely available."

She hadn't released his hand. He almost wanted to laugh. This was the second time in a matter of hours that someone was coming on to him, for the simple reason that they thought Charlie wanted him. Charlie wanted him at the bottom of a well, and he was about to point that out to Olivia when he thought better of it. After all, he had a job to do. If Olivia and Gia wanted to waste their time flirting with him, he could certainly put their attention to good use. He couldn't understand why he'd even hesitate.

"So what were you doing to my daughter?" she continued smoothly, finally releasing his hand and sinking into the chair beside him. "Besides giving her one hell of a hickey. I doubt she's ever had one before."

"Yeah, right," Maguire drawled.

"You think I'm kidding? You obviously don't know Charlie very well. She's frigid. Bona fide, diagnosed sexual dysfunction. She's been seeing some doctor in New York, hoping she'd get over it, but so far no luck. I maintain she just hasn't found the right man, but then, she hasn't asked for my opinion. She won't even discuss it."

Maguire stared at her in fascination. "I don't blame her."

"Oh, then you've met Henry? No, I don't blame her, either. He's attractive enough, but hardly the type to make a girl hot and bothered. You, on the other hand, have definite promise."

"I mean I don't blame her for not wanting to discuss it with you. Do you discuss your daughter's sex life with everyone?"

Olivia laughed, a soft, deep chuckle. "You disapprove of me! How utterly delicious. And no, I don't go chatting about Charlie's total lack of libido with strangers. Just men who look at her the way you were. How'd you manage to hold her still long enough to make that mark on her wrist? I know you haven't slept with her—she doesn't look guilty enough.''

''If I had sex with your daughter I don't think guilt would be her foremost reaction.''

''Arrogant, too, aren't you? I like that in a man.'' She put her hand on his arm, that bleached, smoothed hand. She was probably very talented, very clever with her hands. Unlike Charlie, who was scared shitless of him. ''I like to be outrageous, and I don't beat around the bush. Keep away from Charlie, Mr. Maguire. She thinks I'm the Wicked Witch of the West, but deep down, I care about her. She has enough going on right now and she doesn't need you complicating things.''

''I'm a complicating kind of guy,'' he said in a lazy voice.

''Well, leave her alone. Henry's perfect for her—he's got patience and a deep abiding love for her. He's reliable, financially secure, and he'll take good care of her and he won't make demands. What do you have to offer her?''

Maguire snorted in derision. ''Lady, have you got the wrong end of the stick! I'm here to do a job, nothing more. I'm not interested in your daughter.''

''Then why did you put that mark on her

wrist?'' Olivia said archly. ''I'm only a little bit older than you are, but I've been around. And I don't trust you.''

''All right, since we're being so honest, I'll admit it. I want to shag your daughter,'' he said. Olivia didn't even blink. ''It's a natural-enough reaction—that ice princess act is a challenge to any red-blooded male.''

''So you want her because she's a challenge? Hardly a good reason to screw up someone's life.''

''I'm not screwing up her life, lady. I'm not screwing her. I'm just…flirting a little. No harm in that, is there?''

''With Charlie there might be.''

''So what do you suggest I do? Sleep with you instead?''

Olivia laughed lightly. ''No, darling. You're too old for me. Unlike Charlie I like my men buff and brainless.''

''Henry's not buff and brainless?''

Olivia shook her head. ''Come meet him. I know you'll be enchanted.''

Enchanted was far from the operative word. Olivia Thomas had just thrown him for a loop. The well-preserved dragon lady had an unexpected weakness for her daughter. Unless, of course, she was playing an even more complicated game. Maguire rose to his feet, towering over her. She had an air of fragility about her that was as deceptive as Charlie's air of serenity. Olivia was as fragile as a bull moose. And while Charlie put on a better act, her acquaintance with serenity probably didn't come any closer than twelve-step wall plaques.

He followed Olivia to the living room, not sure what to expect. He knew one thing, though—he wasn't going to like seeing Charlie curled up next to her beloved Henry. For some inexplicable reason he didn't want to see Charlie curled up next to anyone.

He needn't have worried. They sat, side by side on the ancient, sagging sofa, so deep in whispered conversation that they didn't even realize that Olivia and Maguire had come in.

"Tell me that's not Henry!" Maguire muttered. "He looks like her grandfather."

"What did you expect, Maguire?" Olivia whispered back. "She wants safety, not sex."

At that Charlie looked up, a wary expression on her face. She saw him watching her, and defiantly she reached out and took Henry's hand, holding it. She looked as natural as a marionette.

"Henry, dear, this is Mr. Maguire," Olivia said smoothly, dragging him in. "He's an insurance adjuster, assessing Pompasse's estate. Or what's left of it."

Henry rose. He was a thin man, with a narrow,

elegant face, thinning dark hair, a perfect suit and perfect manners. He was taller than Maguire, a fact that Maguire found irrationally annoying.

"Good to meet you, Maguire," he said. "I hadn't realized that Honore had sent someone out already. They told me it would be another week before they could spare someone."

Maguire didn't blink. "With an estate as important as Pompasse's, they made the effort to find someone," he said. Who the hell was Honore?

"That's good," Henry said absently, but his pale blue eyes looked wary. "How are things going? I'm afraid I've been so busy catching up with Charlie that I haven't asked about the estate." Charlie had also risen, standing close beside him, and he reached out and put his arm around her narrow shoulders, drawing her close. She complied, and most people wouldn't have noticed the imperceptible stiffness in her body as she leaned against her fiancé.

"Going slowly," Maguire said. "Certain paintings are still missing, and I've been unable to find Pompasse's records."

"Missing?" Henry's high forehead furrowed in dismay. "How can that be? I assumed they'd have turned up by now. What does Honore say about it? Do you think they've been stolen?"

"I haven't finished my investigation."

"But surely it's time the police were involved? What would you estimate the paintings to be worth? Two million? Three? I'm not sure Pompasse's estate can withstand such a loss."

"I'm not at liberty to discuss it."

"Don't be ridiculous—I'm Charlie's fiancé and her lawyer, as well. I can speak for her in all matters...."

Maguire cast an inquiring glance at Charlie's frozen countenance. Olivia was right—the mark on her wrist was glaringly obvious. It gave him a hard-on, just looking at it.

"We don't need to talk business now, Henry," Charlie broke in, pulling her gaze away from Maguire's. "You and Olivia have just arrived and you must be exhausted. Why don't you get settled and we can discuss this later?"

For a moment it looked as if Henry might argue, but then he smiled down at her with paternal fondness. Maguire half expected him to pat her on the head like a good little girl. "Of course, you're right, my dear."

"Charlie's always right," Olivia spoke up. She'd been leaning against the doorway, observing everything. "Where am I sleeping, Charlie? In my usual bedroom? Or has one of Pompasse's newest pets taken up residence?"

"Your room is ready, Olivia. Lauretta had Gia move to a smaller one."

"That's hardly necessary, darling girl," Henry broke in. "I can share your room. After all, we are engaged."

Darling girl, Maguire thought, ready to hurl. Charlie looked like she would have rather slept with a snake. How she thought she was going to marry a man when she couldn't stand him touching her was beyond his comprehension.

"There's no need. Gia has already moved her things. Maguire is staying in the studio, and you'll be in my old room."

Henry's well-bred features nobly concealed the trace of a pout. "Whatever you want, darling," he said. "Nice to meet you, Maguire," he said, dismissing him like the underling he clearly considered him to be.

"Yeah, likewise," Maguire drawled, watching as Charlie walked from the room with him. Not touching him.

"Lovely couple, aren't they?" Olivia cooed.

Maguire shrugged. "If he makes her happy it's none of my business."

"Now, you strike me as someone who makes everything your business. And you could hardly say the two of them look happy, could you?"

"What's your problem, lady? You want Henry?

I think Gia's going to take a crack at him, but you may as well, too.''

"Gia's going after Henry? What an interesting notion. Who put that idea into her empty little head? No, I don't have to ask. You're a very inventive man, Maguire.''

"Just a working stiff,'' he said modestly.

Her eyes dropped to his crotch level with suggestive slowness, and then she smiled. "I suspect we're in for an interesting time over the next few days. I intend to enjoy it tremendously, especially when we lay that old bastard in the ground.''

"You didn't like Pompasse?''

"I despised him,'' Olivia said.

"Oh, I forgot. You're the devoted mother, aren't you? You despise him for what he did to your daughter.''

"You're a bastard as well, Maguire,'' she said evenly. "I have more than enough reasons to want the old man dead, and I'm not about to share them with the likes of you. Just don't be surprised if I dance on his grave.''

The reporter in him could only hope. Maybe all Pompasse's castoff women would join hands and dance around the old man's resting place.

He had his camera with him. Several, in fact. He'd had them for years, gotten off a CIA acquaintance in the Congo. His favorite was in the cigarette lighter, but since Charlie had decreed no smoking, that was now out of the question.

The other was a pen, small, compact, efficient. He had three tiny disks already downloaded onto his laptop. He'd stay in the background at the funeral, get the grieving widow with her new old man, and make Gregory double his asking price.

Unless Henry poked his long, thin, aristocratic nose where it didn't belong. He'd taken one look at Maguire and sized him up for a commoner, an interloper, someone who didn't belong. The question was, how long would it be before he checked up on him with the mysterious Honore? If he could just hold out through the weekend and the funeral service then he didn't care what happened.

But he wasn't ready to leave, not just yet. Too much unfinished business.

In particular, Charlie Thomas.

"You have a most interesting expression on your face, Mr. Maguire," Olivia observed. "What were you thinking of just then?"

"Your daughter's fiancé," he answered with complete truthfulness.

"Don't let it get you down. I'd back you ten to one."

"I don't want her," he said flatly.

"Don't you?" Olivia said sweetly. "But then, I already knew you were a liar."

* * *

"I don't trust that man," Henry said as they climbed the front staircase.

"Hush," Charlie whispered. "He'll hear you."

"I don't give a damn if he does," Henry said in an even louder voice. "There's something about him that I don't like."

As far as Charlie could remember Henry liked just about everyone. "Well," she said after a moment, "I don't think he liked you much, either." They reached the hallway, and she pushed open the door to the bedroom. "I put you in my room," she said.

"I thought you said we weren't going to share?"

He looked pathetically hopeful, and Charlie felt the familiar guilt wash over her, compounded by the feel of Maguire's mouth on her skin. "You're sleeping in my old room, I'm sleeping in Pompasse's," she said gently.

"Of course," he said, ever the gentleman. "You know I'd never put pressure on you."

"Henry, I'm not sure if this is going to work…" she began, but he caught her hand and drew her into the room, closing the door behind them, shutting them in. She took slow, deep breaths, willing her panic not to show, and she looked up at him.

"Of course it's going to work, my darling girl,"

Henry said gently. "I'm a patient man, mature enough to know how to wait for things. Sooner or later you'll be ready to try again. You yourself said that Dr. Rogerson thought you were making progress."

"Henry, I really don't want to discuss it," she said with a trace of desperation. "Not here, not now."

"Of course not, my love. Not with that Neanderthal downstairs. I don't wonder you're unsettled, coming back to this place and then being subjected to his brutish company. I'm surprised at Honore, sending someone like him. He's not the right sort at all to handle a delicate situation like this one."

"Not the right sort?" Charlie echoed.

"You know what I mean, darling. Not 'our' sort. A little rough around the edges, don't you think? A little too working-class?"

"I suppose so," Charlie murmured uneasily.

"You go away now and let me unpack. I think I need a short lie-down before I face the rest of Pompasse's menagerie. Spending the last twenty-four hours with your mother has been an exhausting experience. I don't know how you survived her."

"She's not so bad," Charlie said, wondering vaguely why she was defending Olivia. For some reason everything Henry said rubbed her the wrong way. She wasn't used to arguing—she tended to let disagreements wash over her. But for some reason she felt like contradicting him.

"Don't be ridiculous, Charlie, your mother's a monster," Henry said indulgently. "But I promise, we won't have to see her once we're married. Once you're settled again she won't be interfering anymore."

"How has she been interfering?" Charlie asked, astonished.

"Never you mind, darling," Henry said. "We'll talk later."

It wasn't the first time he'd dismissed her when she'd asked uncomfortable questions. Henry was a man who preferred the appearance of calm over every other consideration. It had been one of the things that had most attracted her to him.

It was now one of the things that annoyed her.

"All right," she said, letting a touch of coolness creep into her voice. "We'll talk later. In the meantime I'd appreciate it if you'd at least be polite to Maguire. He may not be your kind of person but he's here to do a job, and the sooner he's finished the sooner we'll be rid of him. It'll just slow things down if you interfere."

"I have no intention of interfering, precious,"

Henry said. "I'm just going to do a little research, once I'm rested. Surely you can't object to that?"

Surely she couldn't. And yet oddly enough she did. She didn't want Henry making phone calls to his old boys' network, checking out Maguire's bona fides. Which was ridiculous—if there was something suspicious about her unwelcome guest, then the sooner she found out the sooner she could get rid of him. Which was her main goal in life, wasn't it?

"Of course not," she said. "Have a good rest, Henry."

"Kiss?" he said plaintively, proffering his angular jaw.

She crossed the room and planted a dutiful peck on his smooth-shaven cheek. He was the only man she knew who could travel halfway around the world and still manage to be freshly shaven.

Unlike Maguire's ever-present stubble. His rough beard had scratched her face when he'd kissed her mouth. She'd felt it against her wrist, and she cast a hurried glance at the blazing red mark. Henry hadn't noticed, thank God. But then, Henry wasn't a particularly observant man—he saw what he wanted to see.

"Sleep well, Henry," she said, closing the door behind her.

She was alone in the hallway, and she leaned

her forehead against the wall, taking in a deep, shuddering breath. How had things gotten so terribly confusing? All she had wanted was for Henry to be there, so that she could lean on him, let him take care of things.

And now that he was here she was filled with a vast, unfocused annoyance. Everything he said, everything he did set her nerves on edge.

It was all Maguire's fault, of course. He's the one who'd unsettled her. By putting his hands on her, his mouth on her, he'd stirred up all sorts of troubled feelings.

Oddly enough he hadn't stirred up disgust. The one time she and Henry had tried to make love Charlie had ended up in Henry's black-tiled bathroom, trying to stifle the sounds of her retching. She couldn't even think about sex and Henry's pale body without breaking out in a cold sweat.

And yet with Maguire she wasn't cold and clammy. She was angry, filled with rage and heat and passion....

Not that kind of passion, she reminded herself. She just wanted to kill him. It was a simple, well-deserved reaction.

She pushed away from the wall. She had the oddest feeling someone was watching her, and she looked around, into the shadowy hallway leading to the right and to the left. There was no one in sight, all the doors were closed.

She was getting skittish, she thought, shaking her head. Too much stress. She needed to lie down and listen to some soothing music, something to calm her, bring back that cool wall of stillness she kept around her. The last thing she wanted was to go back down to her mother and Maguire.

She reached for the handle on her door, then pulled it away in shock and disgust. There was something wet and sticky on the doorknob, and in the shadowy light of the late afternoon her hand looked covered in blood.

She didn't hesitate, she simply shoved the door open, and whatever had been holding it closed toppled to the floor with a dull thud.

And Charlie looked down at what lay in her path, and her mouth opened in a silent scream.

14

The portrait lay on its back in the middle of the room. Charlie could just recognize it—it was the very first that Pompasse had done of her. *Awakening,* one of the missing paintings. She had looked even younger than her sixteen years—though it was hard to tell at this point. Someone had slashed the portrait down the middle and covered it with blood.

She backed out of the room, shaking all over. For a moment she couldn't understand why the entire household hadn't come running, and then she realized that she hadn't made a sound. She pulled the door closed again, her hand sliding on the wet knob, and she stared down at the red in horror. She turned and stumbled blindly down the stairs, not even knowing where she was going.

The living room was empty—her mother must have gone to her room, thank God. No one on the terrace, either, and without thinking she headed straight for the studio. She couldn't knock—the red would get all over the whitewashed door. She simply pushed the door open with her shoulder, not caring what she'd find.

Maguire had moved his computer and his CD player into the room, and he was immersed in his work, but this time he heard her approach, and he looked up, an expression of vague annoyance on his face that vanished the moment he got a good look at her.

By that time she was shaking so hard her teeth were chattering, and when he crossed the room and caught her arms in his strong hands she was beyond noticing or caring.

"What's happened?" He shook her slightly when she didn't, couldn't answer. "Charlie? Are you hurt?"

Through her dazed mind she was slightly surprised that he'd even care. She shook her head. "My room..." she said. "Blood..."

He released his hold on her, and for a moment she thought she might collapse. His strength had been holding her up. But she stiffened, trying to stop the shaking.

"You stay here," he said, starting for the door.

He'd left his computer on, but she was past caring. "No!" She shook her head violently. "I don't want to be alone."

He gave her an odd look but simply nodded. He

didn't touch her again, and she led him back through the empty house, up to her bedroom.

"There's blood on the doorknob," she said in a strained voice. "It's on my hands."

"Let me see." Without waiting for her to offer he reached down and caught her wrist, pulling her hand up. The red was still bright, thick on her palm, and she shuddered.

He brought her hand to his face and sniffed it. "It's not blood," he said. "Blood smells different, almost metallic. It's probably paint."

"How do you know what blood smells like?" It was a stupid question, but that was all she could think of as she tried to wipe her hands against her shirt. Her white shirt, now streaked with telltale red.

"A misspent youth," Maguire said, reaching for the doorknob. Most of the paint had already come off on Charlie's hands, and he pushed it open.

The painting was still there, viciously slashed and splattered, but now that she knew it wasn't blood she should have felt marginally better. She didn't. Maguire tugged her into the room and closed the door behind her, then turned to stare down at the painting.

"One of the missing paintings, I assume. Which one?" He sounded only slightly curious.

"*Awakening.*" She was still shivering. The red

wouldn't come off her hands, and she couldn't stop shaking. "It was the first one he painted of me," she said through chattering teeth.

"Never mind," he said. "Let's get you cleaned up." He took her arm and pulled her into the bathroom, and she was in no shape to fight him. He drew her to the bathroom sink and began to run the water, but she simply stared at her reflection in the mirror ahead.

She looked like a stranger. Her hair had come loose, her face was pale, and her white shirt was streaked with blood. No, paint, she reminded herself. She reached up to push her hair out of her face and saw the red on her fingers.

She tried to turn away, but Maguire was behind her. He simply put his arms around her, catching her hands in his and putting them beneath the running water, like a parent teaching his child how to wash her hands. He scrubbed at the paint, using the soap, and she watched the red leave her fingers and swirl down the drain like blood.

Gradually she stopped shivering, the warmth of his body behind her slowly penetrating into her iciness. He felt strong, safe, and she had the strange need to close her eyes and lean back against him.

She didn't, of course. And when the red was finally gone from her hands he stepped back, leaving her cold and unprotected. "Take off your shirt," he said brusquely.

"What?"

"It's covered in paint. Take it off." He didn't wait for her answer, since she just stared at him numbly. He caught the hem of her shirt and tugged it over her head, leaving her standing there in the bathroom in her plain white bra.

At least he didn't mock her or leer. For all the attention he paid she might as well have been a marble statue. "I'll find you something else to wear," he said. "Put that in the trash."

He started out into the bedroom, then stopped, blocking the door.

She'd wrapped her arms around her body in a vain effort to cover herself, but his sudden stillness startled her. "What is it?" she asked. "Is someone in there?" Maybe he'd been wrong about the paint, maybe there was a dead animal, or worse....

"No," he said, and moved out of the way, letting her pass.

She saw it immediately, of course. The word *Murderer* was splashed in red on the inside of the door.

"I—I didn't..." she stammered.

"Get dressed," Maguire said. "I'll clean it up."

She didn't even stop to think. By the time she'd pulled a clean shirt over her head he'd managed to wash most of the paint from the door, leaving only an illegible smear of red behind. She sat down in the chair, watching him as he worked, too numb to do anything else.

"Why would someone do this?" she asked finally.

He glanced over his shoulder at her. "You tell me."

"I don't know. I didn't realize anyone…"

"Suspected you?" he supplied.

"Hated me," she corrected him. "Hated me that much."

"Well, Gia certainly isn't your biggest fan. And the old lady seems to think you're some ancient enemy. I bet if we looked further we could find some other people who aren't too happy with you."

"I don't understand," she said. "I've never harmed anyone—at least, not on purpose. Who could have…?"

"Where's Lover Boy?" he interrupted.

"I beg your pardon?"

"The fiancé. Henry. Where is he?"

"He's asleep next door."

"And he didn't hear the noise we were making?" Maguire asked. "Sounds suspicious to me."

"Henry sleeps very heavily."

"How would you know? Your mother says you've never slept with him."

She jerked her head up in outrage, the last of her panic fading. "I don't tell my mother the intimate details of my sex life, Maguire," she snapped.

"She says you don't have a sex life. Looking at Henry, I can see why. Don't you think you ought to try someone a little closer to your own age, instead of men with one foot in the grave?"

"Leave me alone, Maguire. I'm not in the mood for this."

"You're the one who came and got me. As a matter of fact, why did you? It would have been easy enough to wake up old Henry to provide moral support. Or didn't you want him to see the word on the door?"

"I didn't see the word myself until you showed me," she said in a weary voice. "And I don't know why I didn't go to Henry. It was one of the missing paintings, and you were looking for them. I just went on instinct."

"And your instincts sent you to me," he said in a thoughtful voice. Before she could protest he went on. "You all right now? Stopped shaking?"

She nodded. "I'm fine. I was just...surprised."

"To put it mildly. Why don't you go curl up

next to Henry while I finish up in here? Distract him so he doesn't notice any noise I make.''

"No," she said flatly, cold again.

"He doesn't do it for you, does he? Poor old Henry. Maybe a little Viagra would do the trick."

"Stop it!" Charlie said, desperate. Her last ounce of calm was disappearing beneath Maguire's skillful prodding.

"Well, if Henry doesn't appeal to you, then go down to the kitchen and find someone to talk to while I take care of this mess. I'd rather not have any witnesses."

"I want you to burn it."

"Hell, no. This is still worth a pile of money," Maguire protested.

"It's been ruined."

"You'd be surprised to see what an art restorer could do with something like this," Maguire said. "Go and find Lauretta and talk about cooking. By the time you come back everything will be cleaned up."

"What if Henry wakes up and hears you? How are you going to explain being in my bedroom?"

He grinned at her. "Sweetheart, I leave that up to you."

Without another word she fled, averting her eyes from the ruined painting and the red smear on the doorway. Averting her eyes from Maguire's cynical gaze. She'd run, all right. But not to the kitchen, where she might run into anyone. She needed peace and quiet, some place to restore her hard-won, vanished serenity. Maguire was making her crazy. She'd go up to the ruined church, and not come down till she was good and ready.

Maguire closed the door behind her silently, then reached in his pocket for the camera. He'd been a quixotic fool to clean off the damning word from the door before he could take photos, but Charlie had been so panicked, so distressed, that he'd been uncharacteristically noble. He took some photos of the smear, anyway, contemplating whether he could re-create that damning word long enough for a decent photo. It would make a helluva dust jacket.

In the end he didn't bother. The ruined painting on the floor was dramatic enough.

He took his time, using different angles, propping it against the bed. He took a few shots of the paint-spattered sink and her stained blouse for good measure—he'd learned from Molly that some of the least-expected photos turned out to be prize-winning shots. Though what the hell would Molly think of him now that he'd sunk to the level of spying on the rich and famous? He didn't know whether she would have laughed or wept.

He knew one thing, though. She would have kicked his butt for what he was doing to Charlie. She would have told him what a son of a bitch he was, and he would have listened.

But Molly had died, covering one too many battles, and he'd stopped caring what anyone thought.

By the time he was finished the sky was beginning to darken into the early autumn twilight, and he could hear voices on the terrace below.

He peered out, and they were all congregated out there. Olivia and Henry and Gia, with Madame Antonella holding court. There was no sign of Charlie, but that didn't worry him. She was probably in the kitchen with Lauretta and Tomaso, discussing garlic and pesto. No one would see if he hauled the ruined painting out of the villa to someplace secure.

He still couldn't figure out why Charlie had come to him. And it hadn't been an accident— she'd been heading straight for him and no one else. She said it had been instinct, knowing he was trying to find the missing paintings. It was instinct, all right, but of a much more basic nature. She may not like sex, or kissing, or men. She may not like him very much at all. But she was drawn to him, like a moth to a flame, like an iron filing to a magnet, like a dog to a bone. Which was exactly what he wanted.

He lucked out—no one spotted him as he spirited the ruined canvas down the stairs. He couldn't stash it in the studio—the entrance was down from the terrace and he'd have to carry it straight past the curious inhabitants of La Colombala. Besides, Gia had already proved that the studio was far from secure. He'd pointed her in Henry's direction, and if his glance from Charlie's window was anything to go by, she'd already zeroed in on him, but you never could tell who might decide to pay him a little visit.

Instead he propped the painting behind the house, hidden in the underbrush, hoping that no one would notice it in the gathering twilight. After it was dark and the household was asleep he'd take it up to the old church—there were plenty of dry, empty rooms there to store it.

The question was, who had left it for Charlie to find? It was a good-size painting—about two feet by three feet, and heavily framed. It would take some effort to haul it into Charlie's room without anyone hearing.

And why would they do it? The slashed painting seemed more like a death threat, the scrawled word on the door an accusation.

Of course the police could find out who did it in short order. Fingerprints, questioning, would narrow it down immediately. Too bad he wasn't

about to involve them, but he had his priorities
straight. If the police started investigating Pompasse's death, then half the paparazzi in Europe
would be on the trail. He already had one hell of
an advantage, but he wasn't about to give that up
readily. Besides, it wasn't as if Charlie was in any
particular danger. So someone had put a torn,
paint-splattered painting in her room. Someone
was just trying to spook her.

He paused in the doorway to the terrace, looking
out at them all, wondering who could have done it
and why. Maybe Henry, who was deep in conversation with the fawning Gia. No one slept that
heavily in the middle of the day, even with jet lag,
and he had the most to gain. The painting should
have thrown Charlie into his arms, and he could
have been strong and protective and she could have
been pathetically grateful.

Except that she hadn't turned to Henry. And he
hadn't come to investigate.

Still, it was interesting that it happened the moment he and Olivia arrived at the villa.

Which brought him to Charlie's mother. He
couldn't see any reason why she would have done
it, though she was probably strong enough to haul
the painting around. He wasn't sure whether she
would have had time or not. It would depend on
how long everyone had been there before Olivia

came out to the terrace. Besides, the paintings had
been missing for a while now, and nothing suggested that either Olivia or Henry had anything to
do with that.

No, Olivia was unlikely and Madame Antonella
too old and too spacey. Though, in fact, the act
had been one of almost deranged rage. Still, he
couldn't believe that Madame Antonella would
ever have been able to manage it.

Which left Gia, the obvious choice. Gia, who
hated Charlie and would delight in tormenting her.
He bet if he looked hard enough he'd find a trace
of red paint on her hands.

The question was, why? Sheer malice on her
part? Did she really believe Charlie had killed the
old man? If so, why hadn't she gone to the police?
Fear of scandal wouldn't stop her—Gia would
revel in the attention of the press.

Maybe it was as simple as a war of nerves. Gia
was a better fighter—she had no scruples.

On impulse he headed toward the kitchen, look-
ing for Charlie. But instead he found Tomaso and
Lauretta, hard at work, and there was no sign of
Charlie.

"She's gone for a walk, Signore Maguire," Tomaso told him. "She said she needed some time
to think, and not to hold dinner for her. I wouldn't
worry if I were you. Charlie knows these hills

well—she won't get lost, even in the dark. She'll come back when she's ready.''

Not what he wanted to hear. At least he knew she'd be relatively safe—everyone who might want to do her harm was out drinking Pompasse's liquor and enjoying the Tuscan evening.

Everyone, that is, but him.

His brand of Scotch was on the makeshift bar, and Gia was smoking. Two of his favorite vices, and Charlie wasn't around to complain. He was half tempted to bum a smoke from the little bitch, except that he wasn't in the mood to ask her any favors. He had a score to settle with her.

And the Scotch wouldn't improve matters, either, tempted as he might be. He wasn't about to throw away two years of sobriety at a time when he needed all his wits about him.

He headed straight for Gia. He had to admit she was damned good. She had one hand on Henry's arm, and she was looking up at him out of her dark, melting eyes, speaking earnestly in a hushed voice. Henry was swallowing it whole, basking in her attention, and he probably didn't even remember he had a fiancée somewhere out in the night.

"I need to talk to you," he said abruptly.

"Certainly, old man," Henry began.

Maguire allowed himself an irritated growl. Henry annoyed him already—his upper-class af-

fectations made him feel downright murderous.
"Not you, Henry. Gia."

Gia was smart enough to know she was in trouble. "Maybe later," she said airily, holding tighter
to Henry's arm. "We're just about to go in to dinner."

"Maybe now," Maguire said, clamping his
hand down on her wrist and removing her.

"See here, Maguire..." Henry protested.

"Don't worry, I'll bring her right back to you,"
Maguire replied, dragging Gia off with him.

Gia was cursing him out in Italian, trying to pull
back without making a scene. Olivia arched one
perfectly plucked eyebrow, then turned back to her
conversation with Madame Antonella, dismissing
them. Maguire pulled her through the house, out
the back door and into the underbrush, pushing her
up against the wall.

"I thought you weren't interested, Maguire,"
she said with a silky purr.

"I'm not. Why'd you do it?"

"Do what?" She batted her eyes innocently at
him, but Gia Schiavone probably hadn't been innocent since the day she was born.

"Don't bother trying to deny it," he drawled.
"You're the only one smart enough and mean
enough to do it. What have you got against Charlie?"

Gia stopped pouting. "Didn't she like her little present? She was worried about the missing paintings, so when I found one of them I thought I should return it to her. I was going to drag it out onto the terrace but I thought a little discretion might be wise."

"Very thoughtful of you. Where do you claim you found it?"

"You don't believe me? I *did* find it, but I wouldn't think of doing that to the canvas! I know the value of Pompasse's work—I have a healthy respect for money, even if I hate that pale, overgrown little bitch. The portrait was already destroyed when I found it—slashed with a knife and splashed with paint. I guess someone else hates her as much as I do." Her mouth curved in a satisfied smirk.

"Where did you find it?"

"You're being awfully protective, aren't you? What does it matter to you?" she shot back.

"I'm being protective of the paintings. It's my job, remember? Where did you find it?"

"Near the old barn. It was propped up against the wall, as if someone wanted me to see it. Though I assumed it was Charlie who was supposed to find it. She's the only one around here who goes for long walks. It was a fluke that I was out. But since I figured that it was obviously meant for Charlie, I decided to help things out a bit and deliver it.''

"And paint her door for good measure?"

"It was a nice touch, don't you think?" she said smugly. Reminding Maguire just how much he hated smug little girls.

"So you think Charlie killed the old man?" he asked in a deceptively calm voice.

"I know she did."

Her calm certainty threw him for a moment. "How?" he demanded.

"By leaving him. She took his heart with her, and he could never love anyone else."

"Honey, I doubt he ever loved anyone in his entire life. Are you telling me Pompasse pined away, or do you mean Charlie shoved him down the stairs?"

"How could she do that?" Gia said blankly. "She wasn't even in Italy when he died."

"But you were. Maybe you were in Florence on the day he died. Did you push him down the stairs?"

"Don't be ridiculous. I loved him."

"But you were being replaced, weren't you? Maybe you went to tell him you were leaving him, and he got angry, and you struggled. It was an accident, no one was to blame," he suggested smoothly.

But Gia had already pulled herself together. "You're crazy. I was nowhere near Florence on the day he died. And why the hell do you care?"

"I don't. All I care about are the paintings. I want to know where the other ones are, and I want to find his journals."

"I can't help you," Gia said with an extravagant shrug of her bony shoulders. "And I would if I could. One thing you could say about Pompasse—he took care of his own. If there's any money left then some of it will be mine. I want to make sure the full estate is valued, and I don't like the idea of missing out on the value of those paintings."

"I don't know. Maybe you stole them yourself, then decided to sacrifice one for the sake of your vendetta against Charlie," Maguire suggested. "It still leaves you with at least two priceless paintings."

"Of Charlie." Her venom wasn't feigned. "Not exactly what I want. Trust me, I'm too practical. Don't waste your time with me. Why don't you ask Charlie where the paintings are? She knows this area better than anyone."

He wasn't going to get any more out of her and he knew it. Not at this point. "Go back and work on Henry some more," he said wearily. "It's less expensive revenge than destroying paintings."

"And a lovely notion it is, Maguire. I'm enjoying myself tremendously."

He watched her go, twitching her nonexistent rear, and he cursed softly. He wasn't any further ahead than he had been before.

The problem was, he believed Gia, lying little sneak that she was. And although she admitted dragging the painting into Charlie's room, who had vandalized it in the first place?

Who hated Charlie that much? And why?

15

It still felt peaceful in the ruined church, Charlie thought. Not even Maguire had been able to spoil it for her. Even with the old window and doors completely gone and only a small section of roof remaining, it felt like a safe, holy place.

Several of the old pews were still there, and she made her way to one of them, curling up in the corner with her feet tucked underneath her. It was growing dark, but she didn't mind. Up here she felt protected, at home. Alone, which was the only way she ever had felt completely safe.

Her hands smelled like soap, with no lingering scent of paint. Logically she'd known it couldn't be blood on the doorknob, on her hands, but her heart hadn't listened to logic. It wasn't until Maguire held her and washed the stuff from her hands that she finally calmed down.

How could Maguire's touch calm her? He was the most dangerous of all. And yet for a brief moment, with his body pressed up against her back, she'd felt at peace.

She really must be losing it, she thought. Responding to a pig like Maguire and not Henry. She should do what Henry wanted. She should grit her teeth and get in bed with him, tonight, before any more time passed. It wasn't that she couldn't bear it. She'd survived Pompasse, even welcomed him with a certain tenderness. If the act of sex had seemed slightly messy and degrading, it had brought the old man pleasure, and for that she'd been grateful. He'd given her the first security, the first home she'd ever known. It was a reasonable trade.

She loved Henry—surely she should be able to give him that same pleasure. He didn't expect much from her—not athletics or inventiveness, just acceptance of his body.

But ever since she'd left Pompasse she had been unable to bear a man's touch. Her doctor had suggested that it was simply a case of Henry being the wrong man, but Charlie refused to consider that possibility. Henry was in every way the right man, the perfect man for her. It was only her own coldness that stood in the way, and sooner or later she'd get over it. She had to. Or at least learn how to fake it again.

She'd probably been far too honest with Henry, she thought, pulling her knees up and wrapping her arms around them. He was so solicitous, so careful not to make too many demands, that she felt even more guilty. There were times she almost wished he'd just grab her and kiss her.

But then, Maguire had done just that, hadn't he? And she'd hated it.

Hadn't she?

She leaned her head back against the battered old pew. She didn't want to go back down to the house, but she'd have to, sooner or later. Henry would worry about her. Olivia probably wouldn't notice, but Maguire wouldn't leave her alone. It would take her a few minutes, but she'd pull herself together and climb back down the steep path to the farmhouse. After this morning's ugly scene she had no intention of going by way of Madame Antonella's place. The old lady was getting more and more confused, and Lauretta no longer seemed as capable of calming her. Had Pompasse made any arrangements for her, for the time when she could no longer live there safely? Did they have the same sort of assisted living in Italy that they had in the States? Or would she end up in some depressing nursing home, cursing everyone?

No, Pompasse wouldn't have condemned her to a life like that. He'd always been touchingly devoted to the old lady, the first great love of his life. He never abandoned her in life—he wouldn't have abandoned her in death, either.

Of course, Pompasse had always considered himself immortal. And, in a way, he was. His paintings would live forever, but his body had only been human, and subject to the laws of nature. He was dead, he was dust and ashes now, and in a few days those ashy remains would be buried in the vineyard.

And then maybe Charlie would finally be free.

She needed to talk more with Henry, to see what he'd done on his end. He'd been talking with the lawyers—surely he'd brought things to a point where she could just run away like the coward she was. She had missed Tuscany, missed La Colombala with all her heart and soul, but now that she was back she knew she no longer belonged here. It had been an important part of her life, but that time had passed. She needed to move forward. To find her own home.

For some reason her careful plans for the future no longer seemed so wise. New York had been a haven for five years, but it was no more home than any of the dozens of cities she'd lived in over the years. Home should be with Henry, and yet she couldn't quite imagine it. What had happened to shake her secure belief in her self-ordained future? How could she reclaim it?

She closed her eyes. She was absolutely exhausted, her body still dealing with the vagaries of jet lag and the shock of the last few days. Someone thought Pompasse hadn't fallen down those apartment steps he knew so well, but had been pushed by an angry hand.

But it wasn't her—she'd been holed up in her apartment in New York. Besides, she had no reason to kill him. She'd escaped—or at least she thought she had.

Murderer, it had read, and the red paint had dripped down her door like blood. Someone hated her enough to slash through her portrait and daub it in bloodred paint. Did they hate her enough to do the same to her?

And if everyone was wrong, and Pompasse had been murdered, could that murderer want to hurt Charlie, as well?

She could think of no reason why, and the thoughts went whirling around and around in her head. The wooden pew was hard beneath her curled-up body, but she was past caring. She wrapped her arms around herself in the cool night air because there was no one else she could turn to for warmth and comfort, no one she would let hold her close and calm her. She'd go back to the house later, when everyone was asleep. She'd take off her clothes, go through the adjoining doors and climb into bed with Henry. In the same bed where Pompasse had made love to her.

And she wouldn't say a word. Henry would think she'd been cured, and she'd never tell him the truth. She would make a safe, comfortable life for herself, with babies. She couldn't see Henry as a father, but she could see herself with babies, fat, cheerful babies, at her breast, at her feet, crawling on the dusty floor of a place far away from cities and...

But she would always live in the city. And there'd be no dust in Henry's household. She needed to sleep, at least for a while, before she faced up to her decision.

By tomorrow it would all be simple and clear. By tomorrow she would have slept with Henry and have no more doubts. By tomorrow...

Charlie's houseguests were having a surprisingly good time without her, Maguire thought grumpily. They'd taken Lauretta's explanation without question, and not even devoted old Henry seemed to miss her. Of course, he had Gia doing her best to dazzle him, and the man was easily dazzled. Though if Charlie was as cold as her mother said then the poor old guy probably hadn't gotten laid in a hell of a long time, and Gia was pretty damned tempting.

Though for that matter, Maguire hadn't gotten laid, either, and he hadn't had any trouble resisting

Gia's overtures. But then, he was already distracted by Charlie, a much more complicated proposition.

It must have something to do with his cavemen ancestors, he thought, sitting in a corner watching them. The need to conquer, the need to control, the need to prove to someone like Charlie Thomas that she just hadn't found the right man. So she didn't like sex, right? That's because she hadn't let him try it.

He was full of shit and he knew it. But he couldn't stop thinking of her. Thinking of the things he could do to her, how he could get her to react, and he was sitting there with a hard-on while the girl's mother and a senile old lady were looking at him suspiciously, and he wished to hell he had a book or something to cover his lap. He was like some horny teenage boy, unable to control himself.

Lauretta and Tomaso were trying to get the old woman to go back to her cottage, but Madame Antonella was resisting quite loudly. "I want to stay here!" she cried. "I'm waiting for Pompasse. He promised he would come. He promised he would always take care of me."

"Pompasse is dead, Antonella," Olivia reminded her tactlessly. "Look at it this way—you outlived him."

For a moment he wasn't sure what the old lady would do. A torrent of grief and rage seemed imminent, and then to his amazement the old broad cackled. "True enough," she said. "I'll outlast you all."

"Not if I can help it, you old witch," Gia muttered, but fortunately Antonella was almost as deaf as she was senile.

"Bring me another glass of wine, Lauretta," Antonella commanded grandly. "We must raise a toast to Pompasse."

It was his cue to leave. He wanted to get the ruined painting up to the old church, and he had every intention of taking a little detour by Madame Antonella's cottage. Despite Lauretta's insistence that the paintings couldn't be anywhere inside that small building, he wasn't about to take anyone's word for it.

Once he had the painting stashed he might go for a walk himself. Not that he was worried about Charlie, of course. Everyone insisted that she knew this countryside like a native—that she was perfectly safe alone out there in the dark.

Maybe she was. But maybe Gia was telling the truth, and she wasn't the only one who hated Charlie. And the next little surprise might be more deadly than a slashed portrait and a bucket of paint.

There was a strong half-moon overhead, lighting the way, and he'd always had good night vision. He hadn't wanted to bother with a torch—not wanting to draw attention to his little foray. As far as he could figure out there were as many as a dozen thick journals and, at the very least, two good-size paintings still unaccounted for. They should be easy enough to find if someone had stashed them in the old woman's house.

He set the ruined painting down at the edge of the path leading up to the church and climbed onto the flagstone terrace. For a moment he remembered Charlie's expression when he'd caught up with her this morning. She actually looked frightened of the old lady. But then, Charlie was frightened of everything—men, sex, touching, old women, probably spiders and snakes, as well. For some reason she wasn't afraid of being out alone at night in a place where at least one person had it in for her—but logic didn't seem to be her strong suit. Determination, self-sufficiency were far more important to her than safety.

The house smelled like lavender and mothballs and stale urine, a less-than-intoxicating aroma. It didn't smell of turpentine or paint, however. The rooms were so cluttered he could barely move—there were tables of knickknacks everywhere and more furniture than would comfortably fit in a place twice the size. Antonella wasn't a small woman—he wondered how she managed to move through the crowded pathways. He glanced up at the walls, but they were bare of everything. If Pompasse had ever given his former mistress any of his paintings they were long gone.

He barely made it out of the cottage before Lauretta arrived back with her charge. They were arguing about something, but the sound of their voices was muffled on the night air, and Maguire was too intent on stashing the painting and then going to look for Charlie to pay much attention to a couple of querulous old women.

He might as well admit it—he was worried about her. He wasn't supposed to be swayed by tender feelings—if he started getting sentimental he might think twice about the story he was writing, and then he'd really be up shit's creek without a paddle. Gregory would kill him, and he wouldn't be too happy with himself, either.

Charlie was perfectly capable of taking care of herself. She'd already survived marriage to a creature like Pompasse—and the scandal he was busy stirring up would be child's play for her compared to the real thing.

Unless, of course, she had actually killed the old man.

But he wasn't even going to consider that possibility. He trusted his own instincts enough to know when someone was capable of murder, and that was one area where Charlie fell short. It wasn't that she was incapable of that kind of passion. Beneath that cool exterior raged a blazing heart, he was sure of it. He just couldn't see it channeled into destruction.

He wanted to see her laugh. Had she ever been a child, ever felt playful? She always seemed to be on her best behavior, even with him doing his best to irritate her. What would it take to break through that unnatural calm of hers? Make her laugh, make her cry?

The moon was shining down through the broken roof of the abandoned church, providing plenty of light for him to make his way down into the cellars and put the painting in one of the driest rooms. He didn't even see Charlie until he came back up.

She was sound asleep, curled up on the pew where he himself had stretched out. Her hair had come loose around her face, and a shaft of moonlight shone down on her, like a ridiculous spotlight.

He wanted to laugh at the romantic absurdity of it. He wanted to go over and shake her and wake her up, get her annoyed and fighting again.

He did neither. He crossed the rubble, more quietly now that he knew she was there, but she didn't wake up. He could see the lines of exhaustion on her pale face, and he figured jet lag and the entire mess must have finally caught up with her. She'd be stiff as a board when she woke up, and he ought to give her a good shake and send her back to the villa.

Instead he sat down at the other end of the pew. Even the weight of his body hitting the seat didn't disturb her. She was out for the count, and he stared at her in the moonlight, unable to look away.

She was the strangest combination of opposites. Strong yet fragile. Frigid, yet there was a streak of powerful sensuality beneath her repressed surface. He'd watched the way she touched the flowers, smelled the food, lifted her face to feel the soft breeze against her skin, and he could almost feel her reactions.

She could stand up to her mother, survive a powerhouse like Pompasse, and yet she was afraid of men. It didn't make sense. Nothing about her added up.

He leaned back against the armrest, watching her. So he wanted her—it was no crime, no weakness on his part, he told himself. She was pretty. Gia was prettier, but he wasn't particularly interested in beauty.

Maybe it was just the challenge.

Or maybe it was the look in her eyes and the feel of her body against his when she finally relaxed. Maybe it was the taste of her mouth. What would it taste like if she kissed him back?

She slept for another two hours—by the time she

awoke the moon had sunk low. He'd watched over her the entire time, oddly content. Tomorrow they'd battle again. For now he could keep her safe.

It was dark in the church, and he could tell by her movements that she was awake, that she'd seen him. He caught her before she started screaming, clamping a hand over her mouth to silence her.

"It's just me," he growled.

She relaxed, no longer fighting, and he had a moment to wonder that they both considered him a safe alternative before he released her and moved away.

"What are you doing here?" she demanded.

"Being a proper little gentleman and watching over you while you slept. I stashed the painting in one of the rooms down below—it seemed the best spot to keep it out of sight until we find out where the others are."

"Why?"

"Why what?" he said irritably.

"Why were you watching over me?" She was trying unsuccessfully to pin her hair back, but it kept coming loose around her face and eventually she gave up.

"Maybe I didn't want Pompasse's killer to make you his second course. At least, not until I find the paintings."

She leaned back against the pew. "Why does everyone keep insisting he was murdered? There's been no hint of suspicion."

"Maybe because he was."

"Then why haven't the police been out to the villa? Why hasn't anyone been asking questions? As far I know you're the only one who's the slightest bit curious...." Her voice trailed off. "You're not an undercover policeman, are you?"

He laughed, genuinely amused. "I don't think so."

"Then who are you?"

"You know perfectly well who I am. I'm an insurance investigator, trying to catalog your husband's estate."

"Why don't I believe you?" she said quietly.

Hell and damnation. "I don't know," he said amiably. "Maybe because you're naturally suspicious?"

She ignored his comment. "What time is it?" she demanded.

"After two. You've been sleeping like a baby."

"Why didn't you wake me?"

"Maybe I liked listening to you snore."

"I don't snore. I need to get back to the house."

"Why?"

"I need to get to bed. With my fiancé," she added with a trace of defiance.

If he hadn't been so annoyed he would have laughed. "All right. I'll come back with you."

"I can find my way myself."

"Well, I can't, and I'm sure as hell not going to spend the night up here. I was just waiting for you. By the way, I found out who put the picture in your room."

She was already halfway to the door, but that stopped her. "Who?"

"Who's the logical choice? Your friend Gia. Problem is, she says she didn't slash it. Says she found it like that and thought you deserved a little present."

"Did you believe her?" She'd waited until he caught up with her, and together they started down the pathway.

"As a matter of fact I did. She said she was too pragmatic to ruin an expensive piece of art."

"She is," Charlie said slowly. "Did she steal it in the first place?"

"She says no, she just found it."

"Who took them, then? Does she have any idea where the others are?"

"Not the faintest, love," Maguire said. "I looked around the old lady's cottage. They're not there. I don't think there's room for anything there, even the old lady."

"You're lucky she didn't catch you snooping

around. She always had a fearsome temper. Did you check the paintings on her walls? Pompasse gave her several over the years.''

''None. Just a bunch of cheap garbage littering every available surface. Watch your step!'' he said as she stumbled.

She caught herself before he could grab her. ''I'm fine,'' she said. ''I'm like a mountain goat.''

''Sure you are, sugar,'' he drawled. ''Though I won't argue that you like to butt heads.''

''Only with you, Maguire,'' she shot back.

That's what I'm counting on, he thought, following her down the pathway. It was a strange consolation. She treated everyone else, friend and foe alike, with calm serenity. He was able to get to her as no one else could. He considered that a small victory.

The house was dark, with no sign of life, when they reached the bottom of the path. ''I guess they weren't too worried about you,'' he murmured.

''In case you didn't notice, Henry's light is still on,'' she said. ''He's probably waiting up for me.''

''Maybe,'' Maguire said. ''But if I were you I'd let me go on ahead and check things out. Make sure everyone's where they're supposed to be.''

''What are you suggesting, Maguire?''

''Nothing. You don't want to walk in on anything, now, do you?''

"Go to hell," she said, really angry, and pushed past him, into the hallway, moving up the stairs in the darkness.

She didn't bother being particularly quiet, and neither did he, but it didn't matter. Henry and Gia were making enough noise to drown out anyone's approach.

Charlie had halted outside his door, and in the darkness he couldn't see the expression on her face. Gia was by far the loudest, probably for the express purpose of announcing herself to the entire household, but Henry was wheezing and groaning away in tandem, and for such a large, immovable bed it was making a surprising amount of noise. He had to hand it to Gia—she'd been more successful than his wildest dreams. Henry must have been ripe for the plucking.

He half expected Charlie to slam the door open and demand an explanation. But then, maybe she didn't need one. She turned and walked past him, back down the stairs and out onto the terrace, her eyes bright with unshed tears.

16

The moon had set completely, and the terrace was swathed in darkness. It was only a small comfort. When she'd lived here before, been married to Pompasse, she'd come out here in the middle of the night to hide. But there was no place to hide any longer.

She knew he'd follow her. He loomed over her in the darkness, huge, silent, and she couldn't read his expression. Which was just as well.

"So?" he said finally.

"So what? So Gia managed to get Henry in bed. It's not surprising. She's a beautiful woman, and Henry's been...frustrated recently. It's no wonder he succumbed." She looked up at him, and some of her anguish broke through. "I thought she was going to go after you."

"Yeah, so she told me. Guess you thought you'd kill two birds with one stone by setting her on me. Problem is, it didn't work. I told her I wasn't interested."

"Why not? She's young and beautiful."

"Let's just say I have more taste than that old horn dog you think you're going to marry."

"I'm not going to marry him," she said.

"That's the first sensible thing you've said all night."

"I have no right."

"Oh, for Christ's sake!" Maguire exploded. "Don't be such a bloody fool. The bastard took the first piece of ass offered to him, in your house, in your bed, and you say you have no right. Get over it, lady. You're well rid of him."

"I wouldn't sleep with him."

"So what? A grown man deals with it. He doesn't go after the first bit of pussy that comes his way."

"Maguire!" she said, shocked.

"Don't like my language? I can get a lot more crude. You're better off without him. Tomorrow morning you tell him to pack his bags and get the hell out of here. You're good at doing that— you've had lots of practice with me."

"Yes, but you don't listen," she said mournfully.

"Yeah, but I'm not Henry. Don't make the mistake of thinking we're anything alike." There was a strange undertone to his voice in the darkness, one she couldn't recognize. Didn't want to recognize.

"I don't want you feeling sorry for me," she said.

"I'm not."

"You probably think this is funny."

"Not particularly. Look, sweetheart, it's the middle of the night and even though you took a lengthy snooze you still need your rest. As do I. You want me to go kick Gia out so you can get some peace and quiet?"

"No," she said. "I want to sleep in your bed."

There was a moment of silence. "Isn't that a bit of a drastic turnaround?" he said finally. "Not that I'm unwilling, but under the circumstances..."

"Not with you, asshole!" she said. "I mean I want to sleep in the studio and you can sleep somewhere else. Go up to my room if you want."

"No, thank you. I'm not interested in listening to the moaning, either."

"I'm taking your room."

"Fine. I'll sleep in a chair. I've slept worse places. Though it would help if I had a pack of cigarettes."

"Sorry, I'm fresh out."

He couldn't see her face in the darkness, her doubtlessly woebegone expression. She felt as if the air had been knocked out of her—everything she'd been so sure of had vanished. She'd waited too long. She didn't want to blame Henry—he was only human. And she already knew Gia was an alley cat out to take anything that belonged to Charlie.

"I can see you're brokenhearted," he drawled, and for a moment she wondered what he meant.

She headed for the studio, half expecting him to follow, but he stayed where he was at the edge of the terrace. "Do you need anything?" she felt compelled to ask. "Covers? A pillow?"

"Don't worry your pretty little head about it, sugar. I can find what I need."

"Suit yourself," she said, and shut the French doors behind her, closing him out in the night air.

She didn't start crying until she got into the bed. It was a saggy old double bed—Charlie had no idea where Tomaso had found it, but it enfolded her like an old friend, and she sank into the softness with a sigh that somehow caught on a sob. And once she started she couldn't stop.

She didn't even know why she was crying. Was it for Pompasse? Was it for her seemingly safe future with Henry? Was it for her lonely childhood or her empty present? It didn't matter. She buried her face in the pillow, trying to stifle the sobs that were shaking her body, but the more she fought them the stronger they became, until she thought she might rattle apart from grief.

She was barely aware of the door opening, the

coolness of the air as the covers were lifted. But she felt his body slide up against hers in the sagging bed, his arms go around her, pulling her back against him, and she panicked, kicking out.

"Calm down," Maguire whispered. "It's just me."

"Get out!" she said. Or tried to say. The words were almost indecipherable through her sobs.

"I'm not going anyplace. There are times when a woman needs to be held and this is one of them."

"No!" She tried to fight him, but he was astonishingly strong, holding her pinioned against him.

"Yes," he said. "You need someone to hold you, and I'm your man. Now, go to sleep."

Somewhere along the way her tears had left her. "Sleep?" she echoed in astonishment.

"Yes, sleep. Did you think I was going to have my wicked way with you, love? I'm a right bastard, but even I have my limits, and you're not interested in sex right now."

"I'm never interested in sex."

"So you say," he muttered. "In the meantime, go to sleep. I'm not leaving until you do."

"I can't sleep with you."

"Sure you can. Close your eyes, take a deep breath and try it."

She yanked once more at his restraining arms, but it was hopeless. His grip was like a straitjacket, albeit a relatively gentle one. There was no escaping.

"I hate this. I hate you," she said fiercely.

"Of course you do, love," he said in a lazy voice. "Now, stop arguing and go to sleep."

There was no escape. At least, not until he was asleep. All she could do was lie perfectly still, somehow grit her teeth and put up with the feel of his body pressed up against her back, and sooner or later he'd drift off and she could get away from him.

At least he'd gotten into bed with his clothes on. She could feel the cotton of his T-shirt, though his legs were bare against hers, and...

"What's that?" she demanded.

"What do you think it is? It's not like you never had any. You just didn't like it."

"You're disgusting. Get out of my bed."

"My bed, and I'm not going anywhere. It's a perfectly natural response to being snuggled up to a woman. It doesn't mean I'm going to do anything about it. Go to sleep."

"I don't want..."

"If you keep talking then I'll start thinking of ways to occupy our time."

She shut up, fast. She'd survive this. She'd survive anything—she already had, and this was just one more assault on her fragile serenity.

She took a deep breath, then let it out in a shuddering sigh. The softness of the bed kept her plastered up against him, and the stiffer she held herself, the longer it would take for him to drop his guard and fall asleep. Besides, he was stiff enough for both of them.

The thought shouldn't have been funny. She was just a little punchy by now—too many things happening in too short a period of time. She should be lying here mourning Henry, and instead all she could think about was the feel of Maguire's heat against her back, the steady pounding of his heart, echoing through her own skin.

His breathing was slow and steady, but his hold on her didn't lessen, and she wondered whether he'd be able to sleep with her clamped against him. Probably. The sooner she gave in, the sooner the night would be over.

She closed her eyes, trying to think of something peaceful. Snowstorms and olive trees and ocean waves and heat, reaching into her very bones, soothing her, so that her muscles began to relax and she felt herself sink back against him with a soft, forgiving sigh.

She was going to fall asleep, which seemed like the greatest betrayal of all, and yet she couldn't fight it any longer. She felt drugged, by the night, by the heat of his body, and she was tired of fighting.

"Maguire?" she whispered, just before she fell asleep.

"Hmm?"

She didn't even know she was going to say it until the words came out. "Thank you."

There was silence. And then a little shift, as he tucked her closer to him, spoonlike, and she was even more comfortable. "My pleasure, love," he whispered. "My pleasure."

When she awoke the room was filled with a murky half-light, and for a moment she couldn't remember what had happened. Slowly, almost imperceptibly, she became aware of where she was, what she was doing.

Sometime in the night she'd turned in his arms, facing him. Her hands were under his T-shirt, pressed against the hot skin of his chest, her legs were entwined with his, and when she opened her eyes his face, his mouth, were just inches away, and he was watching her out of steady, calm eyes.

She didn't move. Couldn't. Her body was frozen, her hands trapped beneath his shirt, and yet she wasn't cold. She was hot, burning, a glowing fire radiating outward.

She didn't say a word. They were sharing the

same pillow, and her hair lay tangled around them both. His mouth was so close.

And she knew he wasn't going to bring it any closer. He was going to lie there, watching her, waiting for her to move. Waiting for her to put her mouth against his. Knowing that she would.

It was astonishingly easy and yet the hardest thing in the world. She wanted to kiss him, to feel his mouth. It was that complicated and that simple. And she did what she had to do, moving her head just enough so that her lips brushed against his.

The world didn't end. Her body didn't freeze, her stomach didn't revolt. His lips felt firm, warm beneath hers, and she drew back a bit, to look at him.

He didn't say a word, ever watchful, ever patient. So she kissed him again, a little longer this time, pressing her mouth against his, and her hands clutched at his chest beneath the loose T-shirt, and she could feel the beating of his heart against hers, faster.

She looked at him in the murky shadows, wanting some sort of sign. But none was forthcoming. He was just there, waiting for her, letting her do exactly what she wanted.

And she closed her eyes and kissed him, and he opened his mouth for her, and this time it wasn't firm and dry, it was hot and wet, and she felt a jolt all the way down her body. For half a moment she tried to pull away, and then simply sank against him, pulling her hands from beneath his T-shirt and sliding them around his neck, pulling him closer. She felt his hands skim her face, as if he was afraid to touch her, and then he did, cupping her face lightly, as he met her unpracticed kiss with such profound gentleness that she wanted to weep with longing.

She slid down on the bed, pulling him over her so that he shut out the light, shut out reality. She took his hands from her face and slid them down her body, pressing them against her breasts, and she could feel her nipples harden beneath his fingers, through the layers of cloth, and she could feel that empty yearning in her belly, between her legs, and she was so delirious that she actually wanted someone that she almost laughed out loud.

He rose up on his elbows, looking down at her, and then without a word he pulled off his T-shirt and threw it across the room. Then he reached for hers.

She let him. She even helped him as he skimmed the shirt over her head, then reached for the wispy scrap of bra. He unhooked it with the ease of long practice, and it followed his T-shirt onto the floor, leaving her half naked beneath him, waiting for panic and finding nothing but need.

This time he was the one who kissed her. He pulled her beneath him, and the thin scraps of cotton were the only barrier between them, and she could feel his erection sliding against her. Without thinking she moved, making a cradle for him with her hips, and when she felt his tongue in her mouth her body convulsed with a tiny shiver of shocked pleasure.

She felt his hand move down her body, his long fingers slide between her legs, touching her beneath the damp cotton, and the soft sound she made was half protest, half entreaty. She wanted his flesh against hers, she wanted to feel him, she wanted everything, and when his fingers slid beneath the elastic waistband she almost cried out in relief and anticipation, knowing he'd touch her, knowing she could go someplace in the darkness and shadows that she'd never gone before, and she opened her mouth to tell him yes, when the door from the terrace slammed open, flooding the room with light.

He moved fast, shielding her body with his, hiding her from prying eyes as he turned to face the door. "What the hell do you think you're doing?" he demanded in absolute fury.

"The police are here." It was Olivia's voice, cool, detached. "No one's seen Charlie since last night, and I'm starting to get worried."

"The police are looking for Charlie?" Maguire demanded, keeping her hidden beneath him.

"No, actually the police are here to question people about Pompasse. Turns out they think there's a possibility that he was murdered, after all. They're with Henry right now, but they were very interested to hear about you. I imagine you'll be next." Even from her cramped position Charlie could hear her mother move closer. "You're sure you haven't seen Charlie?"

"I'm sure Charlie's fine. And now if you'd get the hell out of here I'll get dressed and come and talk to the *polizia*. But I don't fancy having an audience around."

"You don't strike me as a shy man, Maguire," Olivia said archly.

"Get the hell out!"

"I'm going. But it might be a good idea if Charlie made an appearance fairly soon. We wouldn't want the police to get the wrong idea."

The door closed behind her, plunging the room back into darkness, and Charlie slid out of bed so fast her knees slammed against the rough stone floor. The pain was welcome, and she scrambled out of the way, trying to cover herself with her arms.

Maguire was sitting up in bed. "Don't look at me like that," he said irritably. "I didn't start it."

"You were about to finish it," she said, her voice not much more than a whisper.

"And you were about to like it," he shot back.

"Get out!" she said.

"Here we go again." His voice was infinitely weary, and if she had anything close to hand she would have thrown it at him. Unfortunately there was nothing in the room but the bed. The damned soft, cozy, comforting bed.

He got out of bed and she closed her eyes, wanting to blot out everything that had happened. A minute later something came flying, and she realized he'd tossed her shirt and bra in her face. He was already dressed, pulling his denim shirt back on, and in the shadowy light his face was grim.

She still hadn't moved from her place in the corner, though she held the T-shirt against her chest to provide more protection. He opened the door, and bright daylight flooded the room once more. It must be midday, she thought miserably.

And then he strode back across the room, reached down and hauled her up against him. "Remember one thing, Charlie," he snarled. "You *liked* it." He put his hand behind her neck and kissed her, hard and full and deep. And then he pulled away, looking down at her.

"Nice knowing you," he said. And then he was

gone, leaving her trembling, her clothes clutched to her chest.

He had every intention of heading straight to the car. He'd already stashed his laptop in there, ready for a quick getaway, but there were three police cars blocking his way, not to mention a handful of armed gentlemen on the terrace. He could have slipped out the back, made it up to the old church and headed out over open terrain, but he'd be screwed without his material. Not to mention that Gregory would cut his throat. Besides, either way, the jig was undoubtedly up. He hadn't broken any laws—he'd just be kicked out of the villa, but he had been running out of time, anyway. And a part of him was glad. He needed to get away from Charlie before he got sucked in too deep. She had a bad effect on him—turning him into a sentimental sap when he couldn't afford to let sentiment get in his way.

It was just as well that bitch Olivia had interrupted them when she had. He'd given Charlie a taste of pleasure, and now that she knew what it was like she could go enjoy it with someone else. Though preferably not with a jerk like Henry.

He could still barely believe what had just happened. She'd come when he'd kissed her, he'd felt her whole body convulse. She had so much bottled-up sexuality simmering inside her she was past ready to explode. She just needed someone who knew how to handle her.

It wasn't going to be him, more's the pity. In a matter of minutes she was going to find out what a shit he really was, and then she'd never look at him again, much less touch him.

Which was fine with him. He didn't need a vulnerable child-woman like Charlie falling in love with him, as she'd be bound to do as soon as he gave her a nice big orgasm. He preferred his solitary life, and commitment was the last thing he was looking for, and the first thing Charlie needed.

Pompasse's women were assembled on the terrace. Lauretta was trying to calm a querulous and confused Antonella, Gia was smoking, and Olivia was staring out over the countryside.

"Have a good night, Maguire?" Gia greeted him smugly. "I did."

"So I gather," he said in a cool voice.

"I know. I heard the two of you come upstairs. I hope poor Charlie wasn't too distressed."

"She survived," he said.

Some of Gia's smugness vanished. "Don't try to convince me you slept with her. I know better."

"Of course you do, Gia," he replied.

"Would you mind?" Olivia broke in. "It's my daughter you're talking about."

Maguire took a quick glance around. His battered Fiat was blocked in by the police cars, but if he was fast he might be able to get out without hitting anyone, which would be a major plus. He was going to have to answer questions sooner or later, but he'd just as soon get the hell out of there before anyone knew exactly who and what he was. Before having to face Charlie once she knew what a liar he was.

Not to mention making his escape without denting a police car in the process.

He went over and poured himself a cup of Lauretta's strong coffee. It wasn't as good as Charlie's. There was something irresistible about a woman who could make a truly great cup of coffee. Hell, there was a lot that was irresistible about Charlie. And he needed to get over it. "So what are the police doing?"

"Talking to Henry," Olivia said. "Apparently he had a lot to tell them."

"About Pompasse? I thought he barely knew the old goat."

"No, Mr. Maguire," Olivia said, meeting his gaze. "I do believe he's talking about you."

17

"If they're not ready for me then I think I'll go for a little walk," Maguire was saying in a lazy voice just as Charlie came out on the terrace. She had pulled her clothes on with shaking fingers, then gone around the back way to enter the house from the other side. For a moment she'd been tempted to just run upstairs, but she could hear voices from behind the closed door to the dining room. Henry's voice, in his rich, modulated tones, and the rapid-fire translator.

She heard Maguire's name, and she didn't want to listen anymore. She would have turned and run back out, but Gia had already spotted her, and her mouth curved in a perfect, catlike smile.

"You will please stay here, *signore.*" One of the policemen had moved to block Maguire's way. "They will be ready for you momentarily."

She felt him look at her from across the terrace, but she ignored him, unable to look into his dark, unfathomable eyes and remember what had passed, or almost passed, between them.

"Where the hell have you been, Charlie?" her mother demanded. "Henry was worried sick about you."

"Sure he was," Charlie said, moving to pour herself a cup of coffee.

"You're still wearing your same clothes," Gia pointed out maliciously. "Where'd you spend the night?"

For some reason they were all far too interested in the answer to her question. Even the police seemed curious. And God knows Maguire was capable of coming up with the truth if she didn't answer.

"I spent the night in the church. I like to go up there and be alone sometimes. You have to admit this house is awfully crowded." She managed a deprecating smile, a ghost of her usual calm. "I must have fallen asleep up there." At least it wasn't a complete lie.

"It's not safe up there, Signora Charlie. You should know that!" Lauretta said. "The stones are crumbling more than you're used to. You could fall and no one would know where to find you."

"Actually that's not true," Gia said. "Now we all know where to find her when she disappears."

There was no missing the undertone of menace in Gia's soft voice, and Charlie could have kicked herself. Not that she truly believed anyone would

want to hurt her, apart from Gia's focused malice.
But still, one of the great joys of climbing up to
the ruined church was knowing that she'd be completely alone, that no one would wander up to join
her. Now they all knew, though she doubted anyone would care enough to make the trek.

Of course, Maguire had already done just that,
and it hadn't ruined the place for her. She allowed
herself a casual glance in his direction, then
frowned. He was surreptitiously moving toward the
edge of the terrace, for all the world as if he was
about to make a run for it.

"Signore Maguire."

The rest of the police had emerged from the dining room, accompanied by a particularly smug-
looking Henry. Considering Henry's occupation
the last time she'd been anywhere near him, Charlie wasn't particularly pleased to see that expression on his patrician features.

Maguire halted, like a deer frozen in the headlights. "Yeah?"

"Mr. Richmond informs me that you're here under false pretenses." The stern-looking *poliziotto*
in the fancy uniform said, clearly the man in
charge. "You told the ladies you were working as
an insurance adjuster, when in fact you're a paparazzo."

Maguire had the gall to look offended. "I'm a reporter."

"For the sleaziest tabloid on the international scene," Henry broke in ruthlessly. "You took advantage of the innocent trust of my fiancée, wormed your way in here just to write an exposé of Pompasse and his sex life. The police tell me I can't have you charged with anything, but I can beat you within an inch of your life."

Maguire strolled right up to him, and Henry took a nervous step backward. "You and what army, mate?" Maguire demanded.

"Oh, my," Olivia breathed, fascinated. "I should have guessed you weren't a bureaucrat."

"It would be best if you left, Signore Maguire," the policeman said solemnly. "But we'll be wanting to talk with you shortly, and we'll be confiscating your notes and photographs."

"Photographs?" Charlie said faintly, the first words she'd been able to utter.

"You won't be confiscating a goddamned thing," Maguire said. "For that matter, there's nothing to confiscate. I haven't been taking any notes."

"His laptop," Charlie said in a strained voice. "You should check his laptop."

"Unfortunately they'll need to get a court order to do that," Maguire said, turning to look at her.

There was no apology, no remorse in his face. "And the *Starlight* has the best lawyers in the business."

"The *Starlight?*" Charlie echoed in horror. She'd managed to avoid tabloids whenever possible, but the *Starlight* was notorious enough for even her to be aware of.

"He's top of the food chain when it comes to rats," Henry said. "But you forget you're dealing with a damn fine lawyer already."

"Please leave," Charlie said, breaking through. "Please." Her voice was calm, steady. She'd wrapped her serenity back around her like a cloak, and nothing could get through.

Without a word Maguire turned and bounded across the terrace, through the maze of cars to his rusty-looking Fiat. He paused as he climbed in the driver's seat, and his eyes met Charlie's for a long, thoughtful moment. And then he was gone.

"Marco, Adolfo, make sure Signore Maguire leaves the premises," the chief policeman ordered. "And Signora Pompasse, if you would be so good as to come this way, we have a few questions for you."

She allowed herself one last glance at the Fiat as it sped down the road. He drove like a bat out of hell, she thought. Maybe he'd even crash before he reached the bottom of the driveway. One could only hope.

She turned to the policeman, a calm, ready smile on her face. "Of course," she said. And followed him into the dining room.

By the time Maguire reached Geppi he'd managed to lose his police escort. There'd been no need to—it had been pure cussedness on his part, but he took great pleasure in the shortcuts and false turns that left the police far behind. He wanted to get back to his ramshackle apartment in Florence in time to download the photos and text, just in case Italian law proved to be more invasive than usual, and he needed to call Gregory and tell him what had happened. It was a setback, of course. Maybe a major one. Maybe he should just trash his material and tell him there was no story.

Yeah, and how far would that get him? Gregory was no fool, and Maguire had been keeping him up-to-date on the stuff he'd been uncovering. Missing paintings, a harem of castoff women, a murder and a world-famous artist were elements too juicy to be ignored. If Maguire didn't give Gregory the goods, then chances were he'd hire someone to take those elements and make something up.

There were a dozen reporters after the same story, and making some kind of quixotic gesture would do little good. Besides, nobility wasn't part of Maguire's makeup. Charlie had chosen to marry the old man, and she'd benefited from it, hadn't she? People make their choices in this world, and then they have to pay the price. So what if Charlie's price was a little too steep? So what if he'd gone in there and upped the ante? It wasn't his problem any longer.

He didn't expect to see her again, which was nothing but a blessing. She annoyed him, she got under his skin, and she made him start thinking about things that had no place in his self-sufficient life.

No, to be honest he couldn't blame her for everything. He'd been burned-out for a while now, ready to chuck it all and head back to Australia. He'd been counting on this story, and the ensuing book deal, to keep him in style for the rest of his life.

He didn't need money to go back to Australia. There were jobs waiting—he could have his pick of newspaper work if he wanted, or he could just go out to the cattle station he owned with his brother and become a rancher and screw everything. Right now that seemed the best bet.

In the meantime, though, he had to finish with this mess. He couldn't just drop it, not until the

questions were answered. Where were the paintings? Who killed the old man?

And what the hell was he going to do if he never
saw Charlie again?

He needed to get back to his apartment and call
Gregory. So why the hell was he circling around,
stashing his battered Fiat in a back alley and sitting
in a café, watching the road to La Colombala?

Charlie did what she always did in times of
stress. Once the police had finished their brief and
respectful questioning, she had headed straight for
the kitchen. By the time her mother strolled in, the
tabletops and countertops were littered with ingredients, and Charlie was kneading bread with a ven-
geance, her face streaked with flour, her clothes
covered with everything else.

"You always were an extremely messy child,"
Olivia remarked. "I should have sent you to the
Cordon Bleu. At least there you would have
learned to clean up after yourself."

Charlie didn't even look up from the dough. "At
the Cordon Bleu you have people to do the dirty
work and the cleanup," she said. "Besides, by the
time I was old enough to go I was already married
to Pompasse."

"To my regret, yes," Olivia said. There was one
tiny section of counter that was uncluttered, and

Olivia hoisted herself up onto it, obviously preparing for a chat. "I remember when we lived in that awful place in the suburbs, when I was married to what's-his-name. Greenwich or Rye or someplace. You were seven years old and I bought you one of those tacky little play ovens. You spent every spare minute turning out tiny little cakes that tasted like cardboard and you kept wanting me to eat them."

"And you were on a diet and couldn't be bothered," Charlie said.

"You're just lucky you didn't end up with an eating disorder, given that you turn to food for comfort at the drop of a hat."

"I wouldn't call this situation 'at the drop of a hat,' I turn to food preparation, not eating, and I came here to be alone," Charlie pointed out coolly, concentrating on the dough.

"I know you did. I didn't feel like leaving you alone. Sue me. What are you going to do about Henry?"

"What do you mean?"

"You know perfectly well what I mean. The entire household does. Are you going to forgive him and take him back, or are you going to break the engagement?"

Charlie glanced at her. "I'm sure you have an opinion on that that you're just dying to tell me."

Olivia shrugged. "I want what's best for you."

"Sure you do."

"Actually, I really do. We never got along, the two of us. I suppose I was just too selfish to be a mother. But that doesn't mean I don't care about you. I worry about you, Charlie. I don't want to see you make another mistake."

Charlie didn't bother to hide her disbelief. "Don't tell me you want Henry for yourself? He's too old for you."

"You still think I wanted Pompasse?" Olivia asked, disbelieving.

"Why else were we here? Why else did you have a screaming, raging fit when I told you we were married?"

Olivia shook her head. "I love how the young always have all the answers. Of course I intended to have an affair with him when we first came to visit. He was famous, he was fascinating, and I was in a celebrity-hunting mood. I never intended to marry him. And I certainly never intended for *you* to marry him."

"I did. And you couldn't stop me."

"I know, Charlie. And I'm sorry for that."

Charlie jerked her head up, the dough momentarily forgotten. "What did you say?"

"I said I'm sorry I couldn't stop you. The man was obsessed with you, and when I couldn't stop it I could only hope he'd treat you like a goddess. Instead you had years of misery.''

"It wasn't misery," she said absently, still concentrating on Olivia's words. "I don't think you've ever apologized before."

Olivia laughed. "Haven't I? Well, I'm an arrogant bitch, there's no denying that. Not anybody's notion of an ideal mother. I'm selfish and greedy and self-absorbed, and I doubt if I ever put your well-being ahead of mine in your entire lifetime."

"I'd agree with that."

"But that doesn't mean I don't love you, Charlie."

Charlie looked at her, her hands motionless in the dough. "And how do you define that love? Isn't love caring about someone, sacrificing for someone, putting their happiness ahead of your own? You've never done that in your life."

"No, I haven't," Olivia said. "But, nevertheless, I love you."

Charlie straightened her shoulders. "I'm touched to hear it."

"You're all I've got, Charlie."

"And whose fault is that?"

"Mine," Olivia said. She slid off the counter in one smooth move. "I just thought I'd mention it, in case it might come in handy later on in life. The fact that your lousy mother loves you."

"Great." Charlie punched the dough.

"Nothing like a touching mother-daughter reconciliation to get me sentimental," Olivia said lightly. "So tell me, precious. How was Maguire in bed?"

"Why don't you find out for yourself?" she shot back.

"Apart from the fact that I don't know where he's gone, I'm not interested. You know me, I like 'em buff and brainless. Maguire's buff enough, I gather, but he's a little too complicated for me. I think you could handle him, though."

Charlie turned to stare at her mother in disbelief. "Are you out of your mind? He's a tabloid reporter! He was lying to us, using us to get his slimy little secrets to splash all over the pages of some disgusting magazine. He probably has pictures of you in the shower."

"And pictures of you in bed. I agree, he's a very bad boy, and he deserves to be punished. But I've never seen anyone look at you the way he does, when he thinks no one is watching."

"I don't want to hear this."

"Of course you don't, sweetie," Olivia said. "You have all the answers. But you know, sometime you ought to consider the alternative. Maybe things aren't quite what they seem." And she left the room before Charlie could reply.

Typical of Olivia. She had a flair for the dramatic, and she always wanted to have the last word, the great exit line. She probably expected Charlie to throw her arms around her and weep gratefully at the thought that beneath her pathological self-absorption her mother had a spark of feeling for her. If she even believed it.

But Charlie had been protecting herself for too long to fall for it. So Olivia was having some sentimental backwash about her only offspring. It was probably just hormonal and would pass as soon as she set her sights on some new young man. In the meantime, Charlie had too much on her plate to start bringing her mother into the equation.

She'd had five minutes alone, letting her anger dissipate into the dough, when Tomaso appeared in the open door, his sun-beaten face creased with concern. "No one's going to want to eat that, Signora Charlie," he said. "Lauretta would tell you that you've put so much anger into making it that it would probably poison people."

"Too bad Maguire's gone, or we could feed it to him," she growled.

"I wanted to talk to you about that."

Charlie sighed. "Not you, too, Tomaso! I've already had to put up with the police and my mother. I really don't even want to think about Maguire, much less discuss him...."

"Not Maguire, Charlie. It's everyone. I think you all should leave, and quickly."

Charlie looked down at the dough. Tomaso was right—she could feed it to Henry and Gia, but she found she didn't even care enough. She dumped the dough in the compost bucket, and for a moment she remembered doing the same thing a week ago, when she first heard that Pompasse had died. Maybe she'd better stop making bread. That, or stop getting upset.

She turned her attention back to Tomaso. "Leave? But why? We haven't even buried Pompasse yet. And where would everyone go?"

"It's Madame Antonella. She's getting very troublesome, *cara*. She hasn't been well these last few months, and the master's death has hit her very hard. You've heard her—she keeps talking about murder, and whores, and the like. I can't be sure that she'll be safe as long as there are strange people around. Once everyone leaves she'll calm down and be fine. But I'm afraid she'll hurt herself or someone else as long as there are so many strangers here. And to *madame*, in her condition, almost everyone is a stranger."

Charlie sighed. "I can't kick everyone out, Tomaso, even if I wanted to. I think part interest in this place was left to Gia. If you really think Madame Antonella has deteriorated that much then perhaps we should find someplace to put her. She's only in her seventies, but at times she seems much older. She needs a kind of home, or assisted living, where she can't hurt herself.''

"Charlie!'' Tomaso was shocked. "Don't let Lauretta hear you talking like that! The master promised *madame* a home for life. He was devoted to her. You can't send her away!''

"I don't want to send her away, I just want her to be safe,'' Charlie said wearily.

"She would never…'' Before Tomaso could finish his sentence Madame Antonella tottered into the kitchen.

Her rheumy eyes slid over Charlie, dismissing her, and fastened on Tomaso. "Where's Lauretta? I want to go home now,'' she said in autocratic tones.

"Lauretta is already up at your cottage,'' Tomaso said in a soothing, deferential voice. "I'll take you up there. Say goodbye to Charlie.''

"Charlie?'' The old lady looked confused for a moment. "Who's Charlie?''

"The master's wife. You remember Charlie, Madame Antonella. She lived here with us.''

Antonella stared at Charlie for a moment, then shook her head. "She's not his wife,'' she said flatly. "Now, stop annoying me. Take me back home.'' Not bothering to wait, she started out the back door to the winding gravel path.

"She didn't hear me, did she?" Charlie whispered, worried.

Tomaso shook his head. ''She's deaf, and we were speaking English. Besides, few things make sense to her nowadays. But I meant what I said. Lauretta and I are worried about her, and there's no way we can move her. The rest of you will have to leave. Soon.''

And he followed the old woman's slow, fragile progress up the hillside.

18

It was going to rain. By the time Charlie finished cleaning up the devastation she'd created in the kitchen the sky had turned a dark, ominous gray. Odd, but in the seven years she'd lived in Tuscany she couldn't really remember rain. They had to have had their share of it, otherwise the crops wouldn't be so plentiful. But whenever she thought of Tuscany, all she could remember was the bright, merciless glare of the sun.

The house seemed deserted, though she knew that was too much to hope for. Lauretta and Tomaso were up at the cottage, getting *madame* settled, trying to calm her querulous fears. Olivia was probably taking her afternoon rest—she wouldn't forego that for love nor money. Particularly for money, which had always held more sway with her mother than so-called love.

Charlie still couldn't get over her mother's odd conversation. Never in her life had her mother told her she loved her, or at least not that Charlie could remember. Olivia wasn't the demonstrative sort, and she'd never been particularly fond of children. She had trotted Charlie around Europe as if she were a partially housebroken toy poodle—watching her like a hawk, cooing over her on occasion, but mostly handing her over to someone else's care. By the time Charlie was twelve she'd lost count of the schools, the countries, even the fathers she'd had. By the time she was fourteen she'd learned to do without anyone.

She'd always thought that was the way she preferred things to be. But for some reason she was getting mortally tired of being so damned self-reliant. Just once in her life she wanted to lose her temper, have a tantrum, stop being in charge of everything.

That was impossible, of course. She was a responsible woman, with people depending on her. It didn't matter that she wanted to jump in her car and go chasing after Maguire to give him a piece of her mind. The lying, treacherous, slimy bastard had used her, and God knows how far he would have gone if her mother hadn't interrupted. Right now the notion of venting her fury had taken on an almost grail-like dimension.

At least Olivia had managed to save her in time, and for that alone Charlie should be eternally grateful. She was just having a hard time summoning that well-deserved gratitude when all she wanted to do was break something over Maguire's hard head.

There was nothing she could do about it but get on with life. Maguire had escaped, and it was just as well. She needed to focus her energy on getting her life back together, not on an infuriating, lying journalist.

She needed a shower and a change of clothes, but she couldn't decide where she wanted to go. Her bedroom upstairs was haunted by the memories of Pompasse and the noisy lovemaking of her erstwhile fiancé. The studio held even stronger ghosts.

In the end she had no choice—her clothes were upstairs. She could only hope that Gia and Henry had taken their activities elsewhere if they were busy continuing them.

They weren't. Henry was sitting in her room waiting for her, and it took all of Charlie's formidable self-control not to turn around and leave. She could handle it, she told herself. She could handle anything.

"This is my room, Henry," she said in a deceptively polite voice. "I don't remember inviting you in here."

"You're angry," he said, an understatement. "I don't blame you. I'm completely horrified by what

I did last night. I have no excuse, no right to ask you to forgive me.''

She waited. She knew perfectly well he was going to ask, anyway. She just didn't know what she was going to answer.

He rose, crossing the room to take her hand in his. He had very narrow, soft hands. Perfectly manicured, always immaculate. Hands that had never done a day's worth of real labor in his entire protected life. He drew her back to the bed, and she let him, letting her hand rest in his, observing her own reactions from a distance.

Odd, but she didn't feel that chill, that fear from the touch of his dry, cool skin. She didn't feel anything at all anymore. Maybe Maguire had cured her. Or maybe she'd just gone beyond distaste into numbness.

He sat down beside her on the bed, gently stroking her hand, and she let him, her attention on the darkening clouds outside, the rapidly approaching storm.

''I need to tell you why it happened,'' he was saying. ''I need to explain to you, so that maybe I'll understand it myself. You have to know how frustrated I was. I'm a man, Charlie, with a man's needs. I've tried to be patient with you, God knows I have, but last night something just snapped. Maybe it was jet lag, maybe it was the way that

Neanderthal was looking at you, maybe it was some crazy self-destructive streak…''

"Neanderthal?" she interrupted.

"Maguire." His voice held all the contempt of generations of Ivy League entitlement. "That ruthless, sleazy journalist couldn't keep his eyes off you. And you didn't seem to mind. I couldn't believe it—you've always placed a high value on yourself, and yet you didn't even notice that man was stalking you."

"Stalking me? I don't think so, Henry," she said calmly. "You were imagining things. I have no idea why you'd be jealous, but I can assure you that Maguire wasn't the slightest bit interested in me, apart from his goddamned story."

"I'm not trying to excuse myself," Henry said, ignoring her protest. "I'm just trying to explain. I'd just flown halfway around the world for you, and you didn't care. You didn't want or need my help. Or me, for that matter. You disappeared, and Gia was looking at me, talking to me the way you used to, as if I were the center of the universe, and I suppose I was flattered. And I admit it, I was attracted. I was tired of being made to feel like I was disgusting. Gia saw me as a man she wanted, rather than someone making impossible demands."

"Gia saw you as someone she could take away

from me,'' Charlie said. ''A new meal ticket with the added advantage of hurting me.''

''She's in love with me, Charlie.''

She turned to look at him. He was absolutely serious, and for once Charlie couldn't think of a single response.

''Well?'' he said after a moment.

''I hope you'll be very happy together,'' she said.

''I don't want it to be this way, Charlie,'' he cried. ''This wasn't what I planned. Let me tell you about the first time I fell in love with you.''

''Please don't,'' she said wearily. The rain had begun to spit down from the sky, beating against the old house. She should get up and close the casement window, but Henry was still stroking her hand as if he thought if he rubbed it hard enough he'd get his three wishes.

''Humor me,'' he said. ''I've never told you this, and it's past time. We didn't just happen to meet at La Chance, you know. I came looking for you.''

''Really?'' She tried to summon an ounce of interest. He wasn't going to release her until he got it all off his chest, and she owed him that much. To hear him out.

''You see, I'd fallen in love with a painting. A painting of you, Charlie. I'd fallen in love with the look in your eyes and the expression on your face. I paid a fortune for the damned thing, telling myself it was an excellent investment because it was a Pompasse, but the real reason was because I wanted you. The girl in the painting. I wanted you to look at me like you looked at the painter. I wanted you in my house, not just the oil and canvas.''

''I've never seen any of Pompasse's work in your apartment,'' she said.

''I didn't want you to see it. I didn't want you to know how…obsessed I'd become. And once I met you I knew the real thing could be so much better. That you could become my Charlie, that you'd look at me with all that need and longing. But you never did.''

''Which painting?''

He frowned. ''Does it matter?''

''Pompasse did dozens of me over the years. I want to know which painting you bought, that you thought captured my soul.'' She already knew the answer, knew it with a sinking dread, but she had to hear him say it.

''It was called *Charlie in Her Dressing Gown*,'' he said.

She closed her eyes for a moment, remembering. Remembering the empty soul that portrait revealed, the naked need and helplessness.

"So you fell in love with the painting and set out to find me," she said calmly. "And you call Maguire the stalker."

He looked affronted. "You don't understand. It was your purity that I fell in love with. That's why I didn't mind when you weren't interested in sex. I thought I preferred you like that—pristine and unsullied. Like some chaste Diana. I didn't realize how human I could be."

"I understand," she said. *Let go of my hand and go away,* she thought. *I can't stand this anymore.*

"I'm not giving up, Charlie," he said, his voice ragged. "We were meant to be together, I've always known it. You will become that girl in the picture again, I can feel it. We can be happy, darling girl, you know we can, and..."

"Henry," she said softly, moving his hand away from hers. "Not now, not ever."

He blinked in disbelief. "You don't mean that."

"Go away, Henry. Go to hell and take Gia with you."

"Charlie!" he said, shocked.

But Charlie was past worrying what Henry thought. "Take Gia and go back to the States. You need someone to adore you and I'm sure Gia will fill the bill, at least for a while. Just support her in the manner to which she's been accustomed and things should be just fine."

He rose from the bed, and she could feel the anger in him. "You're jealous," he said.

"Not particularly."

"Not of me," Henry said bitterly. "I wouldn't be fool enough to think I was ever that important to you. No, you're jealous of Gia. You know that she's a real woman and you'll never be more than a cold, lifeless, frigid bitch. That painting has more warmth than you do."

The last trace of guilt slipped away. "Thank you, Henry," she said. "Now fuck off."

He slammed the door behind him, odd behavior for a mature man, Charlie thought absently. But then, Henry was far less mature than his years might suggest. He was a spoiled boy in an old man's body, and she didn't want any part of him.

The rain was splattering into the room, and the plain white curtains, now soaking wet, flapped in the breeze. She should get up and close the window, she thought, but she couldn't make herself move.

She stared down at her hands almost absently. There was still flour beneath her short fingernails. Better than bloodred paint. She looked up, and the smear on her door was a faint rosy color. And she knew she had to move.

Even the studio offered more respite than this place. She paused long enough to slam the window shut and grab some clean clothes, and then she raced down the stairs, hoping she wouldn't run into yet another person intent on unwanted conversation.

The house was deserted. She was half tempted to climb back up to the deserted church, but even though part of the roof remained to shelter her from the storm, the path itself would be a slippery trail of mud.

Which left the studio. She could take a shower, and even sleep there tonight if she had to. Maguire was gone, with his lies and his tricks and his wicked hands. If anything, she should be grateful to him. In a few short moments he'd proved to her that she wasn't nearly as repressed as she thought she was. He'd touched her, kissed her, and she'd responded. If she could respond to a lying, conniving creature like Maguire, then there was definitely hope for her.

Maybe she should take a cue from her mother and find herself a boy toy. Someone young and muscle-bound without a brain in his head. Someone who existed only to please women, who could teach her to enjoy her body.

Except, when she tried to conjure him in her mind, he looked suspiciously like Maguire.

There was no hurry, she reminded herself, pausing at the French doors leading to the rain-soaked terrace. She was free of one man, and there was definite hope for the future. In the meantime she needed to forget about men and sex and concentrate on the mess that Pompasse had made of his departure. She still refused to believe he could have been murdered, and the police had given her little real information. The past week had taken on an almost nightmarish tinge, and she could only hope that she'd wake up in her own bed in her New York apartment and all of this would be some bizarre fantasy.

That wasn't going to happen. She no longer believed in happy endings and miracles. Nor did the rain look like it was going to let up any time soon. Clutching her clean clothes in her arms, she dashed out onto the terrace and headed for the studio.

She ran inside, slamming the door behind her, shutting out the storm. The huge room was a mass of gloom and shadows, and she tried to remember where the light switch was. She felt her way carefully, running her hand along the wall, when suddenly she realized she wasn't alone.

Something was moving in there, in the shadowed darkness. Someone was breathing, watching her.

"Who's there?" she called out sharply.

The lack of response was terrifying. She began to edge her way back toward the door, slowly, trying to get her eyes accustomed to the darkness, half afraid of what she might see. "Is that you, Henry?" she demanded. "Gia? I know someone's there, I can hear you."

Still no answer, just the faint rustle of clothing as someone moved closer. There was nothing to be afraid of, Charlie told herself. Someone was playing a trick on her, probably the wretched Gia. But no one would hurt her, no one would touch her....

Something came hurtling toward her out of the darkness, like a huge bat, blotting out what little light there was. She tried to duck, and felt the wood glance against her head, felt the wetness that may have been paint, may have been blood. It was a painting, though in the darkness she couldn't begin to guess which one, she could only tell that the canvas had been slashed and splattered, just like the other one.

The door was behind her, and her hand felt the knob at the center of her back, and she fumbled with it, desperate, as the huge dark creature kept coming toward her, a mass of shadows. Something else came flying at her head, but she finally managed to open the door and escape out into the rainy afternoon, hearing it clatter harmlessly to the floor.

She slipped on the wet stone terrace, going down hard, and she scrambled up again. The noise of the downpour drowned out the sound of her pursuer, but panic was still searing through her. She ran down the steps to her car, the rain soaking her hair, her clothing, plastering it against her skin.

She jumped inside and slammed the door, locking it. Waiting, waiting for a dark, shadowy figure to appear out of the rain and try to reach her. Then at least she could see who it was who had sent her into such a mindless panic.

But no one came. She was alone, wet and shivering in the tiny car, but no evil figure appeared out of the gloom to threaten her, hurt her.

She took a deep breath, pushing her wet hair out of her face. Her hand came away red with paint or blood, she didn't know and didn't care. She had two choices. She could get out of the car and try to make it back into the house, hoping that whoever had been lurking in the studio wouldn't reach her first.

Or she could drive away.

The keys were in the ignition, her hands were shaking so much she could barely turn them, but it was a no-brainer. She tore away, her tires sliding in the fresh mud, and drove off down the rutted driveway as fast as she dared. The rain was so heavy she could barely see beyond the windshield, and she was shivering, freezing, crying. It didn't matter. Within five minutes she was off the property, onto the main road that led through Geppi, into Florence. And she didn't look back.

19

Maguire had never had a psychic moment in his whole pragmatic life. Sitting under a leaking awning in the pouring rain was probably the most irrational thing he'd ever done, and yet three hours later he was still there, drinking his millionth cup of coffee, staring up at the villa through the clouds and mist like some forlorn suitor.

Hell, no, like a reporter on a hot story, he reminded himself. That was what made the difference between the good reporters and the great ones—tenacity. Working the story like a dog with a bone, never letting go until he had everything he needed from it.

And who the hell was he kidding? Maybe he'd been a great reporter once, but now he was nothing but a hack, pandering to the worst instincts in human nature. Either way, it was better than wars.

When Charlie's little Alfa first appeared he almost didn't believe his eyes. But there weren't that many sports cars on the roads this time of year—hell, there weren't that many cars at all in the pouring rain, so he definitely recognized Charlie's. She drove through town like a crazy woman, and by the time he'd slammed some *lire* down on the table and gotten into his car she was out of sight.

He could only guess she was heading toward Florence, though he couldn't imagine why. She'd been driving so damned fast he couldn't be certain she was in the driver's seat, or if she was even alone. Hell, maybe she and Henry had patched it up and they were running off to get married.

It didn't matter. He headed out of town after her, his bald tires skidding in the mud.

He caught up with her on the hill just outside of town, amazing considering how much more power her car had than his ancient rust bucket. He could see her fishtailing as she headed up the steep curve, and he sped up, trying to get one more ounce of power out of his old engine. His windshield wipers needed replacing, and he could barely see through the downpour, but Charlie's brake lights were unmistakable as the car slid sideways ahead of him.

"Slow the fuck down," he muttered beneath his breath, but Charlie wasn't listening. The road was getting steeper, she was pulling away, and he considered honking his horn. If she knew he was following her she'd probably simply drive faster. He slammed his foot down on the accelerator, trying to catch up with her, and his tires spun.

She disappeared into the rain and mist, and he swore again, trying to get his stubborn old car to behave. By the time he reached the crest of the hill she was already out of sight.

He kept going, telling himself he was headed that way, anyway, telling himself that nothing would happen to her, telling himself to hurry the fuck up and find her.

When he did he almost missed seeing her. The Alfa was off to the side of the road, halfway up an embankment, the lights spearing wildly into the rain.

He slammed on his brakes, sliding on the greasy surface as he struggled to maintain control of his car. He just barely managed to bring it to a stop a few feet from the Alfa, and he jumped out of the car, willing himself not to panic.

She was sitting in the driver's seat, the window rolled down and rain pouring in. "Go away," she said in her calm, well-bred voice.

He ignored it, of course. She'd been telling him to go away since she first saw him. "Are you hurt? Can you get out of the car?"

"I'm not hurt, I can get out of the car, but I have no intention of doing so. Go away and leave me alone."

"Don't be an idiot, Charlie. You've got two flat tires and you've probably bent the frame. That car can't be driven anywhere, it's pouring rain and getting late. Get out of the damned car and I'll take you someplace.''

''Go to hell, Maguire.''

He wasn't in the mood for this. He hadn't realized just how scared he'd been chasing her up and down these hills in the treacherous rain, and his uncertain temper snapped.

She'd locked the door, but she hadn't closed the window. He reached in, opened the door from the inside and put his hands on her, preparing to haul her out.

''I'll scream!'' she said fiercely.

''Go ahead. There's no one around to hear.'' He yanked at her with just a trace more energy than he needed.

''At least let me get the damned seat belt off,'' she snapped.

''You're wearing a seat belt? I thought you had a death wish, considering the way you were driving.'' She wasn't making any effort to unfasten the belt, so he unfastened it for her, then pulled her out into the heavy rain. She sagged against him for a moment, and his panic was back in full force.

''Are you sure you're all right?'' he demanded. ''You didn't hurt yourself?''

''I'm fine,'' she said, pushing him away. ''I wasn't going that fast when I lost control.''

He had no choice but to believe her. "The Fiat's over there."

"I don't want…"

"I know you don't want, sweetheart. You don't want anything to do with me. But you're on a deserted road in the pouring rain, it's getting dark, and you're stuck with me. I'll take you wherever you were heading, drop you off and then leave you alone."

"Florence."

"Why?"

"I'm getting wet, Maguire. Could we continue this conversation in your car? Since I don't seem to have any choice in the matter?"

He gritted his teeth. He wasn't a violent man, but if anyone could drive him to it, it would be Charlie. He didn't touch her, simply started toward the car, expecting her to follow.

Lucky for her she did. He hadn't realized how small his car was, once Charlie was inside. He'd dumped his laptop and all his papers into the rubbish-strewn back seat, and he waited until she closed the door before he started the engine again.

"Where's the seat belt?" she asked.

"Long gone. I figure if you survived the way you were driving, then a couple of hours without a seat belt won't do you any harm."

"You know what happens in an accident if

you're not wearing a seat belt? You get thrown around the car like a frog in a blender, crushing everyone,'' she said severely.

''Feel free to crush me,'' he said, pulling out into the rainy evening. He concentrated on the road, driving in silence, until they got closer to the next town. He glanced over at her, and then swore.

''You told me you weren't hurt!'' he snapped.

''I'm not.''

''Your head is bleeding. You must have hit it on the windshield.''

''I was wearing my seat belt, remember? And it's not blood, it's paint. Someone…something threw one of Pompasse's paintings at me. Another ruined one, I might add. Not that it matters to you, Mr. Insurance Man,'' she said bitterly.

He reached out and touched her forehead lightly, and she winced. He glanced at his fingertips. ''I hate to tell you, sugar, but this time it's blood.''

He wasn't sure what kind of reaction he expected. Tears, panic, something. She just breathed a rattled sigh. ''Well, it's stopped by now,'' she said, turning away from him to stare out into the rain.

He gave her a few minutes. ''What happened?''

For a moment he thought she wasn't going to answer. ''It was not a good day,'' she said, obviously the model of understatement. ''I decided I didn't want to see or talk to anybody anymore, so I went to the studio to take a shower and a nap. Unfortunately something…someone was there.''

"Who?"

"I couldn't see. There were no lights and the rain had already started. I heard them, sort of shuffling, and I saw a kind of shape. Somebody threw the painting at me, I ran, and here I am. Very simple.''

"Very simple. Why didn't you go back to the main house?"

"Because there was no one I could turn to there.''

"Not Henry? You didn't decide to forgive and forget, kiss and make up and all that?"

"Go fuck yourself, Maguire.''

"I guess not," he said, suddenly feeling a lot more cheerful. "What about your mother? She's not as bad as she seems.''

"So she tells me. Let's just say she's never given me much reason to trust her. I decided to just get the hell away from the place. Spend a night or two at a decent hotel in Florence, then decide whether I'm going back to La Colombala or just flying straight home. I think I've had enough of Tuscany. Though Pompasse would have said that's impossible.''

"And of course he was so very wise."

"Cut the sarcasm. He was right about some things, wrong about others. For a long while Tuscany was home. But it isn't anymore."

"And New York is?"

He could see her thinking about it. At least he was able to distract her enough to forget how righteously pissed off she was at him. "I don't think I have a home." She glanced over at him. "You know what they say—home is where the heart is. I have it on good authority that I don't have a heart."

"Hmm. Had a few words with our Henry, did you? The man's an asshole."

"Thank you for the comforting words but I don't need them," she said. If she was as icy as her voice she'd be heading for pneumonia. He punched the heater button, but as usual only cold air came out. He didn't often need the heater in Italy, but now was one of the few occasions it would have come in handy.

"You're ice-cold," he said mildly enough, ignoring her hostility. She had every right to hate him, and all the apologies in the world wouldn't do a bit of good. Especially since he wouldn't necessarily mean them. No, he had to concentrate on practicalities for the time being, and worry about the future when it got there. "Why don't you reach in back and grab a sweater or something from my duffel bag?''

"I'd rather freeze, thank you very much. If it were up to me I'd still be back in my car, waiting for rescue.''

"Rescue showed up, sweetheart, and it was me. Like it or not, I'm your knight in shining armor.''

"God help me,'' she muttered.

The night was lousy. The rain was pouring down steadily, and his windshield wipers barely put a dent in it. He was soaking wet and the heater didn't work, he could barely see ten feet in front of him, and he was trapped in a car with a woman who despised him and probably wanted to see him dead. So how come he suddenly felt like whistling?

He was smart enough not to. Charlie had been through enough for one day. "We'll be in Florence in another hour if we're lucky. Any idea where you'll be staying?''

"The first hotel I can find.''

"That may be a bit tricky. There's another one of their damned festivals going on right now—just about every room is booked. I was even considering renting out my apartment, seeing as how I didn't think I'd be needing it.''

"But you do need it," she said with false sweetness. "And I'm sure I'll have no trouble finding a room.''

''Nice to be sure of things,'' he said evenly.

She began to shiver. She tried to hide it from him, and he decided to be a nice guy and pretend he didn't notice, but the longer they drove the more she shivered, so that the seat was practically vibrating. The only reason he couldn't hear her teeth chatter was because she had them clamped shut. He didn't blame her—he was freezing as well.

His apartment was on the east side of town, not far from the Duomo, an old, seedy set of rooms in an old, seedy building that had somehow defied gentrification. He drove straight there, avoiding the busier streets, and by the time Charlie noticed he had already started down the narrow alley behind the building where he usually parked.

''Where are we?'' she demanded. He had to admire the fact that there was only a faint tremor in her voice. A less observant man wouldn't realize she was about to turn to ice.

''We're at my apartment. You're going up there, get some dry clothes and warm up, and then we'll find you a hotel room for the night.''

''No.''

''Charlie, you're shaking so hard this old car almost bounced off the road. You look like a drowned rat—try walking into the Excelsior or something in your current condition and they'll set the police on you.''

"I'm not going anywhere with you."

He parked, turning off the lights and car, and sat there in the darkness with her. "You already have. It's late, it's cold, I'm freezing even if you won't admit that you are. And I'm not going to argue. Get out of the damned car or I'll carry you."

"I'd like to see you try," she said, except the effect was ruined by her chattering teeth.

"Sure thing," he muttered, slamming out of the car and coming around to the passenger side. She pushed the lock down, naively assuming his derelict car actually had locks that worked. Since it didn't, he simply opened the door and reached for her.

"Hands off!" she said. "I'll come quietly."

"Good," he said. The rain had softened to a faint drizzle, but the night was still unseasonably cold. He watched with a critical eye as she climbed out of the car in the dimly lit alleyway, but apart from the cold she seemed to be in reasonably good shape. He still wanted to get a good look at her in decent light, to make sure she hadn't been hurt when her car had gone off the road. She had insisted she was fine, but then, she'd lie.

"Nice neighborhood," she said.

"Sarcasm doesn't work when your teeth are chattering. Hurry up."

She didn't dignify that with a response, she simply followed him into the rainy night, her head ducked to avoid the dampness. The old building held four apartments, but he seldom saw his neighbors, and there was no sign of them that night. He made his way up a narrow back staircase, listening to her follow him, and wondered how in the hell he was going to talk her into taking off her clothes. If he suggested it she'd probably hit him.

And she'd have good reason to. He wanted to get her warm. But he was even more interested in getting her naked. Even freezing to death and guilty as hell he was still a horny bastard, all things considered. At least as far as Charlie was concerned.

He'd been a mass of frustrations since he first laid eyes on her, and those tantalizing moments in the sagging bed this morning had brought him to the boiling point. Which was just too damned bad—Charlie was in no condition to be hit on, particularly by him. She'd be lucky if she ever let another man touch her after this morning's betrayal.

Not that it was his fault, he reminded himself, fiddling with the old key and pushing the door open. He switched on the light, then held the door for her, and for the first time he saw his ramshackle apartment through someone else's eyes.

It had high ceilings and large windows overlooking the alleyway where he parked his car. It had a huge bathtub. And that was about it as far as good points. The place was cluttered—he had someone come in and hoe it out every few weeks and, thank God, she'd just been there. Otherwise his discarded clothes would have been scattered all over the place, along with newspapers, filled ashtrays, empty bottles, dirty dishes, you name it. It still looked like a seedy wreck, but it was his wreck, and it was marginally neat.

"Nice place you've got here, Maguire," Charlie said faintly. "You want to open a window so I don't choke to death from the dead cigarettes?"

Her color wasn't bad, even in the lousy lighting of the bare bulb hanging in the hallway. Her forehead had stopped bleeding, but she was still shivering.

"The bathroom's through there," he said, jerking his head in the direction.

"I didn't say I needed to use it."

"There's plenty of hot water, towels, soap. You need to warm up. My sister-in-law left some clothes the last time she and my brother came to visit—she's a little shorter than you but about your size."

"I don't believe it. You can't have a brother. You were hatched from a spider."

"Watch what you say about my mother," he

cautioned calmly. "I was very devoted to me old mum."

"I'm not taking a shower, I'm not changing my clothes. I'll use a towel to dry off a bit and then I'm calling a hotel—"

"Charlie, you don't want me stripping you down naked, do you?" He kept his voice absolutely reasonable. There was nothing he'd like more than the excuse to put his hands on her and strip those clothes from her shivering body. And she knew it.

She glared at him. "Fine," she said bitterly. "When I come out I want there to be a hotel reservation waiting for me."

"Yes, ma'am," he said. "Mary's clothes are in the closet on the right. Take your time."

"Hurry up," she countered in a dangerous voice.

And he gave her an affable grin.

20

She wasn't about to admit to Maguire how desperately she wanted to get clean and warm. Or, for that matter, to use the toilet.

The bathroom was huge—a converted room, and the marble tub looked like a cattle water trough. At least the room was relatively clean—she couldn't believe Maguire would be that neat. He must have someone come in.

The bathroom had doors leading into the bedroom as well as the hall, and she found the closet with no problem, keeping her eyes averted from the rumpled-looking bed. There were a couple of long, casual dresses, but of course no underwear. On the off chance, she went to the massive chest of drawers.

No bras, no panties, of course, but she hadn't really expected them. She grabbed a pair of Maguire's briefs, then stopped as she saw the gleam of metal at the bottom of the drawer.

Not a gun, and Charlie would have been more than happy to have found one. They were plaques, of various sizes, weights, dates. They were journalism awards, prestigious ones. She stared down at them in consternation. What the hell had happened to him, to turn him into a gossipmonger, the lowest of the low?

She heard him moving around in the living room, so she quickly shoved the drawer shut and disappeared back into the bathroom. Locks on the door, thank God, and there was a rickety electric heater on the bathroom floor.

She switched it on, fully prepared to die instantly from electrocution and not particularly minding, but after an ominous crackle it started kicking out heat. As the tub filled with hot, steamy water she stripped off her sodden clothes, then turned to look at her reflection in the mirror.

Maguire was right—no hotel would take her in looking like that. She looked like a crazy woman— blood matted in her hair, eyes wide and fearful. She hadn't brought anything with her—no clothes, no makeup, no...

"Shit!" she said out loud.

"What's wrong?" Maguire called from the living room.

"Nothing," she shouted back. "Call the hotel."

He didn't reply. She had a new problem now, she thought, sliding into the huge tub and letting the blissfully warm water flow over her. In her des-

perate flight she hadn't brought her purse. No passport, no identification, no credit cards, no money.

Still, she had her face. Whether she liked it or
not, the art world knew her face, and Tuscany did
as well, as the favorite model of their favorite
adopted son. It would take a bit of talking, but she
had no doubt she could get a hotel to advance her
credit until she made a few phone calls to...

To Henry? If she had to, she had to. Henry
would take care of things—that was why she'd
wanted to marry him. She'd wanted someone to fix
everything, make everything all right, and Henry
was good at that.

He just wasn't the man she wanted to spend her
life with. For that matter, she wasn't sure whether
she wanted to be taken care of, either. She wanted
a partner, not a father. An equal. Or maybe she
didn't want anyone at all.

She slid her head underwater, feeling the cut on
her forehead sting. It didn't matter—she just had
to get clean.

She was changing. She could feel it, like a snake
shedding its skin, like a caterpillar turning into a
butterfly. She was no longer the quiet, controlled
woman from New York, Pompasse's former wife,
who had forged a peaceful, nondemanding life for
herself. She was back in the thick of it, in the midst
of life and all its messy demands. She didn't like

it—she wanted her serenity back with a need that bordered on desperation.

But she suspected it was gone for good. And a lot of it was the fault of the man in the other room.

She stayed in the tub until the water grew cool, stayed until the room was suffused with warmth from the tiny electric heater.

She took longer to dress than she usually did, probably because she didn't want to go out there again. She was able to get a comb through her tangled hair, avoiding the cut up near her scalp, and her bra was in relatively decent shape. The dress was a little too big, but it was loose and comfortable. Which left the problem of underwear.

She'd grabbed a pair of Maguire's tighty whities. The question was, what would be more unsettling? Going out there with no underwear, or going out there in his shorts? Either way she was too damned vulnerable. She finally decided a layer of cotton, anybody's cotton, was preferable to being naked.

He had a fire going in the marble fireplace. He'd managed to get himself washed and dried while she was hogging the bathroom, and he was wearing a faded pair of jeans with an old sweater. His hair was spiky from the water, and he looked...wonderful.

There, she admitted it. She found him attractive.

There was no crime in it, as long as she didn't do anything about it. He was a liar, a pig, a trickster, but he had the seemingly unique ability to turn her on. She should concentrate on that fact. If she'd responded to one man she could eventually find another, better one. Someone to love, someone to trust, someone to be partners with.

"What are you staring at?" he demanded.

"I'm wondering why this place is so neat. You don't strike me as a particularly tidy person."

"I'm not as bad as you'd think. And I've got a cleaning lady who comes in every few weeks. Lucky for you she came in while I was gone."

"Lucky for me," she echoed dryly. The room was warm and cozy from the fire, despite the clutter and the high ceilings. The vision of that rumpled bed danced back into her brain. She banished it sternly.

"I'll get you a glass of wine," he said. "You look like you could use it."

"I'd rather have whiskey."

"Too bad, love. I gave it up. I only have wine here because you can't live in Italy without having wine to offer. My Italian friends would probably drive me out of the country on a rail."

"First, I don't believe you have any friends, Italian or otherwise. And second..." Her voice trailed off. "I don't remember what I was going to say.

I'd better not have any wine. I don't think I've eaten all day.''

He didn't say anything. He was across the room from her, out of reach, and yet still too close. The room was only dimly lit, and she couldn't see his eyes, couldn't read his expression. But then, she never could.

The silence stretched and grew, until it became an almost palpable thing in the cavernous room. ''I'd better get going,'' she said. ''Did you call the hotel?''

He nodded. ''I booked you into the Villa Bovaria. It's a smaller hotel on the west side of town, but the manager owes me a favor or two. He'll get you in even without a passport, and he'll take my credit card.''

''What makes you think I don't have money?''

''You didn't have a purse in the car with you, sugar. You didn't have squat. I told you, I'm your knight in shining armor. Just say the word and I'll take you over to the Villa Bovaria, get your bill settled and leave you in peace. That's what you want, right?''

''That's what I want,'' she said. Certain she meant it.

''Did you want some wine first?''

''No wine. I just need to get out of here. I make it a habit not to be self-destructive.''

His laugh was both derisive and offensive. "You really think so? You married a womanizing old fart when you were seventeen, you were about to marry another old man even though you couldn't bear to have him touch you. You almost had sex with me this morning. I'd call that pretty self-destructive."

"Not that it's any of your business, but did you ever consider that marrying a womanizing old fart was at least better than the rootless life I was leading? He gave me a home, he gave me security, and he loved me. The good points outweighed the bad for a number of years. But you're right," she added. "Don't worry, I'm turning over a new leaf. Obviously I have terrible taste in men." She looked him straight in the eye.

"Obviously," he said, not flinching.

Another silence, long and strained. He finally broke it. "If I'm taking you to the Villa Bovaria you're going to need your shoes on. Passports and money can be dealt with, bare feet can't."

"Sorry. I'll just be a minute." She dashed back into the bathroom, unearthing her flats from beneath the pile of clothes. She slipped them on, then paused to look at her reflection once more.

She hadn't changed. She still looked like Charlie—tawny hair drying softly around her face, wary eyes, straight nose, pale mouth. She hadn't thought he'd let her go that easily.

It was probably much simpler than she realized. He had been after her for the story. He'd wanted to be able to write what Pompasse's widow was like in bed. Now that she knew who he was, now that he wasn't going to be allowed to do that, he had no need to sleep with her.

He probably liked plump women. Healthy, sexual women who took and gave pleasure cheerfully. Neurotic, frigid women wouldn't be Maguire's style at all.

He'd turned off most of the lights when she came out. There was just the glow from the fire and the lone lightbulb overhead in the hallway, and he was waiting for her, his hand on the switch.

"You're not writing that article, you know," she said, sounding very cool. "The lawyers will stop you—"

"You overestimate the legal system," he said. "But actually I don't give a rat's ass about the fucking story. Someone else can write it."

She didn't bother arguing. When it came right down to it, she didn't give a rat's ass, either.

"Do you want a coat or something?" he asked her. "It's still raining and the night air is cold."

"No, thank you," she said politely.

"You ready?"

"Yes," she said.

He flicked off the switch, plunging them into darkness that the flickering firelight from the living room could barely penetrate. She could be out of here in a matter of moments, she told herself. She would be safe, free.

He hadn't moved. Neither had she. She reached out and put her hand on the tarnished brass doorknob. He put his hand over hers.

She didn't even know how it happened. She turned and leaned her back against the door, looking up at him through the thick shadows. And then the shadows were blotted out, as he placed his body up against hers, hip to hip, chest to breast, mouth to mouth.

She was hungry for it. Hungry for him, when she had thought it was something she'd never feel. He tasted like rain and repentance, of sweet sin and the night air, and she closed her eyes and kissed him back, shivering in response.

He didn't ask, she didn't answer. He pressed his hands on either side of her, holding her against the door, but she didn't feel trapped. She felt entwined, invaded, threatened and yet oddly safe. He put one leg between hers, and she could feel his erection through his jeans, pressing against her belly. She put her arms around his waist, pulling him more tightly against her, and he was strong and solid and warm everywhere she touched him.

He didn't say a word. He picked her up in his arms, and she realized again how very strong he was. And she wasn't afraid.

He carried her through the dark, cluttered apartment, into the bedroom where it was as warm and dark as a cocoon. She liked the darkness, the quiet rustling of her clothing as he pulled the dress over her head, the touch of his hard, deft hands on her skin.

She was standing at the edge of the bed, wearing only her underwear. Her knees were trembling, her whole body was shaking, but she didn't move as he pressed his mouth against the base of her throat, kissing her openmouthed, breathing in her flying pulses.

And then he spoke, breaking through her drugged senses. "Yes?" It was a question, not a demand, asked patiently.

She wanted to hide in the dark, in the silence, leaving it all up to him. She wanted to lie back and close her eyes and let the magic happen, something dreamy and disembodied. But he was standing there, asking her, and she knew she had to answer.

She knew what the answer had to be. A solid, resounding no. She was through with being self-destructive. Going to bed with a liar, a user like Maguire would be the ultimate mistake. There was only one thing she could say.

"Yes."

The room was pitch-black, but he knew she liked it that way. Needed it. He'd gotten her to say yes, to admit she wanted this. But she was still frightened, he could feel it in the hammering heartbeat, the coolness of her skin, the thready pulse beneath.

So be it. He could deal with her fear, lure her beyond her panic into a world of flesh and blood and pleasure. He just needed her agreement.

He slid his hands over her shoulders, hooking his thumbs under her bra straps and pulling them down her arms. He heard her choked gasp, but she didn't protest.

It was the same bra she'd worn this morning, sinfully easy to unfasten. He wanted to see her breasts as he drew the bra from her body, but it was too dark. He'd have to settle for touch.

He kissed the base of her throat again, letting his teeth just brush against her sensitive flesh. And then he kissed her between her breasts, letting his tongue dance over her heartbeat.

He kissed her stomach. It was flat, and he suddenly had the strange, erotic image of her stomach rounded, swollen with his child, and he almost backed away from her, shocked by the power of that unbidden image.

He had his own fears, too. But not enough to make him pull back from her in the rich, beckoning darkness.

He reached for her panties, ready to draw them down her hips, when his hands faltered. It took him just a moment to realize she'd filched a pair of his briefs from the bedroom. And the thought of her wearing them was almost unbearably arousing. Without giving her any preparation he slid his hand down the front of the shorts, touching her through the thick cotton, and she let out a muffled shriek that was pure panic.

"I've changed my mind." Her voice broke the velvet silence—nervous, high-pitched, ready to run.

"Have you?" he asked calmly. He didn't take his hand away from her, and she was too frightened to move. He stroked her slowly, gently through the cloth, taking his time. "Why?" He sounded no more than vaguely curious. He still wasn't quite sure how to handle her—whether she needed tender wooing or brute force, whether she was even ready for this. If he made the wrong move...but he wasn't going to. Making love to Charlie had suddenly become the most important thing in the world to him. He wasn't worried about his own pleasure—he could come just from looking at her.

But she needed to know the pleasure her body could give her. Hell, she needed to know the pleasure *he* could give her.

She didn't try to push his hand away, and he kept stroking her through the layers of cloth. There was something perversely erotic about seducing a woman wearing his underwear, and she probably didn't have the faintest idea how turned-on he was. Just as well—she was scared enough already.

"Why?" he asked her again, his voice almost lazy. The cotton was growing damp beneath his stroking fingers, and he could feel the reluctant tremors of reaction sliding across her body.

"I don't want..." she began, and her voice trailed off as she took a little gulp, a shiver of reaction catching her unaware.

"Don't want what?" She was fighting him, fighting the feeling he was coaxing from her. The underwear was now less a turn-on than a hindrance, and he wanted her flesh on his fingers, her dampness, her scent.

She let out a startled yelp when he touched her a little harder. He wanted to rip the briefs off her with his teeth he was so aroused, but he knew he could make her come like this, standing up, half dressed and terrified, and he intended to do it.

He could feel the opened folds of her flesh through the cloth, and he knelt down in front of her, put one arm around her hips to hold her, and pushed his fingers against her clitoris. She was trembling, and he felt her hands on his shoulders, digging into the sweater. He thought she was crying, but he didn't care. He wanted her to cry, needed her to cry with the sheer power of it.

"Don't fight it, Charlie," he said in a harsh voice. "Do it, Charlie. Do it for me."

She probably had no idea what he was talking about, but it didn't matter. The orgasm took her by surprise, and she let out a low, keening wail that was the most glorious thing he'd ever heard. He leaned forward and put his mouth where his hand had been, up against the thick cloth that was guarding her, pulling her body against him.

He held her that way until her shaking began to lessen. Then he rose and began stripping off his clothes.

"Get on the bed, Charlie," he said, reaching for his zipper. His cock jutted out, thick and heavy with need. "Or I'll put you there."

"Maguire." Her voice was a raw thread of sound.

"No more games. If you've changed your mind you can leave. Otherwise get on the goddamned bed."

She got on the bed, kicking off her shoes and sliding up on it. He didn't need to see her face to know that she was watching with fearful eyes, half terrified of what he was going to do to her.

She lay back, crossed her arms over her chest like a martyred virgin, and closed her eyes. His own eyes had grown accustomed to the dark by now, and he could see her quite clearly. The marks of tears on her cheeks. The pale, defenseless skin, the small, perfect breasts. And the incongruous white of the men's briefs that she still wore.

He felt something crack inside him, though he tried to shove it away. Some kind of ice dam finally breaking.

He came around the side of the bed, sat down beside her and took one of her hands in his. "I'm not going to hurt you, Charlie," he said in a wry voice.

She didn't open her eyes. She probably knew he was naked and aroused and she didn't want to see what she was about to get.

Simple enough. He took her hand, kissed her palm, and placed it on his cock.

Her eyes flew open, and she tried to yank her hand away. He didn't let her, he simply held her there, till she stopped trying to pull away. Her hand gentled, and her fingers encircled him.

"You're too big." Her voice was so quiet he almost didn't hear her.

He didn't laugh, though he wanted to, from relief and pure joy.

"I'll fit," he said. Much as he regretted it, he leaned over and slid the briefs down her long legs. He'd seen her naked, huddled, frightened in Pompasse's paintings. The woman lying in his bed, looking up at him with a dizzying combination of need and panic, was far more beautiful, to him at least.

But he needed to wipe that fear from her eyes, from her face, from her soul. And he needed to do it now.

He slid onto the bed beside her, learning her curves, letting his fingers brush the underside of her small, luscious breasts. Her nipples were hard, but he didn't know if it was from fear or desire. She lay still beneath his touch, that martyred look coming over her once more.

"What have you got against sex, Charlie?" he whispered, brushing his lips against the beaded peak of her breast. "Were you ever hurt? Abused? Raped?" Not the most erotic questions, but he needed to know the answers. If she'd been violated he'd have to be even more careful with her.

"No," she said in a low voice. There was a sexy

catch to it when his tongue touched her nipple. "I just...don't like it."

"Why not?" He liked her hipbones. In general, he liked more flesh covering a woman's hipbones, but this was Charlie and right then she was perfect.

"It was never what I thought it would be," she said finally. "It was never...magic."

He slid over her body, pinning her with his strength, catching her face with his hands and putting his forehead against hers, so she couldn't miss the implacable gleam in his eyes.

"Charlie, love, sex isn't magic. It's not making love on a cloud with angels singing and fairies dancing. It's real, it's human, it's wet and sweaty and nasty and the best thing about being alive. And it's past time you learned that."

He kissed her mouth. He kissed her eyelids and her cheekbones and her nose, and then he pushed himself inside her.

She was wet, and tight, and her fingers clenched his shoulders as she braced herself, obviously expecting the worst. It didn't matter—she felt too good to him. It took all his iron self-control to keep from letting go. He pushed slowly, filling her, taking it slow so that she wouldn't panic. The need to have her was almost primeval, and he had to fight back from the mists in order to slow himself down.

He took a deep, shaky breath when he'd finally sheathed himself completely inside her warmth.

"It fits," she said in a soft, startled voice.

He let his forehead rest on her shoulder, in both relief and tension. And he slid his hands under her hips, pulled her up tighter against him, and began to move.

She came immediately, a small, shattering orgasm that was over too soon. But he'd waited too long for her, and he wasn't about to spend it too quickly. Once the breathless peak had passed, he started to move again, slowly at first, setting an almost lazy rhythm to lull her into a state of security. The second climax had drained her of the last vestiges of doubt and shyness, but she still didn't know what she had in store for her. What *he* had in store for her.

He was moving a little faster now, and he heard that breathless catch in her voice. She was climbing again, and this time she knew where it would lead. And she wasn't sure if she was ready to go there again.

But he was. He wanted her with him. He wanted her convulsing around him as he spilled inside her, and he wasn't going to come without her.

"No," she said. The first time she had said no all night.

''Hell, yes.'' He reached between their bodies and touched her, hard.

She was absolutely silent this time as the climax hit her, clenching around him, as wave after wave of release drained her body.

And he followed her, letting go, holding nothing back.

He couldn't tell who came down first. She lay in his arms, covered in sweat, panting, heart racing, weeping. He always thought it was strange that some women wept when they climaxed. For the first time he began to understand why.

She wouldn't want words and he knew it. Well, at least not the words he'd say. She'd want him to tell her he loved her. And he wasn't going to lie.

Funny, though. He always told women he loved them. Never had a qualm about it if it would get him laid or get him a story.

But he didn't want to use those easy words with Charlie.

He rolled over on his side, taking her with him, and they fit together perfectly. No awkward arranging of arms and legs and tickling hair. She simply went into his embrace and fell asleep.

Leaving him lying there wondering what the hell he was going to do.

21

Maguire was in a thoroughly lousy mood. Charlie slept like a baby in his arms, completely trusting, a fact that annoyed him. Didn't she realize what a jerk he was? What a fraud, what a user? How stupid could she be, to go to bed with him and then fall asleep as if she was in the safest place in the world? No wonder her life was so messed up.

No wonder his life was so messed up, as well. He wanted to sleep, too. He wanted to close his eyes, pull her even closer, breathe in the scent of her, and sleep.

But he hated sleeping with women. He liked sex just fine. Loved it, as a matter of fact. But afterward, once the required amount of snuggling and lies were finished with, he wanted his bed to himself. Which was why he seldom brought women to his apartment. Hard to kick a woman out when she was feeling all cozy and postcoital.

But the damnable thing about Charlie was that he didn't want to kick her out. Didn't want to leave her. He'd already slept with her for an entire night, and he didn't even have the excuse of having sex with her. He'd simply wanted to hold her while she was so miserable, give her some kind of comfort. But he'd slept, wrapped around her.

He wasn't going to make the mistake of doing that again, no matter how much his body cried out for it. He could sleep in a chair—he'd done it before. Or he could simply work all night, catching up on loose ends.

But damn it, he was not going to sleep with Charlie in his arms again. He didn't dare.

He gently slid out of the bed. She reached for him, making a small, protesting sigh, but she didn't wake up. He stood by the bed, staring down at her in the dim light. He'd thought she was beautiful before. That was nothing compared to what she looked like now. Well-loved.

Bad term. Well-fucked is what he meant. He'd given her the ride of her life, and she'd sleep for hours now, just to recuperate. And he could start work on rebuilding his own defenses.

He closed the doors to the bedroom so he wouldn't disturb her. He took a fast, cold shower—she'd taken all the hot water earlier, and then dashed out to his car to get his computer and camera. He hadn't had a chance to upload the digital pictures, and he was curious to see what sort of shots he'd gotten.

He sat for hours at the laptop, uploading the pictures, backing them up on his portable zip drive. He did it automatically—too many years in war zones had taught him the importance of backing up your material. He slid the zip disk into the desk drawer, then flicked back through the last group of pictures.

There was one photo that was nagging at him, and he wasn't sure why. It was a shot of Madame Antonella, Lauretta and Tomaso, and it was a picture full of emotion. Molly would have been proud of him.

Lauretta was doing her usual job of pleading with the old lady. Keeping the old lady in line must be a full-time job, Maguire thought. Lauretta must be run ragged trying to care for a full household, as well. There was something about her face, something that bothered him, and he couldn't put his finger on it.

And that wasn't all. The old lady fascinated him. She was staring at someone or something, and the look of hatred on her face was so intense it was almost diabolical. There was something there, something that was just eluding him, but the longer he stared at the computer screen the blurrier it became.

He didn't dare print it up—the noise might awaken Charlie. He'd take the zip disk into the office later in the day, get it blown up before he printed it, and then maybe he could figure out what it was about the photo that was driving him nuts.

He didn't know whether she had made some sort of sound, or whether it was his sixth sense. But he knew Charlie was awake, and he made the mistake of going to check on her without putting the computer into hibernation.

She was stirring, moving around in the bed, still asleep but restless. And he looked down at her, decided there were some things that were just too hard to fight, and got back in bed with her, pulling her into his arms.

She quieted immediately, and her soft sigh caught on an errant sob that was still stifled deep inside her. She had a lot of crying left to do, he thought, stroking her hair gently. And for a moment he wished to Christ that it didn't have to be over him.

Maguire snored. Oddly enough, Charlie didn't mind. He wasn't that loud, and there was something vaguely comforting about the sound. She rose on her elbows to look at him in the murky predawn light. His face had gone beyond a stubble to almost a beard, his eyes were shadowed with exhaustion, and he was sleeping like a baby.

She found herself smiling down at him. She was

half tempted to wake him again, and she started to move when her body cried out in massive protest. She bit her lip in annoyance.

She wasn't ready to stop. She remembered something he'd growled in her ear in the middle of the night, something dark and sexy and exciting, and she wanted to try it. But her body wouldn't let her.

A bath, she thought. She'd soak in a hot bath for half an hour, then climb back into bed with him. Maybe even climb right on top of him. She was feeling wild and strong and dangerous, and she wanted more.

She listened to his snoring all through her bath, secure in the knowledge that he wouldn't even know she'd left his side. When she climbed out of the massive tub she wrapped one of the big towels around her, ready to head back into the bedroom, when she noticed a strange blue light from the living room.

She pushed open the door. The room was still warm from the fire, and the windows overlooking the alleyway let in the filtered half-light of a new day. And then she saw the computer sitting open on the desk.

No Road Runner and Wile E. Coyote. He must have gotten up in the middle of the night to work.

He'd left her alone in the bed to get to his computer. He couldn't wait to get back to his work.

The sense of betrayal was strong enough, and then she saw what was on the screen.

It was a photograph of Antonella, Lauretta and Tomaso. They didn't know they were being photographed, but Maguire had done a good job. You could practically taste the old lady's fury emanating from the image on the computer screen.

Tucking the towel more tightly around her, Charlie sat down at the computer. She liked technology, and it didn't take her long to access the menu of photos, to see the damning ones of her, looking lost.

The text was already open in another window— all she had to do was click on it. She only read a few sentences—about Pompasse's frigid wife who'd been ruined for men for all time, and she pushed back from the table, closing the computer lid with a quiet little click.

She dressed quickly, calmly. Her clothes had dried, though her bra was still somewhere on the bedroom floor. It didn't matter—she wouldn't wear it again. She'd probably never wear a bra with a front clasp ever again—it would remind her of Maguire's deft hands.

Her shoes were in the bedroom as well, but she decided not to bother with them. Maguire was still snoring, but the last thing she wanted was to risk waking him up. She'd spent most of her life at the villa barefoot—she could drive back up there barefoot.

She pushed open the wide living room windows, looking down at the little alleyway. Maguire's Fiat was still there, and the keys were on the table next to the computer. Thoughtful of him.

She unplugged the laptop, brought it over to the window, and dropped it. The shattering sound as it smashed onto the pavement below was shocking in the early morning stillness, and Maguire's snoring stopped with an abrupt snort.

Charlie grabbed the car keys, not daring to wait a moment longer. She closed the door silently behind her, just in case he'd managed to fall asleep again, and ran down the stairs, out into the wet streets.

She had to avoid the metal and glass shards from the smashed computer. By the time she reached his car her bare feet were icy cold, and she remembered too late that his heater didn't work.

So be it. It wasn't cold enough for frostbite, just bad enough for misery. If she could concentrate on how cold her feet were, maybe it would take her mind off whatever else felt irreparably damaged. Her soul? Her heart?

To her amazement the car started at the first try.

She shoved it into gear and took off, driving over the remnants of the smashed computer, and out onto the early morning roads leading out of Florence, back to La Colombala.

Maguire was pulled out of a heavy sleep by a sound he didn't recognize. A muffled crash, and his eyes flew open, and he was instantly awake.

Alone in the bed. He sat up and saw Charlie's shoes on the floor, but he wasn't reassured. She'd fled, like Cinderella, leaving not one but both glass slippers behind.

He struggled out of bed and pushed open the door to the living room, and a moment of absolute panic knocked the air out of him. The wide casement windows were open onto the alleyway below, and for a second he thought she might have jumped.

And then he saw the computer was gone.

He crossed the room, almost at a run, and looked down into the alleyway below. His car was just disappearing around the corner, and he had no doubts as to who was driving. And directly below his window, smashed into a million pieces, was his state-of-the-art laptop.

He stared at it for a long moment, then lifted his gaze to the road Charlie had taken. And then he did something he hadn't done in more than five years.

He threw back his head and laughed.

He didn't pause long enough to think about it. He headed straight to the telephone and punched in a few numbers.

"Gregory?"

"Who the hell is this?" Gregory's sleepy voice demanded. "It's the middle of the fucking night. Is that you, Maguire?"

"It's 6:00 a.m. and it's me."

"You better have a helluva good story about Pompasse to wake me up like this."

"No story."

There was dead silence on the other line. "You're shitting me."

"No story. Everything was dead boring there. The old man died from a fall, all his ex-girlfriends were cozy, and the best you've got is a little gossip for the back pages."

"But you've got pictures," Gregory said. "You told me you had great pictures."

"Sorry, boss," Maguire said, totally without regret. "I'm afraid my girlfriend threw my computer out the window. Smashed everything to pieces."

"But you backed it up?" Gregory was fully awake now, and sounding in a perfect panic. "Of course you did—you're a professional. You always back things up.''

"Not this time."

There was a long, charged silence at the other end, and Maguire could hear Gregory lighting a cigarette. A deep craving swept over him, but he batted it away.

"I'll tell you what you're going to do, Maguire," Gregory said after a moment. "You're going to get in your car and drag your sorry ass back to Pompasse's villa. I don't care what excuse you make, how many lies you have to tell, but you get back in there and get me pictures and some kind of goddamned story.''

"Can't. My girlfriend stole my car."

Another silence. "Since when have you ever had a girlfriend, Maguire? You're the love 'em and leave 'em type. Besides, what woman would ever put up with you long-term?"

"I don't know, boss. But I intend to find out. You'll have to get yourself another flunky. I quit."

"You quit what? The story?" There was real panic in Gregory's voice now.

"No, mate. I quit the job." And he placed the telephone back on the cradle very, very gently.

Gregory got tired of calling back after about an hour. Maguire made himself strong coffee and told himself he didn't need cigarettes. He stretched back out on the bed, but it smelled like sex and Charlie, and in the end he left the apartment and the ceaselessly ringing telephone and went out to find something to eat.

It was a cool morning after the rain from yesterday, and he sat at his favorite café, drinking dark, bitter brew and thinking dark, bitter thoughts. He'd basically fucked his life over completely, he thought. At least Charlie had been driven away— that was one good thing. She would have done nothing but drag him down. She made him vulnerable in ways he didn't even want to consider. Now that she had taken off he didn't have to even think about her again. About the sounds she made when she came. About the lost, tentative look in her mysterious golden eyes. About the way...

He swore under his breath, attracting the attention of the passersby. He had to pull himself together. He'd been a fool to tell Gregory everything was gone. Even crazier to quit his job.

Then again, he'd been thinking about it for more than a year. It was time to go back home—he could have his pick of newspaper jobs, from tabloid to respectable, and he could be back in the country, near his brother and his wife and their bratty kids. He did happen to like their monster children. George and Harry were two right hellions, a perfect match for Maguire and Dan when they were growing up. He missed them.

Maybe he'd have a few hellions of his own. Maybe it was time he grew up. Maybe it was time he stopped thinking about whether Charlie could learn to love Australia.

He needed to think about something else. Like that photo that was nagging at the back of his mind. Now that he'd lied to Gregory and quit his job there was no way he could saunter into the offices and have someone print him up a copy of that photo. No way he could even access it with his computer smashed on the ground, and he wasn't in the mood to run right out and buy a new one.

He closed his eyes, bringing the picture up in his memory. It was one of his gifts—an almost photographic memory, both for pictures and words, that had saved his butt a million times.

He could see it quite clearly. The harried expression on Lauretta's face as she tried to calm the old lady, the doubtful one on Tomaso's. She looked like Madame Antonella, he realized with a start. Lauretta was younger, stronger, but there was a definite resemblance.

It wasn't that obvious. Maybe it was something as simple as Pompasse going for the same type.

Maybe he hooked up with Lauretta because she happened to look like his first model.

Or maybe Lauretta had already been there, at her mother's side.

He stared at the old lady's face. She was the key to everything, he thought suddenly. The look of malevolence on her face was extraordinary, almost eerie. And there was one more thing that wasn't right.

The wedding ring. In the picture, Madame Antonella, the woman who had been Pompasse's first mistress and never married, was wearing a wedding ring. A wide, old-fashioned band on her strong, aging hands.

It was nothing, he tried to tell himself. Plenty of women wore rings on that finger. Hell, she and Pompasse might have even exchanged rings at one point—what the hell did it matter?

But it did, he knew it as well as he knew his own name. The answers to everything lay in that thick gold band on an old lady's hand.

And he wasn't leaving Italy, and Charlie, until he had those answers and knew she was safe.

It was late morning when Charlie drove up to La Colombala. The place looked deserted. The Rolls was still in the barn, but there were no other cars. Olivia's rental was gone, and so was the small Fiat that Lauretta favored.

There was no one on the terrace, and the table wasn't set. The windows overlooking the valley were still closed against yesterday's rain and this morning's chill, and the sun hadn't yet warmed the flagstones under her bare feet.

The house was silent and still, and she walked through the empty hall to the kitchen, suddenly famished. It wasn't until she was halfway through a slice of buttered bread when she thought about why she had left.

Her appetite vanished. She could hear someone approaching, the heavy, measured tread on the worn tile flooring. She held her breath and then released it as Lauretta appeared in the doorway.

"Oh, Signora Charlie!" Lauretta cried, looking distraught. "Why have you come back here?"

"Is something wrong?" Charlie demanded. "Did something happen to my mother...?"

Lauretta shook her head. "Everything is fine, little one. Your mother has driven Mr. Richmond into town to get airplane tickets. He's going home, and he's taking that Gia with him." She gave a disapproving sniff.

"And where is Gia?"

"Gia's off shopping. She needs new clothes to go to New York, she says. That one always needs new clothes. She won't be back, and you shouldn't be here, either. I told you it upsets Madame Antonella too much. She's old, she needs peace and quiet and no disturbances.''

Charlie made a face. "You know I honor and respect Madame Antonella, but I'm not going to have her drive me away from here. She can stay in her cottage and not see me, but I'm going to stay here as long as I want to." She felt childish and resentful and she didn't care. She was tired of doing what everyone else wanted, and she wasn't going to be driven away from La Colombala no matter how desperately she wanted to go.

Lauretta's face was mournful, and she shook her head sadly. *"Poveretta,"* she murmured. "I tried to warn you."

"Warn me of what?" Charlie demanded. And then she realized someone had come up behind her. For a moment she froze. The shuffling tread, the wheezy breathing. It was the same from yesterday afternoon, in the studio. Whoever had tried to hurt her then had come back. And it was too late to get away.

"I'm so sorry, Signora Charlie," Lauretta was muttering.

She turned and looked into Madame Antonella's face. It was creased with hatred, and in her gnarled, sturdy hand she held a long, vicious-looking knife.

For a moment she froze. And then she turned and made a break for it, dodging past Lauretta toward the kitchen door. Only to be stopped by Tomaso, his familiar face dark with sorrow.

And then everything went black.

22

It was his damned Irish blood, that was it, Maguire thought as he drove hell-bent toward Geppi. He'd spent thirty-five years happily free of premonitions and dark forebodings—the only thing the slightest bit psychic about him were his excellent instincts.

But it was more than instinct riding him today, and it pissed the hell out of him. Something very bad was going to happen, and Charlie was at the center of it. He had to get to her in time, before it was too late, and the damned car he borrowed had about as much pickup as a turtle. It made the Fiat seem more like a Ferrari.

He'd gotten off to a late start, as well—he'd had a couple of things to check up on before he took off, and the Italian records system was not made for easy access. In the end he'd given up—if there was a record of a marriage between Aristide Pompasse and Charlotte Thomas thirteen years ago in the town of Geppi or anywhere nearby, he couldn't find it. But he suspected that it had never existed.

It was late afternoon by the time he reached the

villa. His car was neatly parked by the old barn, and she'd left the keys in it. The day hadn't warmed up much, so he didn't expect to see her sunbathing on the terrace, but neither did he expect the house to look so closed up and deserted.

He called out her name as he entered the shadowy interior, but she didn't answer. No one did. The place was abandoned, even Lauretta's domain, the huge old kitchen, was empty.

He looked out the back door, up at the old cottage halfway up the hill. No signs of life there, either. Maybe Lauretta and Tomaso had taken the old lady someplace. Maybe Charlie had gone off with her mother. Or Henry. He didn't like that idea at all, but it was better than what he was fearing.

He stared up at the abandoned church. Charlie had said that someone destroyed another painting and pitched it at her. That meant there might only be one more painting missing. If it was anywhere it had to be up there, and somehow he and Charlie had missed seeing them. If the old lady had taken the paintings herself she couldn't have lugged them very far, and her cottage was too crowded to hold them. He was guessing there was some other place up beneath the church where Antonella had hidden Pompasse's paintings, maybe behind that huge pile of rubble that Charlie said hadn't been moved in decades. Though he still wasn't quite sure why.

The one thing he knew for certain was that Aristide Pompasse had filed for divorce three days before his death. But his divorce was from one Antonella Bourget Pompasse. Not Charlie Thomas.

He took the steep way up, steering clear of Antonella's cottage. As best he could figure, the old woman had stayed watching, the abandoned wife, for the last forty or fifty years, as Pompasse brought in a parade of women to serve as his mistresses and his models. Through it all she had stayed up in her cottage, waiting.

But Charlie must have been the last straw. He had actually dared to marry Charlie, or at least managed a semblance of a marriage, depriving Antonella of her secret position as favorite wife. She must have hated Charlie intensely.

But as long as she was the only real wife, it didn't matter. It was when Pompasse finally decided to break his true marriage that she acted. Killing Pompasse. The problem was, would she stop there? And why hadn't Lauretta realized what she had done and stopped her? Unless that resemblance went deeper than an artist's preference for the same physical type. Lauretta would protect her own mother at all costs. Maybe even at the cost of Charlie's life.

He had no doubt the old lady really was senile. She wasn't faking it—she was old and crazy and very dangerous. But she wasn't nearly as physically frail as she pretended. Beneath her shuffling, madwoman exterior was a strong, cunning monster.

It was getting dark by the time he reached the church. Someone had been there recently—there were more boards across the gaping hole in the center, and the pew where Charlie had napped had been pushed off to the corner. He stepped inside the ruined church, utterly silent, listening for the sound of voices.

All was quiet but for the rustle of the leaves over the missing roof, the faint soughing of the wind through the shattered building. And then the sound of muffled voices began to rise, just barely audible. He moved into the church, making no sound at all, moving to the very edge of the pit and peering down.

It was almost impossible to see anything but the piles of rocks and rubble beneath the gaping hole. The huge mound of rocks at the far end of the passageway had been moved, exposing a thick oak door. The painting and the journals had to be in there.

It was farther down than he remembered—no wonder Charlie had panicked when she'd made her way across the narrow plank. A fall like that could break a few bones if you were unlucky. A fall like that could kill you if you landed just right...

He never felt it coming. Something slammed over his back, something hard, and he was tumbling headfirst into that deep, endless hole, and the last thing he saw was Madame Antonella standing over him, a heavy piece of wood in her strong hands. And then he hit the ground.

Charlie woke up slowly, cold and damp and shivering. It was pitch-black, and she tried to lift her hand to see whether she was blindfolded, but she found she couldn't move. Someone had pinioned her arms to her sides, her legs together, in the inky darkness.

She was lying on something relatively soft. She was able to move her fingers, and it felt like an old mattress beneath her, covered with some kind of wool blanket. The smell of the place was horrendous—a sickly sweet odor of decay mixed with rodent droppings. Wherever she was, it hadn't had fresh air in years. If no one came to let her go she'd probably die of the stench before starvation.

At least she wasn't dead—yet. She'd had one last thought as she fell to the floor in the old kitchen. She was going to die, and at the worst possible time in her life.

A week ago would have been fine. Everyone

would have wept, but it really wouldn't have mattered one way or another. A year from now would be okay, too. Then she'd be over it.

But she didn't want to die right now, when she was stupidly, crazily in love with that lying, exasperating, treacherous, devious son of a bitch Maguire.

She was crying, and that probably wasn't a good idea, either. She could feel the tears slide down her cheeks, and she turned her head to wipe them on the rough wool beneath her. It was bad enough that she was in love with him. She was damned if she was going to cry over him, as well.

She squirmed again, and the surface beneath her creaked. It was some kind of narrow bed or cot. She reached out her fingers, testing her bonds. It wasn't rope but something thicker, something clothlike and incredibly strong. It was...

Duct tape. Someone had wrapped duct tape around her ankles and knees, around her arms and waist, immobilizing her. She knew where they'd gotten it—she'd sent Tomaso a case of the stuff for Christmas last year when he'd expressed his admiration for it. Under any other circumstances she would have laughed at the absurdity of it.

She still couldn't believe that they had done this. Madame Antonella was one thing—the old lady had obviously gone over the edge. But why in God's name would Lauretta and Tomaso help her?

"Bloody hell." The moan came from out of the darkness. "I think she broke my goddamned arm."

The tears were starting again, damn it. "Maguire?" she asked in a quavering voice.

"You there, Charlie?" He sounded as relieved as she was. "Where the hell are you—I can't see a thing in this pit."

"I can't see you, either. Follow the sound of my voice."

"I'm in a lot of pain here, Charlie," he said in a sour voice. "How about you come and find me?"

"Someone duct-taped me to the bed."

The silence was so long that she wondered whether he'd passed out. "Now, that's worth moving for," he said finally, and she could hear the rustle of clothing, the sound of him inching his way closer to her, accompanied by muffled curses and the occasional groan of pain.

She jumped when his hand found her. A moment later there was a flare of light as Maguire lit his lighter. "Forgot I had it," he said, looking down at her.

The flickering light illuminated him, as well. "You look like hell," she said, hoping he wouldn't notice she'd been crying. He was covered with dust, his shirt was torn, his face was bruised and cut, and he was cradling his left arm. "What happened to you?"

"The old bitch hit me over the head with a two-by-four and knocked me into the cellar hole. I don't know how I got in here—I don't think she's strong enough to drag me."

"Probably Tomaso did the honors. He and Lauretta are helping her."

He flicked off the lighter again, plunging them into darkness.

"Why did you do that?" she demanded.

"To conserve fuel. It's just lucky you stopped me from smoking or there'd be no lighter fluid left." His hand was traveling over her body in a professional manner, checking out the duct-tape bondage. "You know, a man could find this kind of erotic."

"Maguire, there's a crazy old lady trying to kill us, and two not-so-crazy, not-so-old people helping her. This is not the time for sexual innuendo."

"It's always the time for sexual innuendo, sweetheart," he drawled. "Do you know why they're helping her?"

"I don't have any idea. I don't even know why she wants to kill me."

"I do."

She waited, but he said nothing more as he fiddled with something in the darkness.

"Well?" she demanded finally. "And what the hell are you doing?"

"Swiss Army knife, love. Never travel without one."

"You're a regular Boy Scout," she muttered.

"Be grateful. I rather like the idea of you tied up. I could have forgotten I had it." She felt him sawing at the tape.

"Don't you want to turn on the lighter?" she asked nervously.

"I'm afraid I've only got one usable hand at the moment. Don't move and I'll try not to slash your wrists."

She held still as he hacked away at the tape. "Why?"

"Why what?"

"You told me you knew why Madame Antonella wants to kill me."

"Because she's not Madame Antonella. She's Mrs. Aristide Pompasse. Always was, since 1957. You were never legally married to him, because he never got a divorce. She's the widow, not you."

"That son of a bitch," she said after a moment.

"Exactly. Hold still and allow me the perverse pleasure of ripping the rest of the tape off you."

"Back off, Maguire," she snapped. "I'm not in

the mood.'' She was able to sit up, and she quickly unfastened the tape. At least it was attached to her clothing and not her skin, though the bands around her forearms were admittedly painful.

She took a deep gasp of air, then coughed. ''This place smells like a garbage dump,'' she said.

''Er...I hate to tell you this, love, but that's not garbage you're smelling.''

''Then what is it?''

He flicked the lighter on again, looking down at her. ''Let's not think about it,'' he said grimly.

''We've got to find our way out of here before they come back.''

''If they come back.''

''Why are you being so cryptic?''

His laugh was humorless. ''I'm afraid *cryptic* is a little too apt. This place is a crypt, and what you're smelling is dead people. I imagine they left us here to die, as well. If we're lucky.''

For a moment she couldn't say anything. ''And you're such an expert?'' she said finally.

''I know what death smells like. I covered battle zones in my misspent youth.'' His voice was flat, emotionless, and she remembered those plaques in the bottom of his drawer.

''All right,'' she said after a moment. ''So we're locked up with dead bodies. That doesn't mean we can't find a way out. Unless you feel like giving up?''

"No, love. We'll find a way out. It's probably after midnight by now, and maybe they won't come back and check on us until daylight. Maybe not at all. But be careful. This place is collapsing all around us. I imagine the old bitch hopes we'll bury ourselves. And the paintings.''

"The paintings?''

"Look around you.'' He held the lighter up high, sending tiny shards of illumination into the darkness. "We've found the missing paintings. There are about a dozen here—more than we realized. Worth a bloody fortune. The journals were probably here as well—there's a pile of ashes that looks suspicious. She must have burned them.''

"Why?''

"Too incriminating, maybe. I don't know. We're just lucky she didn't torch the paintings.''

"She wouldn't destroy them. They're worth too much.''

"I don't think Madame Antonella gives a damn about the money. I think she's pissed as hell, nutty as a fruitcake, and she's going to cause some major damage to anyone or anything that gets in her way.''

Charlie tried to sit up, then sank back with a howl of pain.

Maguire dropped the lighter, plunging the place back into darkness, and swore. "What's wrong?"

"I've got a headache," she said between gritted teeth.

"Tell me about it," he said. "Now I can't find the bloody lighter."

She sat up again, more slowly this time, and the searing pain in her skull subsided to a quiet agony. "I'll help you," she said grumpily, getting on the ground beside him. Unfortunately she couldn't see him, and she practically landed on top of him.

"Mind the arm!" he said with a choke of pain.

"You're a wuss, Maguire."

He'd found the lighter. He flicked it on again, and they were face-to-face, kneeling in the darkness, closer than she'd realized. "Come here and say that," he taunted her.

For a moment she didn't move. She'd thought she was going to die. She hated him with every ounce of her being. And she'd never seen anyone look so good in her entire life.

"The hell with your arm," she said, and jumped him.

He dropped the lighter again, using his good arm to catch her. He met her hungry kiss with one of his own, and within moments there were entwined on the dusty floor, and she was reaching for his zipper with all the brazenness of a streetwalker.

He stopped her, covering her hand with his. He was fully erect beneath his jeans, and she wanted, needed him.

"Hold on, girly," he said with a muffled laugh. "We'll have plenty of time for that later."

"We're going to die, Maguire," she wailed. "And I want to have sex with you."

"Yes, love, and we will. For days on end, but not here among the dead bodies with a crazy woman likely to walk in on us. Pull yourself together, Charlie." He brought her hands to his mouth, kissing her. "I've unleashed a terror."

"That's what I was trying to do." She reached for his zipper again, but he stopped her.

"Enough of that," he said sternly. "Give a girl a couple of orgasms and she gets all mouthy."

"I was thinking I might like to try that, too," she murmured, trying to move closer.

He let out a low, heartfelt groan. "Stop it, Charlie. A man could get distracted. We need to find our way out of this place before the damned thing collapses around us."

"And preferably before Madame Antonella comes back to finish us off," Charlie added.

"Hush!" he said fiercely. In the sudden silence they could hear someone moving around in the distance, making no effort to cover the noise of their approach.

"Then again," Charlie whispered, "it may be too late."

"Get back on the bed and pretend to be unconscious. I'm going to look for something I can use as a weapon."

"I can help..." she began, but he simply shoved her up onto the cot again, cursing as he banged his arm.

"Be quiet!" he said, rising to his feet and moving away from her, the tiny flame disappearing into the inky blackness.

He barely made a sound, but she was intensely aware of every muffled curse, every swallowed groan, just as she listened to the footsteps getting closer and closer. No voices, though—if it was only one person, between the two of them they should have at least a fighting chance.

Maguire appeared out of the gloom once more, an old broomstick in his hand. He saw her doubtful glance and he shrugged. "It was the best I could come up with."

"Let me look..." she started to get up but he pushed her back.

"You don't want to go back there, Charlie. Trust me," he said in a gruff voice.

Charlie swallowed. "I already saw the paintings."

"There's...something else besides."

"Whatever's causing the smell?"

"Yes."

"And I don't want to know?"

"You don't want to know. But they've been there a very long time—it's probably no one you ever knew."

"They?" It came out in a whispered shriek.

"Don't think about it," he said.

They could see the light now, spearing through cracks around a rectangle in the nearby wall. It was some sort of door, though Charlie couldn't tell if it was stone, wood or metal.

"What about the Swiss Army knife?" Charlie whispered.

"I think the broom will be more effective," he said. "Hush."

Someone was trying to open the door. Both of them held their breath, and Maguire had the broomstick raised like a weapon, ready to bring it down on the head of whoever walked through that door.

It creaked open, slowly, noisily, and the light from beyond was momentarily blinding.

"Charlie? Are you in there?"

It was Olivia. Maguire dropped the broomstick and grabbed her flashlight. "Jesus Christ, what are you doing here?" he demanded.

He'd trained the full power of the light on her,

and she glared up at him, affronted. "Looking for my missing daughter, thank you very much. I got back to the villa and the place was deserted. I saw lights up here and I decided to come and see."

"You decided to come and see?" Charlie echoed in astonishment. "It's a steep climb, not a casual stroll."

"Don't I know it," Olivia said languidly. "I've destroyed my Ferragamos, my fingernails are ruined, I've lost a contact lens and I'm in a thoroughly bad mood. I prefer being the center of attention, not running around trying to rescue my daughter. What the hell is going on here?"

"Where's Henry? Gia?"

"I left them in Geppi. They're flying back to the States tomorrow—I figured you were well rid of him. After all, you've got Mr. Outback Tabloid Reporter here."

"Stuff it," Maguire growled.

"So what's going on? And what is that godawful smell?"

"You don't want to know," the two of them said in unison.

"Let's get the hell out of here," Maguire added. "We can talk later...."

It was too late. Lauretta appeared behind Olivia, a stoic expression on her plain face.

"Lauretta!" Olivia greeted her gladly. "Just the

person I was looking for. We need help getting these two idiots back to the villa. Don't ask me what they're doing up here—some kind of kinky love play, I suppose. Charlie, let Lauretta take your arm and we'll get you out of this nasty little pit.''

Charlie didn't move. Olivia stared at her. ''I'm not in the mood for this, daughter dearest. I come charging up here to rescue you and find you don't need rescuing at all. Get off your butt and we'll go back to the villa and Lauretta can fix us something nice to eat.''

''I don't think so,'' Charlie said.

Olivia turned back, slowly, to stare at Lauretta. And at the gun in Lauretta's capable hand.

23

She had to admire her mother. Olivia simply blinked, her calm unshaken. "Well," she said. "And would you like to explain the reason for this, Lauretta?" she demanded sternly. "Give me that gun." She held out her hand peremptorily.

Oddly enough, her commanding tones almost worked. Lauretta looked confused for a moment, and she started to hand her the gun. And then she stiffened. "I'm sorry, Madonna," she said.

"I am not pleased," Olivia said in icy tones. "Not pleased at all. Why do you want to hurt my daughter?"

"You don't understand, Contessa," Lauretta said, using her mother's one-time title. "I have my own family to protect. I made a solemn vow to the master. I promised I would protect his widow, see that she's taken care of. I have no choice but to do what she asks."

"Who the hell are you talking about?" Olivia demanded. "You're holding a gun on his widow."

"No, Mama. He was married to Antonella all this time. Never to me," Charlie said.

"That son of a bitch," Olivia said bitterly.

"My sentiments exactly," Charlie agreed.

"On top of that, Antonella happens to be Lauretta's mother," Maguire broke in. "But Pompasse wasn't her father, thank God."

"Why thank God?" Charlie questioned, momentarily distracted.

"This whole scene is sick enough, but I'm afraid incest might be just a bit over the top," Maguire said.

"Enough!" Lauretta said in a firm voice that sounded like Madame Antonella's when she was being dictatorial. Strange, but now that Charlie knew the facts she couldn't believe she hadn't noticed the resemblance before. "I was hoping I could make it easier for you, Charlie," Lauretta added plaintively. "I helped you leave five years ago, I tried to get you to go this time, but you wouldn't listen. My mother is determined, and I couldn't change her mind. I thought I could at least make it quick for you." She gestured with the gun.

"Kind of you," Maguire drawled, "but I think we'd rather take our chances with the old lady."

"You don't know what you're dealing with," Lauretta murmured. "She killed Pompasse, you know. She found out he was going to divorce her, put her in a home, so he could come after Charlie again. He thought Charlie suspected that they'd never been properly married and that's why she left him. He could never believe that anyone would really leave him.''

"Other women left him," Charlie said. "There were models, mistresses who just disappeared..."

"No, they didn't. Even my own daughter didn't leave him," Lauretta said sadly.

"Your own daughter?" Charlie echoed.

"They're all here. Madame Antonella brought them here. Even my poor baby Luisa.'' Her voice broke. ''They're all in the back of this tomb. As you will be. It grieves me, but there's nothing I can do.''

"Nothing you can do?" Olivia repeated in horror. "She killed your daughter and you're helping her?''

"She's my mother," Lauretta said simply. "And I promised Pompasse I would always watch over her and keep her safe. Especially when we knew what she had done. That was the only reason she never hurt you, Charlie. Pompasse insisted I keep her drugged so she wouldn't realize what was going on. He couldn't bring himself to punish her, but he had to stop her from hurting anyone else. He used to like to set her off against his models.

He called it putting the cat among the pigeons. Until she started killing them."

"But why didn't he turn her in?"

"The master would never do that!" Lauretta protested, shocked. "And he knew I would never let him. He told her she had a choice. She could take pills that would calm her, or she would be put away. She chose to take the pills, and she never came near you. But when we took her to sign the papers even the pills didn't work. She got away from us. And we found her in Pompasse's apartment, crooning over his dead body."

"This is too macabre for words," Olivia said sharply. "I'm going for help." She started past Lauretta, only to have the woman backhand her across the face, knocking her against the crumbling wall.

There was an ominous rumbling, as rocks and plaster spilled down into the dimly lit tomb. "You're not going anywhere, Contessa," Lauretta said firmly. "Tomaso is bringing *madame*, and there will be an end to this. I'm sorry for your sake that you came back. It is sad to lose a child. I have borne the pain myself, but at least I didn't know until it was too late."

"You sick bitch," Olivia hissed.

"Olivia," Maguire said in a warning voice. "She's got a G-U-N. Don't do anything stupid."

"They're coming," Lauretta said sharply. "Show some respect for the widow."

They made a stately procession into the mouth of the old crypt. The mad old lady was dressed in her finest, though she had food dribbled on her black satin. She was wearing diamonds, the diamonds that Pompasse had given Charlie, the ones she'd left behind when she'd run. They were far better suited to the old lady than to a young girl.

Tomaso was supporting her, a miserable expression on his face. He was part and parcel of it all, Charlie thought, but not happy about it.

"Get the hell away from my daughter, you old hag," Olivia snarled, starting to get up.

"Lauretta, kill her," Antonella said promptly, and before Charlie could even scream Lauretta fired the gun.

In the dim light she couldn't make out her target, and Charlie could only hope she'd missed. The explosion was deafening, and the wall behind her began to crumble, a slow rumble of noise and rubble and dust. Maguire grabbed Charlie and dragged her backward, into the darkness, away from the plumes of dust. As it began to settle, Charlie could see that some of the roof had given in, and the faint light of stars were overhead.

"Not with the gun, you stupid whore," Antonella said icily. "You'll bring the whole place down around us. Give it to your stupid husband and then snap her neck.''

Lauretta was looking abashed. She handed the gun to Tomaso, who held it as if it were something unclean. ''Mama,'' she said, ''I cannot...''

''It's easy,'' the old lady said. ''You've killed chickens and sheep—you can certainly kill a worthless creature like this one. You just give the neck one sharp twist and it's over.''

''Madame Antonella,'' Tomaso said miserably. ''You cannot want us to do this. Signora Charlie has never harmed us. She's a good girl....''

''Send your foolish husband away, Lauretta,'' Antonella said sternly. ''He will only interfere.''

Tomaso retreated, but just to the doorway. He looked guilty, miserable, and totally incapable of stopping anything.

Ignoring Olivia, Madame Antonella advanced on Charlie. She smiled, exposing her impressive new dentures, and combined with the smell of the place, Charlie felt her stomach start to roil.

''Thought he loved you, didn't you?'' she said. ''Thought he'd marry you, leave you everything. But you were never married. Pompasse had only one wife, and that was me. He will only have one widow.''

''Of course, *madame*,'' Charlie said softly.

"You know I have always had the greatest respect for you...."

"Silence!" the old woman hissed. "You thought you'd tricked me. Like all the others. But I took care of them, and I'll take care of you. They'll never find you, any of you, and they'll never find your paintings. I couldn't take all of them, but I got enough. You'll all be entombed together, with the other ones, and I won't have to worry anymore. It'll be over."

"What others, Madame Antonella?" Maguire spoke up suddenly. "Who are they?"

"Shut up, Maguire," Charlie whispered. "I'm trying to reason with her."

"She won't be reasoned with, love," he said in a loud voice. "So tell me who those women are. The dead bodies in the back of the tomb? Lauretta says they're some of your earlier victims."

"My daughter knows my secrets," Antonella said smugly. Charlie wanted to kick Maguire, until she noticed Tomaso's reaction. He'd had no idea exactly how bad things were—news about the dead women in the crypt had clearly come as a shock to him, and he was staring at his wife in renewed horror.

"Tell us who they were," Maguire said, his voice soft and admiring. "You must have been very clever to get away with this. I like a woman who's both beautiful and smart.'' He was flirting with her, Charlie realized in shock. And the old hag was responding with ghoulish girlishness. ''How did you do it?''

The old lady preened, responding to Maguire's practiced charm. ''I told you, it's easy. You just snap their neck. Fast, and relatively painless. They didn't even know it was coming. I brought them up here to see some of Pompasse's hidden paintings. I always used to take them when he wasn't looking. He never could find them.'' She smiled with remembered fondness.

''And you killed them all?'' Maguire prompted. ''The women who wanted to leave?''

''Don't be foolish. It was the ones who wanted to stay who were a danger. Those were the ones I killed.''

''Even the young one?'' Maguire prompted her. ''What was her name?''

''Luisa,'' Antonella replied calmly. ''The little slut. My grandchild, and his own child. He took her into his bed when she was fifteen. I killed her when she was sixteen. Lauretta was not happy with me, but she helped me, anyway. She had promised Aristide.''

''Damn,'' Maguire muttered. ''I really didn't want incest.''

''No!'' It was no more than a whispered moan

of pain, but it was the first sound Tomaso had made. "No. Not my baby."

Lauretta threw him a pleading look. "It was too late for me to stop her, Tomaso. She had already done it. I had no choice but to protect my mother...."

"She killed our daughter, and you protect her?" Tomaso's voice suddenly thundered in the underground chamber. "What kind of creature are you? You are worse than she is, a monster." Before she realized what he was doing he raised the gun and fired, straight at her, the weapon sparking in the darkness.

"Oh, shit," Maguire muttered. "Move it." He shoved Charlie toward the back of the tomb, then grabbed Olivia and hauled her after him as the entire place began to rumble.

Lauretta was clutching her stomach, staring at her husband in shock. "Tomaso?" she said in a piteous voice. The old woman was screaming in the background, filthy imprecations in a dozen languages, and Tomaso turned patiently, pointed the gun at her, and fired again.

She went down like a felled ox. Before she even hit the ground the roof collapsed in on them with a rumble that must have rivaled the bombs that first shattered the place in World War Two, burying them where they stood.

Maguire shoved Charlie against a wall and covered her with his body. She heard a muffled wail, and she tried to break free, to make sure her mother was all right, but Maguire was immovable, and the roar of the collapsing stone was deafening. She really was going to die this time, she thought, and she didn't want to die without telling Maguire she loved him, but even if she screamed it he wouldn't hear her, and besides, he was better off not knowing. At least he wouldn't die smug.

It took her a while to realize that the roaring had stopped, though her ears still echoed with the noise. The thick dust was like smoke, swirling around them, and Charlie pushed Maguire away.

"Mama!" she screamed.

There was a dusty cough from the area near her knee. "Right here, darling." Olivia's voice came from the darkness. "I'm fine."

"Thank God," Charlie breathed. "Maguire...?" She reached out for him again, and he let out a yelp of pain.

"I'm surviving," he said bitterly. "Though I'm not sure I want to."

The dust was slowly settling. The night sky was brilliant overhead, the moon shining down brightly on the pile of stones in front of them. Half the remaining church had collapsed, and the old pew lay across the pile like a headstone. Tomaso, Lauretta and Madame Antonella were buried beneath it, crushed by the stone.

"Jesus," Maguire breathed. "Will you look at that?"

"They're dead," Charlie said.

"Not that. Look behind you."

She turned. The other half of the crypt had caved in as well, crushing Pompasse's stolen paintings, crushing what remained of the women Madame Antonella had killed. The only place left standing was the small area where Charlie, Olivia and Maguire had taken shelter.

"I don't believe it," Maguire said, shaking his head. Dust and bits of stone fell onto his shoulders. "It's a bloody miracle."

"I think I'm going to faint," Charlie said in a wavery voice.

"Forget about it. I can't carry you with this bum arm. You've made it this far—you can make it back to the villa."

"Besides," Olivia said, struggling to her feet. "If anyone's fainting it'll be me. I've been through quite enough today. It's not in my nature to be a heroine, and I think I've done quite splendidly, but now I need a hot bath and a rest cure. And some healthy young man to take my mind off my aches."

"You can't have mine," Charlie said.

"Yours, eh?" Olivia murmured. "I don't think he knew that."

Charlie looked up at Maguire. He had a bemused expression on his face, as if he wasn't quite sure he liked what he was hearing.

"Definitely mine," Charlie said firmly.

"We'll have to discuss that," Maguire said. "In the meantime, let's get the hell out of here."

The climb back down the hillside was endless. Despite Olivia's jauntiness she was in worse shape than she had admitted. A shard of stone had cut into her leg and she was bleeding down her silk dupioni pants and into her Ferragamos. Maguire couldn't carry her, but he used his good arm to support her down the treacherous path, and Charlie had no choice but to follow after them as best she could in her bare feet.

Their slow pace had one advantage—they had time to come up with a reasonable story. No reason for the police to know what really happened, Olivia had argued persuasively. Think of the scandal. There was no bringing Pompasse back, and besides, he'd deserved what Madame Antonella had dished out. If the three of them just stuck to the same story it would all be over quickly, with a minimum of fuss.

And Maguire said nothing.

The villa was ablaze with lights, providing a precious beacon to guide them down. The *polizia* met them partway up the hill, a strong young sergeant scooping Olivia up in his manly arms and carrying her the rest of the way down. Another one tried to help Charlie, but a dangerous glare from Maguire had him backing away apologetically.

"Did I tell you I called the police before I came after you? I had a feeling something was wrong. Such a terrible accident up there at the old ruin," Olivia murmured from the young man's arms. She sounded as if she were enjoying herself tremendously. "Very farsighted, don't you think?"

Maguire said nothing.

They took him away from her, before they had a chance to speak. They took her mother, as well—both of them needed the hospital. Which left Charlie to come up with the answers, when all she wanted to do was curl up in a little ball and go to sleep.

It was almost dawn before they finished with her, finished with their endless questions, but they seemed to believe her. Almost dawn before the ambulance came back, bringing her mother. Only her mother.

"Where's Maguire?" Charlie demanded abruptly.

"Yes, I'm fine, so nice of you to be worried,"

Olivia said sweetly. "An ungrateful child is sharper than a serpent's tooth or something like…"

"'How sharper than a serpent's tooth it is to have a thankless child.' King Lear. Where is he, Olivia? Why didn't he come back? Was he more badly hurt than I realized? Did he tell them the truth?"

"You called me Mama up in that chamber of horrors," Olivia said calmly. "I rather liked it. You haven't called me Mama in years."

"Where is he, Mama?"

"He's fine, dearest. He went back to Florence. He said you wouldn't be needing him anymore."

"He did?" She didn't know whether to be depressed or furious.

"If I know Maguire he's probably in a hurry to file the story of tonight's macabre little escapade. He didn't say a word to the police, but you know how untrustworthy these people are. You do have wretched taste in men, my sweet. First, that ghastly old man, then a tabloid journalist."

"You forgot Henry," Charlie pointed out forlornly.

"Henry is eminently forgettable," Olivia said. "Are you going to let him do it?"

"Let him do what?"

"Let Maguire get away with it. Let him write his tabloid trash?"

It took a moment for it to sink in. "No," she said. "Of course I'm not."

"Then you'd better go after him, hadn't you?" Olivia said in a dulcet voice. "You can take my car if you want."

"That's all right. I'll take Maguire's. I'm used to it by now."

This time she grabbed her purse and a heavy sweater on her way out the door. She was halfway across the terrace when she stopped. She turned back to see her mother standing in the door, watching her.

She sprinted back across the terrace and enveloped her mother in a bear hug. "Thanks, Mama," she said.

Olivia's smile was slightly crooked, and her beautiful blue eyes were shiny with tears. "My pleasure, love. I've always wanted to be a heroine."

24

His shoulder hurt like bloody hell. It didn't help having seventeen messages on his answering machine, all from Gregory. He went from threats to bribes to pleas, and Maguire deleted each one at the opening words. No messages from anyone else, but then, why should he have expected it?

Charlie would be sound asleep by now, dreaming innocent dreams and thanking heaven she'd escaped, not from a crazy, murdering old woman, but from a man who was no good for her. She'd run away the first time, and if he hadn't come after her she would probably have been happy never to see him again.

Well, she wouldn't. He was getting the hell out of Italy, heading back home for the first time in fifteen years. Thomas Wolfe said you couldn't go back home again. Maguire intended to prove him wrong.

He'd find himself a nice big Australian girl and have babies. Maybe he'd forget all about Charlie Thomas. In a year or ten.

He had a hell of a time packing with only one arm. They'd set his shoulder, and it was no more than a hairline crack, but it still hurt like crazy, and he had it strapped to his body to keep from using it. Just as well—if it had been free he probably would have punched the wall.

He threw his clothes in his suitcase, then on impulse tossed in her shoes and bra. He wasn't sure why—maybe some crazy sentimental streak. Maybe he could hold them hostage and force her to come to Australia and get them. And maybe he'd finally lost it for good.

He had the zip disk in his hand, staring down at it. He'd be a total fool to toss it—he could count on it as his old-age security. It could come in handy as blackmail material if things got dicey. Or he could simply print off the pictures of Charlie and stare at them.

He'd told Olivia he wasn't going to write the book. It was a long wait at the hospital, more than enough time for Olivia to give him a piece of her mind and then some.

"I warned you, Maguire," she'd said. "She's a precious girl, and I don't want you smashing her heart."

"I'm never going to see her again," he'd said. "Scout's honor. I'm dropping the book and heading back home and I never want to hear Pompasse's name again.''

For some reason Olivia didn't look pleased. ''You care, Maguire. Be a man and admit it. She's afraid, you know,'' she'd added. ''Afraid she'll turn out like me.''

She'd managed to lure him into the conversation, against his better judgment. ''What do you mean?''

''She's afraid that if she lets herself love someone she'll be just like her mother. Going through men, pathetically self-absorbed. She doesn't realize that she's nothing at all like me. She's a person who gives, not one who takes. And it's all right for her to take, every now and then.''

''Don't look at me,'' he'd growled. ''She won't want anything to do with me once this is over.''

''You really think so, Maguire?'' she'd murmured. ''Maybe you're not quite as clever as I thought you were.''

They'd come to stitch up her leg then, and he hoped to hell they didn't numb her before they used the needle. No wonder Charlie was such a pain in the butt. But he believed Olivia—Charlie wasn't anything like her mother. Except in her ability to be annoying.

He looked down at the disk in his hand. He was damned if he was going to be sentimental. He'd hold on to it—you could never tell when something like this might come in handy one day. He was about to tuck it into his pocket when he heard the door open. He hadn't bothered to lock it—he seldom did. He was big enough to take on most of the unsavory characters that haunted his neighborhood, and most of them knew to leave him safely alone.

It was no unsavory character. It was Charlie standing in his doorway, furious, glaring at him.

He wanted to grin, but he didn't. She'd come after him. Maybe she hadn't thought better after that giddy time in the crypt. Maybe she was ready for him, after all. "What?" he said in an irritable voice. "What is it this time?"

"You aren't writing the story," she said, walking into the room and slamming the door behind her. It made a nice solid thump. He liked a woman who slammed doors. Hell, he liked everything about Charlie, including her glower. She'd gone from a pale, colorless mouse to a holy terror, and the truth of it was, he was stupidly, damnably in love with her. And he was going to have to tell her so, whether he liked it or not. But not until he was forced to.

"There's no story to write, sweetheart," he drawled instead. "You trashed my computer, remember?" He shoved the zip disk into his pocket.

"You aren't going to write about last night, either. I don't know whether the police believed what we told them, but they're closing the investigation."

"Gullible of them," Maguire observed. "And you expect me to sit on the story of my life, just because it's a little messy?"

"You're not writing the story."

"All right. I told your mother I wouldn't, anyway. I'm surprised she didn't tell you that."

She looked startled, as if she hadn't expected him to be so amenable. "That's not exactly what she told me, but then, my mother can be quite surprising at times," she said after a moment. "You know you'll probably lose your job."

"Already lost it," he said cheerfully.

She looked at him speculatively. "Then how are you going to support me?"

He blinked. "I beg your pardon?"

"Fine," she said breezily, moving past him. She spied his open suitcase on the bed. "You're packing? Where are we going?"

He managed to pull himself together. "We're not going anywhere," he said sternly. "I'm going back to Australia."

"If 'we're' not going anywhere then why are my shoes and my bra in your suitcase?" she asked in a dulcet tone.

He started to shrug, but his shoulder screamed in pain. "Souvenir?" he suggested. "I like to keep a little something from every woman I've nailed."

She crossed the room, coming up to him. She looked beaten down, exhausted, nervous and uncertain, and more alive than he'd ever seen her. She flashed him a bright smile. "Sorry, pal. It's not that easy. You promised me we'd have days to make love once we got out of that tomb, and I expect a man to keep his promises."

"I was just trying to distract you," he said.

"Consider me distracted. You're not getting rid of me, Maguire. Let's face it, I'm a cold-blooded, heartless woman and you're the only man who's ever managed to turn me on in my entire lifetime. I don't intend to let you get away." Some of her bravado faded slightly. "Unless, of course, you don't want me?"

He was within two minutes of taking her on the floor of his apartment with most of their clothes pulled out of the way. But he wasn't going to give up without a fight. "Do I really have to support you?" he countered.

"Just while I'm having babies," she said. "The rest of the time I can cook. You'll have to marry me, though."

"I like a woman who can cook," he said thoughtfully.

"I'm a very good cook."

"I like a woman who steals cars. Molly would have approved. Sometime I'll tell you about her. She would have liked you."

"Do I need to be jealous?"

"Not of Molly, love. Where did you leave the car?"

"It's in the alley. I don't ever want to drive that junker again," she warned him.

"We won't need it in Australia. We're better off with a four-wheel drive. I like a woman who isn't afraid to say what she wants."

"I'm here," she said. "And I want you."

"Charlie," he said, pulling her up against his body, ignoring the pain in his shoulder, "you've got me."

And he bent down and kissed her, letting the computer disk drop in the trash.

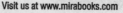

From bestselling author

JoANN ROSS

Alexandra Lyons has always been spirited
and independent. But everything she
believes about herself is thrown into
question when she meets Eleanor Lord.
The powerful matriarch is convinced that
Alexandra is Anna Lord, her long-lost
granddaughter and heir to a family dynasty.

Has Alexandra's life been a lie? Is she really
Anna Lord—or the victim of an even
darker hoax? The truth lies buried in the
past, in a dark explosion of jealousy,
betrayal and murder, and remains as deadly
now as it was nearly thirty years ago.

LEGACY of LIES

"A sizzling, sensual romance sure to keep
hearts pounding after the last page is turned."
—*Romantic Times Magazine*

On sale July 2001 wherever paperbacks are sold!

MIRA®

MJR821

What will happen if they find her?

JUDITH ARNOLD

LOOKING FOR LAURA

When irrepressible Sally Driver—owner of a New Age coffee bar and mother of a sassy five-year-old—is packing up her late husband Paul's clothes, she discovers a stack of letters. Cloying, unbearably flowery love letters from someone named Laura. Now she wants answers…and she hopes Todd Sloan will have them. Todd was Paul's best friend, but he's never heard of this Laura. Now he wants answers, too! Together, Sally and Todd start looking for Laura…but find unexpected passion along the way. Now should they let go of the past—or keep searching for answers to questions that may no longer matter?

> "*Looking for Laura* will have readers looking
> for more of Judith Arnold's books."
> —*New York Times* bestselling author Debbie Macomber

Available August 2001 wherever paperbacks are sold!